Praise for *The M*

"This book is glorious and magical, moving and compelling, and fresh throughout. *The Moon Won't Talk* portrays fantastical worlds seen only by the lucky. It is at once a meditation on love and courage, and a page-turning novel for young and adult readers alike. Fall into its dreamlike spell."

—Beth Castrodale, author of *I Mean You No Harm*, *In This Ground*, and *The Inhabitants*

"In *The Moon Won't Talk*, author Morgan G. Howell joins the pantheon of Southern writers, blending wit, legend, and social commentary in a coming-of-age tale that includes a mysterious mathematical formula, an old lost love, a new forbidden romance, and ghosts! Set in the 1960s South, *The Moon Won't Talk* is a story of both its time and ours, a riverboat ride that does not disappoint."

—Steven Mayfield, award-winning author of *Treasure of the Blue Whale*, *Delphic Oracle*, *U.S.A.*, and *The Penny Mansions*

"A coming-of-age tale set in a whirlwind summer of ghosts, Cajun magic, lost love and painful bigotry, Morgan Howell's *The Moon Won't Talk* will hook fans of supernatural and Southern fiction. Howell seamlessly blends genres to craft a tale of tolerance and the enduring power of love. The endearing protagonist of Morgan Howell's *The Moon Won't Talk* speaks with the wisdom of youth and the wit of a poet in this coming-of-age story teeming with ghosts, naive young love, mysterious neighbors, and dreamy days spent fishing beside the river. Howell's supernatural bildungsroman is sure to transport readers back to the wonders and growing pains of their own boyhoods."

—Ellen Parent, author of *After the Fall*

"Morgan Howell's fantastical coming-of-age tale reveals its author as the real wizard: He conjures an American village of the 1960s, not as nostalgia might soften it—with warmth and joy only—but with all the shameful customs and painful social and economic realities of the era. Though this Eden is not one, it is on the verge of urgently needed change that will start it and its residents down the road to the future. Teen readers will experience both shock and wonder as a young man named George finds his humdrum, small-town summer magicked into a wild eruption of truth and amazing possibility that offers him the chance to lead the revolution he and his flawed Eden need."

—Carolyn Jack, author of *The Changing of Keys*

THE MOON WON'T TALK

Morgan Howell

Regal House Publishing

Published by
Regal House Publishing, LLC
Raleigh, NC 27605
All rights reserved

ISBN -13 (paperback): 9781646035144
ISBN -13 (epub): 9781646035151
Library of Congress Control Number: 2023949029

All efforts were made to determine the copyright holders and obtain their permissions in any circumstance where copyrighted material was used. The publisher apologizes if any errors were made during this process, or if any omissions occurred. If noted, please contact the publisher and all efforts will be made to incorporate permissions in future editions.

Cover images and design by © C. B. Royal

Regal House Publishing, LLC
https://regalhousepublishing.com

Printed in the United States of America

To Rosemary, friend, editor, selfless nurturer,
and, last but certainly not least, beautiful, patient wife.

1

If you move, I'll pull the trigger."
I'd never had a gun pushed into my body before, but there was no doubt in my mind that the hard steel below my ear was just that—a gun. My knees trembled, threatening to give.

"Another inch down and you'll be meeting dead relatives, son." His voice was cultivated—free of the Southernism that marks most folk in Eden. I grimaced and stuck the fingers of my left hand into the knothole that helped bring about my predicament, my face hot with shame and panic. Beads of sweat rolled from my armpits as a yellow butterfly fluttered over my head. I thought of William Chandler at church on Sunday, advising that fishing was always good while the fragile creatures were floating about.

Then, there was Miss Ginn. The last time I cut her grass she had advice as well. Miss Ginn always had advice. *You're going to get into big trouble running around town spying on folk the way you do, you little pervert.* Miss Ginn had a lot of room to talk with her ever-present birding binoculars. I moved, ever so slightly, to glimpse the owner of the voice and gun.

"Ah, ah, aaahhh, put your nosy little eye right back up to the knothole there and tell me what you see, youngster," he said, forcing my head back with the gun. I stuck my eye to the hole.

"What do you see?"

"A yard."

"What else?"

"Nothing."

"You're about to die for spying on a yard?"

"Oh God," I whispered. I closed my eyes and wished for Kansas, Dorothy style. My little voice had warned me, but I'd done what I always do. I shut it down, justifying my actions because that's what I wanted.

"You're in a spot. You could run, but then I'd shoot you in the back. You might get to spend the remainder of your days in a wheelchair, drooling on yourself. You can sit on the porch with Miss Ginn's dear brother—I believe they call him Pug—and drool in concert, so to speak."

I was fourteen. In recent months I'd become increasingly convinced that I knew everything worth knowing about life. What a difference a spying episode can make. Pug was, indeed, Miss Ginn's disabled brother. Whoever was pressing the gun to my head was no stranger, and this realization brought his identity.

The Edenites would love it. A murder would beat adultery, weekend violence on Bangalang, or illegitimate children hands down. I closed my eyes again and saw my name on the obituary page of *The Weekly Observer,* right there in black and white with the old people, perhaps a freak accident, and those taken by disease. "George Parker, local Peeping Tom, killed Sunday, April 24th, 1966, while indulging his perversion."

I'm not a crier for the most part, but tears threatened with stinging power. I shouldn't have been spying on my odd neighbor. I shouldn't spy on *anyone,* but I was having trouble viewing my transgression as a killing offense.

He'd been working at a painting on an easel. I'd never seen an easel, an artist's smock, or a beret, live and in person. Suddenly, he stood upright, looked around a bit, and then disappeared into his house. I assumed to use the bathroom or retrieve more paints.

Yes, I've heard the one about assumption and what it can do, but I'm fourteen, remember? I know everything, and my strange new neighbor had turned my sneaky little game around with perfect execution.

"I'm going to ask you once more. What's so fascinating about a hole in a fence, Spy Boy?"

"Nuh-nothing."

I listened to his even breathing. He was no doubt enjoying

the drama playing out on a lazy Sunday afternoon in our sleepy small town. I was not.

"I believe that you Edenites have a saying. Isn't 'he needed killing' a common defense for offing Peeping Toms?"

I gritted my teeth. I hated the phrase *Peeping Tom*. A sudden end might be a lot less humiliating. "The boy," I stammered. "I was looking for your son."

"Son? There is no son." Something had crept into his voice—frustration, or perhaps a twinge of suspicion. "There's only me in my great big house, Spy Boy. If you were better at your job, you'd know that."

"I saw him," I insisted, "gazing from a second-floor window while I was playing with Buster one day. I heard the music and when I looked up, I saw him."

The would-be murderer's response was to ignore my response. "I wonder how spying would hold up in a murder trial. I know how well it holds up in wartime." Discussion of the boy who'd spied on me first wasn't going to happen.

He'd given himself away, and I was growing more angry than afraid. I turned to look at my executioner, my next-door neighbor. I blinked. Blinking is my mind's way of betraying to the world that I'm confused, stymied, or just plain stupid.

"Gerard Free, at your service," he said. "I must tell you that those tears aren't very becoming on a spy. Perhaps you should stick to playing with Barbies."

I stared at the big hole in the end of his big gun and wiped another tear. Mr. Free smiled with disgusting smugness; his pencil-thin mustache twitched, and his clear slate-blue eyes glittered. He was as cool as a man can be, and as sharp up close and personal as he was at a distance—artist's smock and beret, or no artist's smock and beret.

His pale eyes bored into mine, and I felt as if he were reading my thoughts all the way back to birth. I looked at the ground. "I'm sorry, Mr. Free," I muttered.

"You don't have to be sorry, young man."

"I don't?"

"No, in a bit you're going to be dead. You'll no longer have to worry about idiotic parents commanding that you do things you don't want to do, or teachers with pesky homework who don't have a clue, or old women who don't know what they're talking about when they warn you about the perils of spying on folk."

"Please don't kill me, Mr. Free." The plea came out like a child's whine—a boy-child who plays with Barbies.

"Son, I don't want to kill you. It's just that I have to."

"N-no, you don't. Why do you think such a thing?"

"Why, it's in the rules, of course."

"What rules?"

"The International Code of Spy Conduct dictates that all enemy combatants and sympathizers caught behind enemy lines must be summarily executed."

"But I'm not behind enemy lines. I'm in Miss Ginn's back yard. I'm in Eden."

"Each is a minor technicality, Spy Boy, I assure you."

He dug in a pocket of his smock with his free hand, produced a gold case, and then leaned in close to me.

"Open that for me, please."

I smelled oil paint, Old Spice, tobacco, and a hint of alcohol. I let go of the knothole and collapsed against the fence with a heavy sigh, took the case, and opened it with trembling hands. Two neat rows of cigarettes lay inside.

"Well, don't just stare at them."

I retrieved a cigarette but fumbled it immediately into the grass. "Careful, they're Gauloises. You don't buy those at the Piggly Wiggly."

"Yes, sir," I said, gingerly plucking the foreign cigarette from the grass while he removed a collapsible ebony holder from his smock. He extended the holder and poked it at me. The holder was another of his fascinating affectations. I'd only seen them on television.

"Put the cig in and don't break it. What sort of name is 'Piggly Wiggly' for a grocery store anyway?"

"I don't know," I answered, attempting to insert the cigarette with trembling hands. "It's just a name. It's always been the Piggly Wiggly."

"You Southerners are an absolute riot." He waved the pistol at me again. "I'm done talking here, and I'm done having you spy on me at every turn. Would you like a smoke? A condemned man is entitled to a last smoke."

"I don't think I should, Mr. Free. Mom would kill me."

"*I'm* going to kill you, Spy Boy, not your mother," he reminded me, raising the pistol to a point between my eyes.

I squeezed my eyes shut and waited. I heard a 'snick', but nothing happened. His weapon had misfired. I bit the back of my hand to keep from throwing up and opened my eyes. A happy little flame danced from the tip of the gun with which he gleefully lit his fancy cigarette. He exhaled luxuriously and grinned, exhibiting perfect white teeth.

I wanted to curse him but smiled despite myself.

It hadn't been difficult for Mr. Free to sneak up on me. The wooden fence I used for cover separated his property from the Smith house behind him. Mr. Free's house sat on a corner lot, bordered on its east and west by Main and McAlister Streets respectively, and by a six-foot-high brick wall that ran up to the Smith's wood fence at the rear of his back yard, separating his house from ours. Miss Ginn lived on Lafayette Street beside the Smith house and behind me—unfortunately.

A wrought-iron fence with brick columns separated his front yard from the sidewalk that ran parallel to Main Street. When Mr. Free moved into the widow Jowers' house, mystery came with him. I rode my bike up and down the sidewalk a hundred times in a not-so-subtle attempt to catch a glimpse of our enigmatic new resident.

While sitting with my face hidden behind a Spider-Man

comic at Mr. Allen's barber shop, I'd learned that Mr. Free and Sarah Jowers were related in some way. Supposedly, he was a Yankee. I was the only one in the shop who believed there was about as much Yankee in Mr. Free as there was in me, but I chose silence and Spider-Man rather than an opinion. I was also the only one in the entire town of Eden who believed that Mr. Free didn't live alone.

Mr. Jowers had built the brick wall up to within about a foot of the Smiths' fence. On our side, the gap at the corner of the fence is covered by ivy and, from a distance, the fences appear connected.

My father calls Mr. Free's wall the Great Wall of China. It serves as the boundary between the last of the grand old Eden homes and what passes as the middle-class neighborhood. While standing in our back yard, all you can see of Mr. Free's place is the second floor. That's where I had seen the boy.

By all appearances, my victim appeared to take a break, or forgot some artist's tool. While I waited attentively for him to return to his painting, he was gathering his .45 caliber cigarette lighter, walking out his front door, down the sidewalk toward my house, and rounding the Great Wall of China. He walked the length of the wall, undetected by my parents, who were no doubt doing what they always did on a Sunday afternoon, watching television, reading, or snoozing in the den.

In less than a minute from disappearing into the bowels of his house, Mr. Free was standing behind me with his deadly cigarette lighter. My illusion of being undetectable by the average Edenite while pursuing my furtive hobby was shattered handily by a suspected Yankee who wore smocks and berets—a man who planted flowers that were the envy of every woman in Eden, a man who knew all about *covert operations*. I wasn't pleased in the least, but I *was* fascinated.

"That's real funny," I said, alternating between anger and shame with no way to control the gyrations. He ignored my discomfort with detached coolness. He sat cross-legged in the grass and smiled. "Tell me, George, why would a young man in a thriving metropolis such as Eden spend his time spying on his neighbors?"

"How do you know my name?" I asked, far more demanding than my situation gave me a right to be.

He shrugged and inhaled from his ebony holder, directing the plume of blue smoke skyward with his lower lip when he exhaled. "It's a small town. All one has to do is listen. Between the post office and your wonderfully quaint little Piggly Wiggly food store, one can hear practically anything worthy of hearing, and a great deal that isn't."

He was a quick study in the ways of a small town. Most of what I knew that I wasn't supposed to know I learned at Mr. Allen's barber shop and while tagging along behind Mom at the Piggly Wiggly. I made a mental note to spend more time in the post office. Most adults are more than happy to pretend that an inattentive kid isn't there. In a small town, gossip is hands down more addictive than booze and cigarettes.

Mr. Free didn't wait for me to answer. He removed his beret and wiped his forehead with the back of his smock sleeve. "It's hot as blazes out here, Spy Boy. How about we enjoy a libation?" he asked as he rose and disappeared into the ivy. I stood and followed but stopped at the green gate.

"What's a libation?" I asked into the ivy, shooting a glance toward the back of Miss Ginn's house. I was a goner if she had her binoculars out. I'd be cutting her grass for free for the rest of my life.

"You'll never know unless you screw up a bit of courage," he replied from the other side.

This was it—the forbidden moment—the moment all prior forbidding was intended to prevent. The apple glistened beneath a summer sun, beckoning with sweet promise.

I glanced back at my house, then slipped through the ivy with a joy in my heart that had escaped me since the day my father and I got my first kite airborne. Refusal to follow the mystery man into his lair wasn't among the remotest of options.

2

I burst through the ivy into the forbidden zone and was greeted with a smile and a thumbs-up. Shivers of excitement raced from the hollow of my neck to my heels. In three minutes, Gerard Free had moved me from the grip of terror to anger, to the glee of Saturday night at the Pavilion in Myrtle Beach and pizza by the slice. Despite the warnings from those responsible for my well-being, I was irreversibly lost.

His lawn, like his house, was beautiful. The grass, a rich, deep green, was immaculately trimmed and soft as pile carpet beneath my bare feet. Mr. Free was the first resident of Eden to install a sprinkler system, yet another peculiarity that solidified his place as our first extraterrestrial. No one in his or her right mind applied fertilizer and sprayed perfectly good water on grass that would have to be mown. Not even Mayor Harmon or Dr. Ulmer watered their lawns.

Red, white, and pink impatiens bloomed in beds of mulch along the Great Wall and the wooden fence. Crepe myrtles, laden with fat pink buds, swayed in a gentle breeze. Hummingbird feeders glowed like rubies. My mother couldn't have wrought such artistry had she cut off her own mother's green thumb and worn it around her neck.

A gigantic live oak spread its arms over Mr. Free's patio. The oak was so old its lowest limbs had dipped into the ground and reached for the sun again. The townspeople called it The Oak and it had long been a magnet for children. Before I was born, Mrs. Jowers and the town council had banned climbing it. After Mrs. Jowers passed away, I sneaked over one night and climbed the prohibited tree to its top.

Beneath the oak's canopy, an expanse of red brick tile about twenty-four feet square was surrounded by pots of flowers whose names I didn't know. Wrought-iron furniture fitted with thick padding sat beneath a gigantic green umbrella in the cool shade.

The patio and the fine lawn hadn't existed before Mr. Free's arrival. He'd rolled into town one weekend, and for months on end, the only people who saw him were the folk who worked at Eden Hardware and Lumber, the Piggly Wiggly, the post office and, of course—me.

Mr. Free didn't waste a minute acknowledging or contemplating Eden society's actions or thoughts. He restored a wonderful old home to its former splendor single-handedly and then moved into the yard to match the efforts spent on the house. He asked no one for help, and no one offered, but my mother, sweetheart that she was, did break down and take him a homemade apple pie.

With classic small-town paranoia regarding the sacred and vulnerable social status, she hadn't actually welcomed him to the neighborhood. She left the pie in a rocking chair and knocked on the front door. It's not easy being a stranger in a tiny Southern town.

I stood before his easel with wrinkled brow, trying to envision what was coming to life on the canvas. "What's this supposed to be?"

"It's the beginning of the end, young man, a portrait of the love of my life. I intend to finish it this year."

The painting was large, about four feet square. I saw a room with floor-length windows. Beyond the windows a full moon rose out of an oak-lined road. A yellow hibiscus sprouted from a white vase, and there was a post bed, but I saw no love.

"Shouldn't there be a woman?"

"She's coming, Spy Boy. She's coming any moon now." He ignored my puzzled expression and gestured toward one of the cushioned chairs. "Please, have a seat."

I looked from the painting to the chair, then back at Mr. Free. "Don't make me shoot you, Spy Boy."

He laughed at my exasperated expression. It was a genuine, infectious laugh that hinted of goodness in the man who owned it, no matter what the people of my small town thought. I did as I was told, and he clapped with delight.

"Excuse me for a moment, please," he said, rising and adding a little bow.

He returned minus his smock and beret. Instead, he wore a starched white button-down with the sleeves rolled up. Yellow suspenders were attached to crisply pressed khakis, and he'd donned brown and white wingtips. He was muscular, slender, and as graceful as a dancer.

A silver tray balanced in his left hand. He lowered the tray to the table before us and made quite the show of filling glasses with ice, Coke, and, where it was appropriate, Bacardi rum. I watched the gracious exhibition with awe and took note. He kept sodas in his house, and he used linen napkins. He had nice glasses. The only place I'd seen a real ice bucket was on *The Edge of Night,* my mom's favorite soap opera. At dinner after church, I drank from a jelly glass, and we ate our fried chicken and mashed potatoes from mismatched plates and utensils made of stainless steel. The nicest glasses I ever drank from were the tiny communion glasses at church.

"A toast," he said, raising his glass. "To friends in strange places, and to Jolie Benoit."

I took my glass carefully in hand and raised it. "To friends in strange places," I repeated, unable to stifle a grin. I'd been loathing the approach of another lonely, boring summer. Instead, I'd landed smack in the middle of wonderland.

He took a sip of his libation and leveled his piercing gaze on me. "Tell me something, Spy Boy."

"Okay."

"Why aren't you supposed to be here?"

The man's intuition was intimidating. I allowed a darting ruby-throat to pull my eyes away as it maneuvered for a place at one of the many feeders. "I don't know what you mean," I lied.

"You know exactly what I mean," he said, his voice stern. He sipped from his drink again and smiled, his eyes clear and full of confidence.

I drank from my own glass, once again averting my eyes. I studied the woodwork beneath the giant umbrella overhead. I'd never seen a yard umbrella, either. Mom had one umbrella that she used for going to church and funerals in the rain. Mr. Free had nice things.

"Spy Boy?"

I braced myself and met his gaze squarely. "Because everyone thinks you're strange. Everyone thinks that you're a Yankee."

This outburst made my stomach roll. I didn't have conversations with adults, much less strange adults. On occasion, I went with my mother to see her 'female doctor' in Florence. My mother referred to Dr. Johnson as a 'female doctor' because 'gynecologist' sounded too much like 'vagina' to suit her.

Anyway, trips to Florence constituted my encounters with strangers. Even then, we didn't actually have verbal exchanges. Except for the occasional playground scuffle, my world was easy and quiet. I knew nearly everyone within the boundaries of Eden, at least everyone who attended the Methodist church downtown—about everybody save for the 'illiterate Baptists,' as Pop referred to them. Conversations with adults consisted of how old I was now, how my parents were doing, and what grade I was in. Occasionally, they asked what I wanted to be when I grew up. People talked at me, not to me.

"Well, I *am* strange, Spy Boy, but I'm damned sure no Yankee, and there's no reason on earth to be afraid of me."

It was my turn to laugh.

"What's so funny?"

"You held me at gunpoint with a cigarette lighter. You've never spoken to me in your life, and you held me at gunpoint. How'd you know I wouldn't run away screaming bloody murder?"

"I just knew. I have a sense about such things." He took a swallow from his glass and smacked his lips. "This is the quintessential adult libation, young man," he said, holding his glass up, turning it this way and that. "The only thing in the world finer than a beautiful woman is a little Coke with rum in it."

He fitted another Gauloises Caporal into the ebony holder and squinted into the distance as he leaned to retrieve a Zippo from his pocket.

"I've forgotten who said it," he said, raising the Zippo in the air. "No, wait a minute, I'm pretty sure it was Sinatra. Yep, that's who it was." He flipped the top on the Zippo and winked at me. "'I feel sorry for people who don't drink. When they wake up in the morning, that's as good as they're going to feel all day.'"

"Where'd you read that?"

He arched his eyebrows, rolled the wheel on the Zippo, and smiled. "Who said I read it?" he asked with another laugh. His laughter sounded so nice I couldn't help but join. I sipped more Coke and silently agreed with my new friend. It'd be hard to find anything that tasted better.

"Why do you spy on people?" he asked, touching the Zippo's flame to the tip of his cigarette, and inhaling.

I looked down at my glass and watched the tiny bubbles float to the surface. "Because I'm bored. Eden is so boring during summers I think I'm going to die sometimes."

"Don't you have any friends?"

"Can't say that I do," I said, deciding to reverse the roles. "Mr. Free, who's Jolie?"

His blue eyes locked onto mine and he nodded. "Jolie Benoit is the love of my life. She left me some time ago, but I believe that she'll soon return. As for friends, well, you have one now, and I have a feeling that your summer is going to be anything but boring." He leaned across the table, his hand extended.

I eyed the steady hand for a couple of seconds, and then took it firmly in my own. He squeezed, and a shock ran up my arm, settling in the hollow of my neck at the base of my skull like a tiny bolt of lightning. I shivered all over.

"Friends," he said, shaking firmly.

"Friends," I repeated, wondering what on earth had just happened to me. I'd pushed my luck far enough for one day. I finished the Coke and rose to leave.

"Visit anytime you feel the coast is clear, Spy Boy. Use the secret knock, so I'll know not to get my gun."

"What secret knock?"

"Why, *shave and a haircut*. What other secret knock is there?"

I was about halfway across the lawn when he spoke again. "Spy Boy." I turned. Sunlight filtered through the oak and lit his smile. "It was nice of your mother to leave the pie."

I've always believed he followed that with, "Welcome to the summer of your life," but that's just the way my head works sometimes.

3

Eden is a Southern town for which the word *sleepy* was coined. Her roots can be traced to an Indian settlement where the natives found the Black River easiest to negotiate. From the small settlement, footpaths snaked into the forests, darkened by tall pines, and meandered beneath moss-draped oaks into swamps where cypress trees towered and alligators slumbered in the sun. Game was plentiful and many things were traded throughout the years in Eden by many unusual types of people—not all of them good.

No one knows how Eden's name originated, but local historians suspect it was shortly after the eradication of indigenous Native American tribes, when churches came to the little settlement that perched on the bluff of Black River.

The roar of cannons released on Fort Sumter made things difficult for a while, but Eden fared better than most. Her sister city to the south, Charleston, received the lion's share of the federal government's attention, and things were good until sail switched to steam.

The past doesn't die, despite the efforts of ministers with biblical names and mayors with deceptive smiles, especially in a place where evil once lived. Those looking for remnants of bygone magic that might prove useful may ride into town on big white stallions or sitting behind the wheel of a big white Cadillac convertible.

Eden's streets are wide and protected by live oaks that have been smiled upon by the fates. For the most part, the beautiful old trees have been spared the onslaught of hurricanes, lightning storms, hail, wind, fire, drought, and, as mentioned, war. They've endured the scampering hands and feet of generations of little Edenites, provided cool shade and protection from the rain and wind for every critter brave enough to take advantage of their sturdy kindness. The people of Eden love the oaks the way a dog loves a scratch. They're born and buried beneath the shadows of the old trees. None of them remember the Indians. Asphalt sidewalks wind their way past homes with lawns carpeted with St. Augustine. In spring, azaleas burst onto the stage with pink, red, and white glory. Dogwood and bay laurel do their best to compete as wisteria weaves its innocuous way into places it shouldn't, a tapestry trying in vain to hide things that can't be hidden. I knew that darkness lived in my town, but it was like being born into a crazy family; the world is what it is, and the darkness had never threatened me.

Nearly all of Eden's finer old residences have been passed down through the generations to the chosen in families born to preserve and cultivate wealth. Except for Andrew Thomas's house, the cream of the crop from the glory days was located along the river.

Andrew owned a Queen Anne Victorian built by his physician father on the highest plot of land in Eden. The three-story beauty sported a turret tower that housed the oddest collection of colored bottles I'd ever seen.

Neckbone Rodriguez collected the bottles but nobody in town knew why, nor did they know why Andrew hung them in the turret room windows. The bottles sparkled in the sunlight like a jewel collection and glowed like soft amber in the moonlight. Pop once told me that a town would tolerate almost any sort of behavior if enough money came with it. Mr. Andrew had more money than God.

Andrew was a big man who dressed in white Mark Twain suits and was a bona fide WWII war hero who walked the streets at night with a Confederate Calvary sword resting across his shoulder. I'd seen him standing in the cemeteries on moonlit nights talking as if he was giving a speech at the Rotary Club. He was scary as hell and no kid I knew would darken his door for candy on Halloween night or consider a *trick*.

The caste system of Eden is simple and, for the most part, permanent. If you live in one of the homes built before the first of the larger ships ground its keel into the mud of the bay, you're a blue blood, or you share the name of bluebloods buried in Eden's oldest cemeteries, even if the gods of wealth didn't continue to smile upon your family.

If you live outside the 'old district' to the east, you're middle class and expected to live quietly and be happy in the shadows of the upper tier. My family managed to lay claim to the middle-class section of town by the skin of its chromosomes.

If you travel Main Street through downtown, cross the Black River Bridge and the railroad tracks, you enter the trash-strewn world known as Bangalang, Eden's version of the slums. It's also the home of tough-as-nails kids led by Butch Sinclair, the Billy the Kid of small-town bullies—my very own personal tyrant, and holy terror to any other kid from my side of the tracks that happens his way.

4

What are you going to do today, young man?" my mother asked, scraping eggs from a cast-iron frying pan that had belonged to her mother's mother. Bacon smoke swirled blue in the morning sunlight beaming through the window set over the sink.

She was my mother, but I could see her beauty, a 'turn your head to watch her walk down the sidewalk' kind of woman, if there was a hint of male in you.

I thought of Mr. Allen, one of Eden's two town barbers. He handed out Super Bubble with every haircut, and I'd forgotten mine. I returned for my bubblegum, unbeknownst to my unwary barber. "I'm tellin' you fellahs, she looks like Elizabeth Taylor, or I ain't the best damned barber in the South." He turned to see me with my hand in the bubblegum jar and flushed beet red. I grinned and took two pieces.

"I think Buster and I are going fishing," I said, thinking that she did look like Elizabeth Taylor, and that Mr. Allen was the dirtiest old man I knew.

"You going to catch us a mess for supper?" she asked, placing my plate before me with the same smile that worked magic on Mr. Allen.

I shrugged. The best fishing was on Mingo, but to get there I had to navigate Bangalang. I'd rather have a stick in my eye than face Butch Sinclair during summer vacation. "Maybe I'd better have a backup plan," I answered with a frown. "I'm going to try fishing on the north side today."

"Aw, you know everybody goes to Mingo this time of year. Are you avoiding the crowds again?"

"Well, Mom, the fishing is usually better where there isn't a party going on." My explanation made good fish sense, but I could see she wasn't buying. I fished to avoid people, and she knew it.

"Okay, how about fried chicken and mashed potatoes if you don't come through, my little fisherman?"

"With gravy?"

"Of course, with gravy," she said, tousling my short-cropped hair.

I finished breakfast while Mom made a peanut butter and jelly sandwich for my lunch. "You know, you ought to try hanging out with the rest of the kids a little this summer, George. You might make a friend, maybe even two."

I watched as she wrapped the sandwich in wax paper and placed it in a brown paper bag with a blue pig printed on its side. She sliced an orange with patience and the easy grace that mothers who love being mothers have. I rose to put my plate in the sink, and she turned to embrace me. She smelled like Ivory soap, fresh-washed clothes, and hairspray. I wanted to break away for the sake of teen rebellion but cheated and breathed deeply of motherly essence instead.

"George, did you hear me?" she asked gently.

"Okay, Mom, I will."

"No, you won't."

"Mom, come on."

"I'm just saying that you shouldn't ignore kids your own age in a town this small. It isn't healthy. You may grow up and live here just like your father and me, God forbid."

I gave her the sort of expression that comes with smelling something dead. "I'm feeling faint just thinking about it."

"Don't be a smartie, George. You made friends in Cub Scouts, remember?"

"Yes, ma'am," I said with a sigh.

Buster was waiting by the back door alongside Lightning, my bike. Except when I sneak him in, Buster's almost always by the back door, or underneath the porch by the back door. He's a brindled, deluxe model, Heinz 57, black-with-jagged-brown striping that goes back to a memory of when I was crawling on his back because Roy Rogers showed me how. Buster's probably the chief reason I have so few friends. With friends like Buster, a boy just doesn't need that many more.

A car hit Buster a couple of years ago, leaving him with the ability to prick one ear to attention, while the other refuses to respond. It'd be safe to say that Buster isn't in the Lassie class of intellect, but he hasn't come close to being hit by another car. Buster's the rare form of perfection that I won't have to lose to understand. I know exactly what a boy and his dog, God's perfect pairing, means.

I got my pole and tackle box, then dropped the orange slices in my cricket bucket, tossing a few rolled-up comics in the basket along with my sandwich, water, and fishing stuff. If I wasn't catching any fish, I could at least do some reading. Buster and I rolled out of town in a northerly direction. I was disgusted with myself for not having the guts to deal with Bangalang and Butch, but not so disgusted that I'd turn around and head in the direction of Mingo Creek.

Buster loped along behind. He'd traveled with me like this since Christmas when I got Lightning, a twenty-six-inch Murray that sunlight danced on the same way it dances on the river.

About a mile out of town, I took a right down a slow grade into a grove of trees and onto a shaded sandy road. I didn't actually know where I was going.

Pedaling was difficult, so I got off and pushed. Cool sand sifted through my toes. Birds flitted about in the trees and sunlight dappled the road through the leafy canopy. The aroma of wet, fertile earth hung heavy in the air.

Buster kept darting off into the woods, chasing the visible and the invisible. His excited bark echoed through the woods, tinged with the frenzy that comes with running free. From time to time he burst onto the road to check on me, dripping wet and muddy, his slick red tongue pouring from one side of his panting mouth. He barked at me with one ear pointed skyward and the other bent in two.

"You're an idiot," I said. He responded with another bark,

his bright eyes concentrating on mine, his tail whipping like an antenna in the wind, and then he dove back into the undergrowth. Fish or no fish, I hadn't wasted this morning.

Shortly, I came to a cow pasture. An old Ford coupe rested on rusty wheels in the grass, its hood open as if it had coughed its motor into orbit.

Relics like the old Ford fascinate me and I stopped for a study. Who'd driven it? Where had it been before losing its heart? Had it hauled bank robbers, bootleg whiskey, or famous people? Had kids, now grandparents, made love in its backseat?

"You ain't going to catch any fish today, Bubba," a strange voice said.

I jumped like I'd been shot in the ass with a BB gun. I'd been going about my way under the impression that Buster and I were alone on the planet. I looked around but saw no one.

"You ain't crazy," came the voice. "I'm talking to you." I shaded my eyes and peered into the woods.

"Some spy you are," the voice said. "I'm up here."

I scanned the trees. About fifty yards to my right, standing on a fat limb in the top of a pine that soared a good seventy feet into the air, was the strangest-looking boy I'd ever laid eyes on—the boy in Mr. Free's second-story window.

He was bone thin with curls of bright red jutting from beneath a leather WWI aviator's cap. He gave me a freckle-faced grin that was minus a prominent tooth. He sported knee-high leather boots, a worn leather bomber jacket, and a pair of dark goggles.

An odd contraption that looked like the guard from a window fan was strapped to his back. He wore a harness with chains attached like those that held up the porch swing at home. The chains were fixed to the U of the handle of a huge yellow umbrella resting across his shoulder.

"I know you," I said.

His grin faded. "No, you don't."

I shrugged. There were lots of questions to ask this kid, but the boy in me went for the meat. "How'd you get up there?" I asked. He was, undoubtedly, the greatest tree climber I'd ever seen.

He extended one of his booted feet. Spiked steel braces were strapped to the boots, the kind that power company linemen wore. "Climbed up like a monkey with these babies." I'd never heard such a strange accent. Envy washed over me like a wave at Pawleys. "What in the world are you *doing*?"

"I'm about to take flight, Bubba. Looks like it might be wager time," he said, grinning down at me. "I been in a lot of trouble for betting, Bubba, but once more prolly ain't gonna hurt nothing."

"My name's not Bubba."

"I know your name, George."

Something touched my leg and I looked down at Buster. He was staring up at the crazy kid with just as much curiosity as I had, his one active ear doing every trick it knew. "How do you know my name?" I asked.

"I get around, Bubba. You want to bet, or you just gonna stand there and jabber?"

"I don't have anything to bet," I said.

"Well, it don't matter. Just as well I bet myself. Makes paying off easier." He pointed at Buster. "That there dog says he wants to see some action."

"Well, you were gonna fly whether I came along or not," I said, suspecting that he was where he was because he knew I was going to be in this place, as well as when.

"Right you are." With this he reached underneath his right arm, grabbed a handle, and pulled. A quick succession of burping sounds erupted, and blades whirled inside the cage mounted to his back.

"Holy crap," I said. Buster barked, his tail thumping against my leg.

The kid pulled again, and the burps rolled out but nothing happened. "Patience, Bubba. This thing don't always want to come to life, it being mechanical and all."

I didn't utter a word. I'd seen crazy kids before. Bangalang was full of them, but I'd never seen one of the Bangalang kids come anywhere near a stunt like this. This sort of thing took imagination.

The little motor finally roared to life. It sounded exactly like my grandfather's Homelite chainsaw with its feisty, popping rhythm. Red raced the little motor a few times and the blades pushed leaves and limbs as they whirred into invisibility.

The very strange, very skinny kid gave me quick thumbs-up and opened the huge umbrella. At this point, he lost balance. "Oh my Lord," I whispered and knelt to put my arm around Buster. Abandoning the attempt to regain his footing, he revved the motor into a growling buzz and jumped.

The inevitable didn't happen. Red floated over the pasture with easy grace, a broken grin on his face and a maniacal cackle competing with the din of the ferocious little motor.

I burst into delighted laughter and applause, but the show proved short-lived. The umbrella's mechanism folded upward like in the cartoons and circus acts. Red fell like a brickbat, landing on his back atop the old Ford with a resounding wallop.

Dust billowed from the rusted hulk. Broken parts of flying machine whizzed past Buster and me like shrapnel, a razor-sharp piece removing a nick from my right earlobe that felt like a bee sting.

"Holy shit," I exclaimed, pinching my ear between thumb and forefinger.

"Ooooooooooh," Red moaned.

"Are you hurt?" I asked, blinking, and reddening instantly from the absurdity of my question. It was a wonder he wasn't dead.

Red's head rolled toward me, and he pushed the goggles up on his forehead. Green eyes made me take a stutter-step backward. I don't mean that muddy sort of green that people have. I mean bright green, like the green in a crystal marble with a twirl the color of lime-flavored Kool-Aid inside.

"What in the hell do you think, Bubba? I think I broke my damn back, but it ain't the first time. It's gonna hurt like hell till I go completely paralyzed." He raised his right hand at the elbow and began to count on his fingers. "I can't remember if I counted for the weight of the motor and prop. I jumped off the church roof a dozen times with this umbrella and had no trouble at all."

I mustered a silent gaze of stupidity by way of response. This was my first broken back experience. He'd slammed down onto the roof of the old car hard enough to drive it another inch in the ground.

Oddly enough, Mr. Free and his mischievous smile occurred to me. If my crazy neighbor hadn't held his cigarette-lighting gun to my head Sunday, this episode would be freaking me out.

"Tell me what to do," I said.

"Do I look like a doctor? I'm a damned aviator, Bubba. I don't have a clue what to tell you to do." He pronounced aviator *a-vee-a-TOR*, and I grinned again but only for a second. I didn't like smiling at someone with a broken back.

"How old are you?" I asked.

"You're kidding, right?"

"Well, you cuss like a grown-up."

"It's a good thing I got a broke back," he said, trying to sit up. He halted the effort immediately, his face a mask of pain.

"Why's that?"

"'Cause, otherwise, I'd have to beat your ass for being so stupid."

"You don't have to be rude."

"I know I don't hafta."

"I need to get help. I don't think I ought to move you."

"So, now *you're* a doctor?"

"No, I'm not a doctor," I said, finding his flippancy amazing. There was nothing to keep me from picking up a nice, heavy stick and flailing the snot out of him.

"Okay, I know exactly what you need to do, Reverend George."

"Get a doctor?" I said, wondering how he was connected to Mr. Free.

"No, you need to take that path where the pasture ends and follow it down to the river. I think you'll find what you're looking for down there." He grimaced, raised his right hand, and pointed.

I had to look twice to see the opening. I would have walked right past it. "Okay, I see it. Then what?" When the aviator didn't answer, I looked back, and he was gone.

I stood motionless, staring at the vacated roof of the car, listening to the pounding of blood against my eardrums. A crow flew over and cawed at Buster and me. The crow lit in the tree that the aviator had jumped out of not a minute before.

"Buster?" I said, looking down at my dog, my voice small and afraid. Buster gazed at me with his patient, bright eyes, his spittle-dotted tongue lolling from his mouth. "Buster, did you see that boy crash into the roof of the car?" He wagged as if he understood but said not a word.

A taste like nickel and vinegar rose on the back of my tongue and I bent over, spewing Mom's wonderful breakfast at my feet. This was worse than Mr. Free's gun. Mr. Free's gun had been fake, which meant that he was playing a crude joke on me. But this flying boy hadn't been there—I didn't *think*.

I touched my forefinger to my earlobe and drew back a tiny dot of blood. *How would an imaginary boy whom you made up know to point out a path that you didn't know was there?*

The path led to a clearing on the river. Buster drank at the water's edge, then shot off into the woods again. Sunlight spattered itself on a beach of pale brown sand through river birches swaying in a soft breeze. It was a perfect fishing spot because it allowed for swimming, and it was all mine.

Black River winds a snaky path toward the Atlantic. She is a wonderful, dangerous creature and she rarely offers the ease of access to her mesmerizing embrace that a beach provides.

Of the magic in my life, and there is plenty—Mom, Pop, dog, sunlight, and nature—the Black River touches the part of my spirit closest to the Maker. She's a mysterious, untamed beauty with secrets hidden in the silence of time. She's mother to a world of breathtaking wildlife and she provides a home for one of my favorite creatures of all, the red-breast bream.

If you disrespect the river, she'll take your life without so much as an extra shimmer at sunset to acknowledge that she knew you, played with you, or murdered you for carelessness.

I leaned Lightning against a tree, removed my T-shirt, waded in to about thigh high, and sat down. Water the color of strong tea cooled and soothed. I closed my eyes and listened to the music of the woods and creatures that fed from the river's edge.

"I believe you're in my swimming hole, white boy," a voice said from behind me. I opened my eyes and tried to remember if I'd seen any *No Trespassing* signs. All I could see was my new friend dropping from the sky like a hickory nut.

The voice was feminine, nice, and didn't sound threatening, but that didn't mean she wasn't holding a twelve-gauge at my back, *and* she'd called me *white boy*. The woods around Eden are loaded with game, as well as people who know how to kill it. The option that she couldn't hit the backside of a barn because she was a she wasn't comforting.

"I...I'm sorry," I said, wondering where in the heck Buster had run off to. The girl had sneaked up on me like Vance Baker's grandkids sneak up on him to inspect his pockets and draw on his face with Magic Markers when he's passed out on the front porch.

"Whatcha doin' down here?" she asked.

"Fishing."

"That's the strangest looking fishing I've ever seen."

"I'm trying a new technique. I'm holding a baited hook between my legs."

She giggled. It was a nice sound, and I smiled. "I just bet you are," she said.

I turned for a glance, and my mouth fell open. There were girls in Eden whom I was beginning to appreciate as pretty— lots of them, in fact—but as my eyes roamed this one from tip to toe, I realized that I'd never before seen a girl so alluring.

Her skin was the color of the caramel my mother uses to

make Halloween apples. Her lips were full and formed with the ability to make a boy think about kissing when she spoke. Her straight white teeth worked in conjunction with her mouth to form a smile that lit her round face with radiance. Light brown eyes, the color of dark amber, twinkled behind a pair of round gold-rimmed glasses. She wore a snug-fitting T-shirt and a pair of short, faded cutoff blue jeans.

The utter lack of control over my eyes made me uncomfortable, but I was powerless to stop their shameless hunger. She appeared perfectly proportioned—her arms, legs, and breasts that pushed at the thin material of the cotton tee with pride and a definite disdain for gravity formed a package so sweetened with seduction that this fourteen-year-old male couldn't even pretend to ignore it.

"You like me, don't you?"

My cheeks flushed purple all the way to my ears, and I forced my spellbound eyes into the trees.

"And he's shy," she teased.

"Maybe," I said. I didn't know how to talk to a girl. I hardly knew how to talk to anyone my own age. "It's just…"

"Just what?"

I looked at her again. "It's just that you're so beautiful," I blurted. I would've turned redder if it was possible.

"Well, shy and sweet makes a pretty nice combination, white boy."

"Why do you call me that?"

"Because you are."

"How old are you?" I asked.

"I'm sixteen. Why do you ask?"

"I don't know. I seem to be asking that a lot lately. I guess you sound older."

"I have an old soul, which probably makes me older than sixteen, but they still measure it in birthdays."

I didn't know what this statement meant, but I figured it would come to me in time. "I'm sixteen too," I lied. It wasn't a very big lie. I'd be fifteen in August.

"Nice to meet you, Sixteen. I'm Iris."

Iris. It was a beautiful name for a beautiful girl. I grew quiet, slowly regaining the ability to concentrate on the world around me. A basket lay on the ground at her feet. Next to the basket sat my silent, ever-so-innocent Heinz, staring at me with all the puppy righteousness that he was still capable of mustering.

"I see you've met my guard dog," I said. Buster hung his head and whined.

"What's his name?"

"The cur's name is Buster," I said.

She bent to scratch one of Buster's ears and his tail took off. "Buster and I have things in common. Don't be too rough on him."

I had a powerful craving for a caramel apple and found myself wanting to lick this girl to see what she tasted like. Not only that. I mourned the death of whatever once made me stick my tongue out at girls, but I was grateful that the last of this idiocy had just died at the hands of a beauty named Iris.

"I've never seen you before," I said.

"I don't go into town often, sometimes with Daddy," she said, her smile fading.

"Maybe we could get some ice cream or go to the movies," I hopefully suggested.

She extended her leg and dug in the sand with her big toe. Her foot was delicately arched, and her ankle slender, swelling with flawless curvature into a calf that I imagined would flex with irresistible attraction atop a stiletto heel.

"Maybe," she said. "You don't even know me, and you've already asked me on an official date. You like what you see, not what you know."

"I don't have to know you," I said, gaining a tad of confidence.

"Why not?"

"That's what dates are for, and Buster likes you. That's all I need to know."

Her smile returned and she dropped a leather satchel that

I'd barely noticed by the basket and waded into the water. She sat by me and gazed into my eyes. She was even prettier up close, and I prayed to God not to say anything stupid. Her curly brown hair, strands dyed near blond by the sun, smelled like honeysuckle, and I wondered again what she would taste like.

"I don't have any friends," she said. "Folk come around the store, but I don't know anyone that I would call a friend."

"The store?"

"My granny owns a store down on the river."

I knew the place she was talking about, and her white boy reference suddenly made sense. Her granny was Sugar Hannah; folks called her Shug for short, a name that conjured more mysterious tales and rumors than New Orleans's infamous Marie Laveau. Iris carried heavy baggage, which went a long way toward explaining her apparent fearlessness. It would bring trouble unlike any I could imagine, but I decided in a blink that I didn't care who Iris's grandmother was. I didn't care who any of her people were.

"You're too pretty not to have any friends."

"Pretty only gets you so far, Sixteen," she said. She kept glancing over at a cluster of wax myrtles that hid our little beach from river traffic. I wondered if we were being watched.

"I wouldn't know. I've never been pretty. I'm not even very nice-looking. My name's George," I said, extending my hand and cursing myself.

"Isn't that a girl's name?"

"It most certainly is not," I huffed.

"Don't be so easy, George," she said, bumping me with her shoulder. She stood and turned, her sweetly curved buttock and buttery-smooth thigh inches from my face. Blood rushed to my groin and my cheeks flushed crimson again.

She looked down at me. Her wet shirt outlined her breasts, and her nipples jutted like small brown thimbles. She smiled. "Lotsa men look at me like you're looking at me, George, but none of them actually like me."

"I…I'm not a man," I stammered.

"You got all the right parts," she said and walked back up to the hill. She opened her basket, removed a towel, and began to dry off. I tried not to lick my lips.

"What's in the satchel?" I asked.

"Pretty things," she said, opening the satchel and removing a yellow ribbon. She tied her wavy mane back and smiled. "There's also a hot air balloon, an exotic island with strange creatures, and a submarine."

I'd never been in love before, so I wasn't sure what it felt like, but I'd never actually wanted to take a girl home with me to keep. "How'd you fit all that in there?"

"I would think a comic book reader would already know the answer to that question," she said, reaching into the satchel and pulling out a book. "*The Mysterious Island*," she said. "Do you know it?"

"I don't think I do," I said, disappointed to admit as much.

"Bet you know another, *20,000 Leagues Under the Sea*."

"Holy cow, that's Jules Verne? Is it as good as *20,000 Leagues?*"

"It's better."

"Is not."

"Don't be a snot."

"Excuse me?"

"You admitted to not reading it. How can you say it isn't better than *20,000 Leagues?*"

I shrugged. "Maybe because I don't want it to be."

"That's a good enough answer. I didn't want it to be either."

"I bet it's in the library. The next time we meet, I'll give you a report."

"Just read your comics and leave the serious stuff to me, Sixteen."

"Nothing wrong with a comic. I learn a lot from them."

"Like how to fly and spurt spider webs from your wrists?"

"Who's being the snot now?"

She dropped her book on her satchel, eyeing the wax myrtles again. "I got to collect my catch," she said.

"What catch? I don't see a pole."

She rolled her eyes and waded back into the water almost to her neck, where she untied a string from a lower limb. To my surprise, she dragged a catfish that weighed every bit of ten pounds up onto the beach. I was finally able to take my eyes off her without extraordinary effort.

"That's a big one," I said, impressed with the catch.

"Come on, it's a baby."

"It looks plenty big to me."

"That's because you spend all your time fishing for bait."

"Bait?"

"Those pretty little red breasts, they're bait fish. Don't even try to tell me you don't fish for bream. I saw your pole, and your orange slices." The big cat flopped around a bit, so she dragged it farther up on the bank.

"Okay, you win. I fish for bream. I wouldn't have a clue how to catch a cat that big."

She dug into her satchel again and removed a little cloth bag with a drawstring. She untied the string, poured circles of silver into her palm, and then extended her hand. Sunlight danced on polished stainless steel. "They're circle hooks, Sixteen. You slip on a chunk of your baitfish late in the afternoon, tie them off, and collect the treasure the next day. The cat has fought all night, so there isn't much to landing him. Hold out your hand."

I did as I was told, and she dropped two hooks into my palm. "Set the hooks before dark and check them early the next morning. It's cruel not to check them early."

"But you weren't here early."

"This is my third trip. I usually load my basket around seven in the morning."

"Right."

"The hook's a secret, Sixteen. Granny makes them. You can't tell anyone, okay?"

"Okay," I said, my mouth open in awe, pretty much the way it was when I first laid eyes on her. I had something in my hand that had been crafted by Shug Hannah herself.

She put the catfish in her basket, her book back in her satchel, and turned to me. "You're nice, Sixteen. Really nice. You'll see me again. I don't stay in the woods all the time, but you may not be the same person you are here when next we meet. I know how people are."

"Maybe you don't know people the way you think," I said.

She stepped in close and kissed me lightly on the lips. Just like that I was relieved of sweet-sixteen-and-never-been-kissed worries. She moved her mouth close to my ear. "Set the hooks during a full moon. They work best then. And take care of you," she whispered, her lips grazing my ear.

5

Buster was gone. I swayed slowly on our front porch swing reliving the last time I'd seen him—Tuesday, while eating a peanut butter and jelly sandwich. A hungry dog is the most attentive creature on the planet. Buster had elevated begging to an art form. I could never eat all of anything when he was present with his dog eyes and keep a clear conscience.

A lone female had galloped by with a pack of his cousins in hot pursuit and Buster hadn't hesitated to join them. I called for him but he never looked back, peanut butter or no peanut butter. As he grew smaller in the distance I thought of Iris and shook my head. I understood completely.

I tried to remember the longest I'd gone without seeing Buster, which was probably when we went on vacations, usually to the Smoky Mountains in the fall. Even then, it was me leaving Buster, not the other way around.

A copy of *The Mysterious Island* rested on the swing by my side. Iris was right, the book was better than *Twenty Thousand Leagues Under the Sea*, but I couldn't concentrate. This was a bad sign in and of itself, and it made me angry with Buster—between the moments that I was trying to hold back tears.

"You're getting new neighbors, George, did you know that?" I knew the voice that pulled me from my miserable Buster reverie well.

"Hey, Mr. Hugh, how are you today?"

"Doing fine. Are you enjoying summer vacation?"

It was the first in what would be a long series of questions about summer vacation from Eden's adults. "Yes, sir, lots," I answered, wondering why adults had such a challenging time making conversation with kids and vice versa.

If I'd known Hugh McVey better, I would've known that he struggled with conversation because he was shy and because, with certain people, he wanted to make sure that he said the right things.

"Catching any fish?"

"I went Monday, but I didn't catch anything." *I got caught, but I didn't catch,* I thought, seeing Iris standing in the sunshine in my mind's eye. "How do you know I'm getting a new neighbor?" I was supposed to be a spy and didn't know someone was moving into my neighborhood?

"There's a truck down at the old Snowden house. Looks like a young family. I saw little girls riding tricycles in the yard. They looked like twins."

Mr. Hugh has dark eyes. He's tall and slender with thinning hair, a large thin nose, and a bulging Adam's apple. He wears pressed slacks, and in the summer a white, short-sleeve button-down with a tie and polished black or brown wingtips. In the cooler months he wears a sports coat. I know this because every day since I developed a memory, he's repeated the same routine in similar dress on his way back and forth to work.

Hugh McVey is different than most men. I think it's his gentle way. He's quiet almost to a fault, but he treats everyone who comes into his store as if he or she is the most important customer he has. Mom says he's so quiet because he's sad, and that he's sad because he lost his children. He's the only adult that I've ever seen visit Pug Ginn. From time to time, I'll ride my bike past the Ginn's place and see Mr. Hugh sitting quietly in a rocker, watching the traffic pass by with Pug. Mr. Hugh will wave, and Pug will drool.

At the end of every summer since I can remember, Mom and I have gone to Mr. Hugh's department store to buy school clothes. I like Mr. Hugh the way you like people without question in a small town.

"I hope you have better luck with the fishing, George," he said and gave me a little wave. "It was good talking to you." He looked at me the way my father sometimes does when he's telling me that he loves me but doesn't want to say it because in the South that's the way men are.

"Maybe someday we could go together, Mr. Hugh." I don't know why I said this. It just came out.

The invitation stopped him in his tracks. "That sounds nice, George," he said, blessing me with a rare smile. "Really nice." He turned to go on his way, and I watched him walk toward town, his head down.

Buster was only a small part of my troubles. I was in a quandary over Iris too. As Mrs. Patterson, my sixth-grade English teacher would say, I was *conflicted*. If it hadn't been for Buster disappearing, meeting Iris might have been the only thing I could think about. The mysterious girl was a spell caster. She was also an exotic, forbidden blend of the colored and white races. In other words, she was a great deal of trouble—bad trouble.

I understood what she'd meant about meeting in a different time and place. I watched and listened to the people in my world. I knew the sort of reception Iris would get if I invited her to church or to a party, not that I was ever invited or would go to a party.

I set the swing into motion, bringing a comforting rhythm from rusty chain hooks, and opened *The Mysterious Island* for the tenth time. I needed to escape into Verne's world to avoid the tendrils of fear enveloping my heart. I didn't care if my dog was out having a little fun. I cared about whether he was coming home.

"There's someone close who can tell you where your dog is, Bubba."

I almost jumped out of the swing. My redheaded aviator was standing on the top porch step, grinning like a drunkard.

"How's your broken back?" I asked. I debated bolting for sanity's sake, but he'd used the magic word—*dog*.

"All healed up," he said with a gracious bow. He wore a pair of red silk boxers and a yellow cape, but no shirt or shoes. His aviator goggles perched atop his leather cap and his protruding red curls blazed in the sunlight. He drilled me with his eerie green eyes. I noted the odd designs of the scars sprouting from his chest and shoulders. The boy had known a great deal of pain in his day.

"I know you aren't really there," I said.

"That ain't a very healthy habit, Bubba."

"What ain't healthy?"

"Lying to yourself like that. I know I'm here, and you know it too."

"I'm not crazy," I said, sounding crazy simply as a result of denying it. I wondered if I looked as crazy as I felt.

"Maybe, maybe not. A man who lies to himself so easy can't say one way or the other, now can he?"

"What's your name?"

"My name is Francois Dulcet. I hail from the Crescent City, and I am an aviator extraordinaire."

"Why are you here?" I asked. I wanted to ask where the heck Crescent City was but was loathe to confirm my status as a small-town hick.

"I'm here because you have something most people don't, George."

"And what might that be?" I asked.

"Imagination. You have a wonderful imagination, but that isn't the only reason I'm here today. I know how you can find Buster."

"How'd you know about Buster?"

"I already told you, Bubba, I get around."

"Why would you help me with my dog?"

"Because I was asked to help you."

"Who asked you to help me?"

"Hunh—uhn," he said, wagging a skinny, crooked forefinger. "Too many questions for such a young one." He gave me a big grin; the gap where a front tooth once sprouted daring me not to stare and making me smile at the same time.

"Where's my dog?"

"I can't tell you that."

"You are a frustrating aviator," I said, pronouncing the word the way he did. I was by no means a fighter, but this kid had a way of getting my dander up. I wondered if he was real enough to punch in the mouth. "Didn't you just say you were here to tell me how to find Buster?"

"Yes, tell you *how*, not where. Someone else has to tell you where."

"Well, who might that someone else be?"

"His name is Pug, Pug Ginn. All you have to do is ask him."

My face clouded with anger. "That isn't funny, Francois."

"It ain't supposed to be funny. You have to ask him at night, during the next full moon. Ask him then and you'll find out where Buster is."

"George? George, who on earth are you talking to?" my mother asked, pushing the screen door open far enough to give me the mother's eye. I looked from her to Francois. He was gone—vanished into thin air—just like smoke from a castaway cigarette.

"Nobody, Mom. I wasn't talking to nobody."

"I wasn't talking to nobody," she repeated with a shake of her head. "Mrs. Patterson would love that one, wouldn't she?" She waited for me to answer, but I blinked at her instead.

"George, honey, I know you're worried about Buster, but he'll come back home in his own time. This is a Mother Nature thing. You understand that, don't you?"

Brother, did I ever.

"Read your book. I'm going to bake you some chocolate chip cookies."

I followed Mom inside and stopped at the phone table to check the calendar. The moon was going to be full again on Tuesday, the ninth. Iris had told me to set my circle hook during a full moon. I thought about Buster and Iris, and Mr. Free and Francois Dulcet, my imaginary whatever. It was a weird summer already but good.

I walked into the kitchen to watch Mom make cookies. "Mom?"

"Yes, dear."

"What happened to Pug Ginn?"

She scooped a cup of flour from the big tin in the corner, set it on the countertop, and turned toward me, wiping slender hands on a worn apron. Her loving expression morphed into motherly curiosity.

"Why the sudden interest in Pug?"

"I was just wondering if he's always been that way. He can't even read a book."

No one knows you like your mother until you get married, or so I've been told. She studied me with beautiful blue eyes full of answers to questions that hadn't been asked. No matter how I phrased my reason for asking about Pug, Mom knew that more was afoot than concern for an elderly, invalid neighbor.

"Pug's in his sixties, maybe older. He's been like that as long as I can remember, but when I was growing up, your grandfather told a story about what happened to him. The man with the crazy gray hair came to see Pug and not long after that, the Pug everyone knew back then became the Pug everyone knows today."

"The man with the crazy gray hair?"

"That's what your grandfather called him. He's told the story numerous times through the years because it was the first time he'd ever seen a chauffeur-driven limousine. Lord, I'm surprised you haven't heard it.

"He and old man Irby Cox were sitting out front of Claude's Shell station enjoying a grape snow cone. Daddy saw the car first, sunlight bouncing off its gleaming black paint like it was built of mirrors. The fancy vehicle pulled up to the pumps at Claude's with its big engine purring. Daddy said his snow cone melted on his hand and he didn't realize it.

"As he and Irby stared, the rear window whispered down and a kindly-looking old man with crazy gray hair stuck his head out, 'Young man, would you know the address of a Mr. Pug Ginn, by any chance?' he asked.

"Irby ignored the man, but Daddy stood and walked over

for a closer look. He was cautious about giving up information on a friend to a complete stranger, so he asked the man with the hair his business.

"'I need to ask him a question of significant importance. We have a mutual interest.' Daddy didn't quite know what to make of this, but the man seemed harmless as well as polite. Besides, they'd find Pug's soon enough, with or without his help. Being careful not to touch the limo, he bent over and gave directions.

"The man with the crazy gray hair didn't write anything down, just smiled and nodded while Daddy talked. All this took place sometime in the early to mid-thirties if I remember correctly."

I gave Mom a few blinks. This was one of the most fascinating stories from Eden's past I'd ever heard. Mom had hooked me but good. "Who was the man, Momma?"

"Daddy said he looked like Mark Twain. Who do you think it was, George?"

I made a face and rolled my eyes. "Why on earth was Albert Einstein looking for someone in Eden, South Carolina?"

Mom clapped flour caked hands. "My young man is so smart."

"Mom, please."

"Well, I'm not certain, but I think it might have had something to do with Pug's figures."

"Ma'am?"

"Daddy said there was a time when Pug could figure out how to build a spaceship if he had a slide rule and a big enough piece of paper. He said the boy could figure any kind of math there was. Some claimed that Pug invented his own math. Of course, you know how Daddy is. The man loves a tall tale better than Peter loved the Lord."

Mother knew her men. My grandfather—everyone calls him Doc except Mom—once told me that he talked Robert E. Lee into a cease-fire that would allow for the planting of spring gardens. He swore it was one of the reasons we lost at Gettysburg and made the claim with a straight face.

I wondered what Francois Dulcet would think of what my grandfather called 'poetic license,' even though he was no more a poet than Buster. I also wondered about people who explained that Pug's constant finger-counting was an involuntary muscle reaction.

"Mom?"

"Yes, dear."

"What was the question?"

"The question?"

"What did Albert ask Pug?"

"I have no idea, George, but your grandfather always wondered if he'd played a part in Pug's situation."

I walked back out to the porch, set the swing into squeaky rhythm, and opened *Mysterious Island*. During summer, our windows were up unless it rained. The smell of baking cookies made my mouth water and stomach rumble as I read about Verne's engineer, Cyrus Smith. What might a man obsessed with figures do with numbers, and what might the numbers do to the man? After supper that night, we watched a *Gunsmoke* rerun, ate fresh-baked cookies with milk, and went to bed.

One of the neatest things about being a kid in a small town in summer is prowling the streets alone in the dark. Eden was mysterious at night, thrilling to my senses. There was something in my little town that I believed only I could feel. I didn't know what the 'something' was. I just knew it was there. Eden at night could chase away boredom like Buster could chase a woman—even during the long summer months.

I dropped silently from my window. Tonight, wasn't about spying. Tonight, was about Mr. Free.

6

The grass was cool and damp beneath my bare feet. In the distance a dog rolled out a lonesome howl. I wondered if it was Buster.

I studied a cloudless sky spattered with stars. One of the twinkling lights spent itself in a glorious arc and the lonely dog howled again. I wished for Buster to come home so that he could chase Lightning, beg for sandwich pieces, and sit beside me on the back steps. He'd often lean into me so that I'd put my arm around him, the bricks warm beneath my rear, Buster warm against my side. We'd sometimes sit in the stillness of this magic for hours, and I came to know without question that in all the world there's nothing finer than a dog.

I stood at the corner of the Great Wall of China and studied the rear of the Ginn house. Tuesday night I was going to have to go over and ask Pug about Buster. It was a ridiculous, stupid thing to do. Francois Dulcet was playing me for a fool. Or, worse, I was crazy as a loon, and so far, no one had noticed but me.

Another long, boring summer had been upon me until Mr. Free, the Aviator, and Iris suddenly appeared. Reading and fishing will only go so far to relieve the boredom of a summer with no friends in it. I was not so naïve that I viewed the appearance of each as coincidence, but I was incapable at the moment of connecting the dots. That's what the remainder of the summer was for.

I slipped through the ivy at the corner and moved quickly toward the muted kitchen light, choosing shadow cast by the giant oak, the forbidden nature of my actions bringing shivers of delight in the soft warmth of night. Patio stones kissed the soles of my feet with stored sunlight.

I stepped up to the door and rapped out the secret knock. Not ten seconds passed before the door opened and there stood Mr. Free in yet another of the many reasons the townsfolk thought him so strange—an expensive, custom-tailored suit. Mr. Free had treated us to a variety of colors most of the men of Eden wouldn't be caught dead wearing. Tonight, he wore a purple suit with black shirt and yellow tie. A red carnation perched in a buttonhole of his lapel.

He opened the door with his free hand. In the other was the ever-present tumbler. "Spy Boy, what a wonderful surprise. Please, step into my parlor," he said, the ebony cigarette holder clenched in white teeth.

This was it. Since the big white Cadillac rolled into Eden, I'd wanted to visit this exotic man just to sit near him and taste the world through words born from memory of far-off places and adventure. Unlike my fellow citizens, I found tailored suits, Panama hats, and Cadillacs an unbeatable combination.

"You look great, Mr. Free," I said, my words followed by an immediate blush.

"Thank you, Spy Boy. I try, God knows I try. A gentleman never knows who might drop by." He tilted his head and squinted. "Why the red cheeks? If you think something in your heart, you should say it so long as courtesy rules the day. Thoughts from the heart are illuminating, be they light or dark."

"I just didn't want to sound stupid, that's all," I said, looking down at my bare feet, which made me feel even stupider. They were dirty and grass-stained and wouldn't be truly clean again until a Saturday at the beach or after school started back.

He turned serious. "It's late, young man. Do your parents know where you are?"

"No, sir."

"Then, perhaps of greater import, do you know where your parents are?"

"Yes, sir, they're tucked away."

"How sweet. May I offer you a little Coke?"

"That'd be great." He moved from cabinet to refrigerator

and back in his spacious kitchen with an easy grace that I'll never have. I was born clumsy and have gone downhill since. His kitchen was appointed like everything else in his life. The countertops were tiled in gloss black and were home to a commercial-grade mixer, blender, and block of knives that would make any chef proud. A spice rack sat in a corner and stainless-steel pots hung above a gas range set into an island in the middle of the floor, a spotless expanse of alternating black and white squares gleaming as if they were wet. A white porcelain sink with chrome fixtures glittered beneath an overhead fluorescent lamp. Rows of bowls, plates, glasses, and saucers sat behind frosted-glass cabinet doors.

"My mom would love this kitchen, Mr. Free." She wouldn't just love it; she'd probably give one of Pop's body parts for it.

"Perhaps you could bring her over some day."

I smiled and looked away. "Maybe," I lied.

He chuckled at my discomfort and opened the huge white refrigerator. A cold mist rolled out, revealing row after row of little Cokes.

"Damn, that's quite beautiful, isn't it, Spy Boy?" He pulled a Coke from the depths of the refrigerator and turned toward me. The man bore a striking resemblance to Clark Gable. It was this realization that brought one of my 'aha' moments and the reason so many of the men down at Mr. Allen's barbershop said bad things about a man they didn't know.

He cracked open a tray of ice, made my drink, and then freshened his from a bottle of Bacardi and an open Coke sitting next to the spice rack. He put his cigarette out and placed the holder inside his coat.

"Did I interrupt you?" I asked.

"Yes, you did. It's eleven p.m. and I was plotting the overthrow of the government. I'm convinced that America would work better with a dictator at the helm. So long as that dictator is me, of course. However, I don't suppose one more night with democracy intact will hurt."

"You sure do dress nice for plotting."

"A full moon approaches, Spy Boy. You never know what one of those might bring. One's attire speaks volumes."

"Volumes about what?"

He rolled his eyes and emitted a weary sigh. "It's good to see you, Spy Boy. Would you care for a tour of the remainder of my abode?"

"Heck, yeah."

"By the way, there's a key to the back door in that little mailbox with 'leave a note' painted on its side if you ever need to get in and I'm not here."

I smiled. To be trusted is a wonderful thing.

He led the way through swinging doors onto the polished hardwood floor of a large dining room. A chandelier of diamonds and ice hung from the ceiling over an enormous oak table with a silver candelabra holding center court. Crystal and china nestled behind the beveled, leaded glass of an enormous cabinet on the opposite wall. Not only was Mr. Free fascinating, by Eden standards, he was rich.

"Whatever you do, don't spill Coke on these rugs, Spy Boy. They cost more than the Piggly Wiggly."

"What the hell?" I said, stopping dead in my tracks. I eyed my Coke as if it'd suddenly become a serpent. Mr. Free had just cursed me. The possibility of spilling something on a rug that cost more than Pop's car would become certainty.

Mr. Free turned and gave me a curious look. "Excuse me?"

"Why would you pay as much for something to walk on as you would a grocery store?"

He waved the question away. "Don't take everything so literally. Just be careful with your drink. The rugs are Persian, and they wouldn't understand." I studied the ornate designs and rich, dark colors. My feet sure liked them.

"Come, come, they are, after all, only rugs."

"They aren't just rugs, Mr. Free. They cost more than most of the houses on Bangalang, maybe more than my house."

"Think of them as investments, Spy Boy, not frivolous spending." He took a few more steps and repeated the word 'Bangalang' to himself.

"If you say so," I said.

Stained lamps of elaborate brass design cast soft yellow light on hand-crafted furnishings of mahogany, pine, and oak. Smaller lamps set into the wall above paintings accented places I'd never seen, things I didn't recognize, and people I didn't know.

"Is that a chess set?" I asked, captivated by the ebony and ivory carvings on a table near a window.

"Yes, it is. Do you play?"

"No, but I can fly," I answered.

Mr. Free stopped and removed his cigarette holder from inside his coat. "I once had a good friend who claimed he could fly, Spy Boy. In fact, I've done some flying of my own."

"I can't fly. Don't take everything so literally."

Mr. Free gave me a curious little smile and fitted a Gauloise into his holder. "Touché."

We exited the den through a set of tall French doors into a subtly lit room that hinted of mystery and exotica from every nook and cranny. Except for the interior wall, dominated by a large fireplace, glass-fronted cabinets ran from the polished wood floor to the ceiling. At desk height the cabinets extended into the room to provide counter space for a marvelous collection of artifacts and oddities.

Knives and guns, old photos and bones, exotic masks and large teeth from God-only-knew-what animal, pipes, feathers, and necklaces made of beads, silver, and gold were on display. As with the paintings, I saw things that were unrecognizable.

Watching over the amazing collection of artifacts and treasures were row after row of leather-bound books with gilded imprints on their spines. More beveled glass protected the fine collection that awaited hungry minds. A Victrola sat in one corner, the shelves to its left and right laden with records. In the corner opposite the record player, the painting on which he'd been working sat on an easel.

A large ceiling fan gently stirred air perfumed with the musk of old paper, ink, and leather. Model airplanes hanging by nearly invisible filament moved gently about.

"Oh my," I whispered, embarrassed by my poorly concealed awe. The room held more magic than any paradise of escape and adventure either I or Mr. Verne could've dreamed up.

"Oh my is correct, is it not?" Mr. Free asked with a satisfied grin. "It's too bad that no one visits. Just think, Spy Boy, you're the only person in Eden to lay eyes upon my secret treasure room. I may have to kill you for real."

"Where did all this stuff come from?"

"It came from a life well-lived, from places scattered about the globe in times of chaos, strife, and danger." He inhaled tobacco smoke and smiled.

I walked over to the nearest shelf where a strange-looking pistol lay. "What kind of gun is that?"

"It's a German weapon, Spy Boy, a Walther P38. I took it from a friend one stormy winter night. Sadly, he no longer had a need for it."

"You mean…"

He nodded. "Yes, that's exactly what I mean."

I studied the pistol. All pistols are dangerous, but the Walther is a particularly menacing-looking weapon. It had once belonged to a real live German, just like on *Rat Patrol*.

"How many men do you suppose it killed?"

"None."

"What do you mean, none?"

"Well, a man does the killing, Spy Boy, not the weapon. You can stand here and watch it all night long, and it won't kill anyone or anything."

"You know what I meant."

"Perhaps, but did you?"

I wasn't going to get a straight answer. I turned toward the record player. "What sort of music do you listen to, Mr. Free?"

"Only the best, Spy Boy, only the best."

I thought of the rock and roll that blared from WKYB, the local radio station. "Who makes the best?"

"The Big Bands, of course. The love of my life and I danced away many a night to the big bands. Perhaps we'll give them a listen soon."

"Is that the music I heard that day?"

"What day, Spy Boy?"

"The day I saw the boy in the window," I said, walking over to the painting, which bore the image of shapely feet, ankles, and calves. Iris came to mind. Even with so little done, it was obvious that Mr. Free was a talented man.

"I don't know about the boy but that's probably the music you heard, only it wasn't coming from upstairs."

The odd tone I'd heard when I mentioned the boy earlier had returned. "I know a girl with skin like that," I said.

"You're developing an eye, Spy Boy, and if you know a girl like the one you'll eventually see in that painting, you're a fortunate young man. Remember, beautiful skin does not the woman make."

"It doesn't hurt, though, does it, to have skin like that?" I asked.

"Not one bit, not one single bit," he agreed with a chuckle. "Come sit with me."

Two leather wing chairs were placed before the fireplace. A reading lamp hovered over each with a table between. He took the chair on the right, crossed his legs, and sipped from his adult libation. I heard the soft whisper of the books the instant I settled into the chair's embrace.

"This is wonderful," I sighed.

Mr. Free puffed on his cigarette and smiled. "Much more so with quality company."

It was a nice compliment, and I found myself overcome with the obvious—Mr. Free was an exceptionally nice man. I scanned the shelves slowly. "Have you read all these?"

"Of course not. Do I look like a bookworm to you? I've read quite a few. The rest I'm saving for those dreary winter days when cold rain patters on the roof, those days that cause you to argue with aching bones and muscles when it's time to plant the spring garden. Books are written for escape, that of the writer and the reader. You light a fire, stir a drop or two of water into a fine Southern bourbon, open your book, and travel."

"Well, we don't have a fireplace and I never tasted any bourbon, but I know what you're talking about with the traveling part. I'm on an island with Captain Nemo at the moment."

"Nemo as in Nautilus Nemo?"

"Yep."

"Ah, you're on the mysterious island. It's better than *Twenty Thousand Leagues*, you know."

I couldn't help but grin. His appraisal of *The Mysterious Island* seemed a perfect time to broach the subject. "Mr. Free, I have a problem."

"That would explain a lot."

"Sir?"

"The knocking on my back door at eleven o'clock while I was plotting the overthrow of the government. You aren't just visiting, are you?"

"Sort of, but I still have a problem. We can talk about it later if you'd like."

"I like that about you, Spy Boy."

"Like what?"

"You're naturally honest, but nearly as important as honesty is your courteous way. You're a considerate human being when you aren't spying on others. Considerate folk are rare these days. Tell me your problem."

"There's a girl."

Mr. Free leaned toward me and arched his eyebrows. His blue eyes bored into mine. "In any topic worthy of discussion there should always be a girl, Spy Boy."

I didn't necessarily agree with this, but it would work for the time being. "She's… She's different."

"Those are usually the most interesting."

"She's mixed. Do you know what I mean by 'mixed'?"

He erupted into laughter. "But, of course, I know," he said, his voice sounding much like my new acquaintance, Francois Dulcet.

"How did you do that?"

"Do what?"

"How did you make your voice sound that way?"

"That's the way I sound when I don't sound this way, Spy Boy. It's known among the more refined as an accent. In this instance, the speech of New Orleans."

"I thought you were from New York."

"I am from New York, but I was born and raised in the Crescent City, the Big Easy."

There it was. The Crescent City and New Orleans were one and the same, and the coincidence needed attention, but not now. "I like this girl, Mr. Free."

"Then she must be quite beautiful indeed."

"She's the most beautiful girl I've ever seen, and she kissed me."

"Was she beautiful before or after she kissed you?"

The question made no sense at all, and Mr. Free read the confusion in my eyes. "They are witches, Spy Boy, these creatures called woman, and they have powerful magic. A kiss has blinded many a poor man."

"I don't think she's a witch, but lots of folk might think so. Anyway, she was beautiful before she kissed me."

"Very well, but I must say, thus far I see no problem with your problem."

"I want to ask her to the movies one Saturday."

"And the problem is?"

"I already told you. She's different."

"Oh, it's the mixed blood thing."

I looked into Mr. Free's eyes, attempting to transmit the complexities of being seen in Eden with a girl like Iris. Discussing Iris's heritage with my mother and father presented a borderline impossible situation. I loved my parents and they loved me, but there were some things you just didn't do in a small Southern town.

I slumped in my chair. I didn't know how to state my case. I didn't know how to take Iris to the movies, either. The coloreds sat upstairs in the balcony, a place I'd always longed to sit, but was never allowed. Where on earth would Iris and I sit?

"Spy Boy," Mr. Free said, puffing on his cigarette. "Are you asking me for advice?"

"I guess I am," I answered with a shrug.

"You and I both know how it works here. Someday, perhaps things will change. In fact, I firmly believe they will, but it hasn't happened yet." He paused and studied me through a cloud of blue smoke. "Do you know how people change the sort of things you want changed?"

"No."

"They change them one person at a time. You might be the first person. You can be a crusader, or you can choose to do something besides go to the movies, something that you both could enjoy that might cause a little less controversy."

"I suppose you're right. I don't know what to do. If I'd gone fishing on Mingo it wouldn't even matter."

"Mingo?"

"Mingo Creek. It's the best fishing hole around, but I was afraid to go through Bangalang to get there."

"Why are you afraid to go through this place called Bangalang?"

"I'm afraid of Butch Sinclair."

"And who might Butch Sinclair be?"

"The biggest, meanest bully in the South—maybe in the entire world."

"I think I see your problem, George."

"I don't know if I want to know."

"You're having problems with your backbone. Or, as an old friend of mine would say when he was trying to talk me into participating in his latest death-defying stunt, 'You need to grow a ball sack, Bubba.'"

The accent and crassness with which Mr. Free spoke sounded so much like Francois Dulcet that I sat back and stared. "Do you know Francois?" I asked.

"Who?"

I almost responded, *Francois the ghost.* If I told Mr. Free I was seeing a ghost, this could be my first and last visit. "Where do I buy one?"

"Ball sack or backbone?" he asked with a laugh. "Can't buy either, my boy, but you can grow them. Sometimes you have to make one or the other grow right there on the spot."

"I'd love to know the secret to that little trick."

His smile faded. "Believe it or not, in the years to come, there'll be times when you look back on Bangalang and Butch Sinclair and wish you had it so easy. I know, that sounds a bit bleak, but that's the way life works.

"You're asking about serious things, and I'm not going to talk to you as if you were a child or my son. I'm going to talk to you straight, the way a man talks to a man, a friend to a friend. Is that fair enough?"

I nodded in the affirmative and sipped my Coke. Mr. Free was on a roll, and I liked it.

"Don't turn away from something that'll bring regret. You might save your skin at the moment, but you'll lose a little piece of yourself every time you walk away. You'll fool a lot of people about a lot of things in the years to come, but you'll not fool the man in the mirror. If I see your character properly, and I rarely misjudge character, the man in your mirror is always going to be your harshest critic.

"You're taken with this young girl, and you're afraid of a certain bully. If you didn't have what it took to handle either, I'd advise you that you were outgunned."

"Mr. Free, I don't think I can grow a ball sack while Butch Sinclair is sitting on my chest."

"Yes, you can grow one. You might even have help, who knows?"

"Nobody's going to help me in this place," I said, disgusted with how alone I was in a town full of kids my own age.

"Things aren't always as they seem, Spy Boy. This is a unique little town. I've been to many strange and exotic places. Eden is where I was told to come, and I felt something here as soon as I passed the 'Welcome to Eden' sign."

"Who told you to come here, Mr. Free?"

He looked at me as if he were seeing me for the first time. He kept gazing for so long that I squirmed. "Perhaps we'll talk about that at a later date," he finally said. "As far as your current romantic and enemy territory dilemmas, you're going to have to have faith. But you need to have faith in yourself first, and remember: nothing you ever get in this life worth having will be easy to achieve."

I trudged home with the air cool on my skin and the night creatures humming an enchanting symphony. Mr. Free hadn't reached into his pocket and pulled out a magic bullet, but I felt better. Before I crawled back through my window, I looked skyward. The stars twinkled brightly, and the moon was almost full.

7

The next day I pushed my mower over to Miss Ginn's and cut her grass. The job was worth every penny of five dollars, but she'd only pay two. She reminded me, once again, that if I upped the price, she'd be forced to do the right thing about my *nasty little habit*. Resisting the urge to stick my tongue out at her, I dragged my rickety old mower back to the house with two crumpled dollars in my pocket.

It was day seven and still no Buster. I sat on the back steps with a Superman comic and thought about the prospect of sneaking around Miss Ginn's house tonight. The moon would be full, and she might be moving from room to room in her darkened house with those "bird-watching" binoculars at the ready. I wondered if she had a gun. It was a silly thought. Everyone in Eden had a gun in their house—or two, or three.

As I pondered the ramifications of getting caught peeking into an old woman's bedroom window at night, I was interrupted by the distinct thump of a basketball bouncing off asphalt. I perked to attention.

Cindy Turner was approaching with her best friend. Tall, but well proportioned, she was addicted to the sport of basketball, and she practiced year-round if she could get someone to play with her. Though it was true that I thought Iris was the most beautiful woman I'd ever met, Cindy Turner was not hard to look at.

As with most of Eden's female population, Cindy didn't know I was alive after my mom stopped hiring her to babysit. While I pretended not to notice her, she walked to the rear of her house, dropped the basketball by the back doorsteps, and went inside.

As often happens in situations like these, my little voice spoke up. *Don't do this. It's wrong.*

I debated with the voice. It recommended that I read my comic and forget what I was thinking. *But she's been practicing baskets with friends and was no doubt weary, sweaty, and longing for a hot shower,* I countered. It was broad daylight. What I shouldn't do was climb the oak out by the sidewalk while she showered. Nor should I take up position in the tree and wait, perhaps to spy her wrapped in a towel—or better yet, to spy her wrapped in nothing at all.

It was the typical angel versus devil debate, and, as usual, my near-speechless angel, the little voice, lost. There were times when his input amounted to no more than that of a deaf-mute at a football rally.

I gave Cindy time to grab a snack and knock around doing whatever girls do when they come home to roost for the night. Then I stood, tucked the comic into my back pocket, stretched, yawned, and sauntered casually up the sidewalk. When I reached the oak just outside her bedroom window, I checked to see if the coast was clear, and then shinnied up the tree like a monkey.

Cindy kept the lower curtains of her window closed, but the Turner's house was built high enough off the ground that she felt comfortable leaving the upper curtains open. If I climbed up to the third limb, lay flat, and was patient, I could see right through to her bathroom door.

Sure enough, after about twenty minutes, she exited with nothing on but her skin. "Holy moly," I whispered to myself, unable to stifle a stupid grin. Just as I was thinking that all was well with the world and that I was about the best spy to ever take up the profession, the Superman comic slipped from my back pocket. It hurtled toward earth, spinning end over end with its flimsy, colorful pages spreading like wings, growing until it suddenly looked as large as the Hindenburg. My eyes darted toward Cindy's windows, and I watched as she caught the falling comic from the corner of her eye.

Cindy's face went slack. Her eyes moved from the curtain line to the tree limb where I lay like a vile serpent. I watched expressions of fright, confusion, and anger come in rapid succession, anger being the most prevalent of the three. I needed to escape, but the fury on her face stuck me to the tree limb like a warm wet tongue to a frozen flagpole. Faced with imminent death, I found that despite Mr. Free's encouraging little speech last night, I was still quite incapable of growing a backbone or a ball sack. I closed my eyes and sighed with resignation.

"Oh God," I whispered, "please help me out of this mess, and please don't let the shit hit the fan." My eyes were still closed when the Turners' back door slammed. My little voice sent a meek 'the shit's hitting the fan' from the recesses of my conscience.

"You sneaky little bastard," Cindy hissed. Her mahogany brown eyes smoldered into mine. "Get your ass down from that tree this instant."

Please help me disappear, I thought, still afraid to open my eyes.

"You better pray that I don't kill you, you little shit. Open your eyes, George Parker. I'm talking to you. How long have you been doing that?"

I opened my eyes to see her standing beneath me, barefoot and wrapped in a towel, her damp mane clinging to the creamy skin of her neck and shoulders. Brimming with vindictive righteousness, she held the basketball to her shapely hip with her right hand.

Despite my compromised position, I let my gaze drop to the top of the towel, where it was held in place by her ample bosom. She was gorgeous and wet, and I made a serious error in judgment. I licked my lips.

"George, I asked you how long you've been doing this?" she hissed.

"Maybe five minutes?" The deceptive response came so smoothly that I decided to layer on a tad more. "I swear," I added with all the innocence I could muster.

"A peeping Tom *and* a lying little shit," she said, cocking her arm. I opened my mouth to protest just as she let fly with the basketball. The orb came at me in slow motion, growing larger and larger until it hit me with tremendous force on the left side of my face. I hit the ground back first with a heavy thud and rush of air, my lungs collapsing like burst balloons.

She retrieved her basketball, then returned to stand over my shuddering, prostrate body, her right index finger pointing down like a gun. "If you *ever* do that again, I'm going to break both your legs and drag you up on my back porch for Daddy to finish you off, George Parker. Do you *hear* me?"

My lungs refused to inflate, but I could nod, and nod I did. I couldn't see out of my left eye and my nose and left cheek were completely numb. Spots were dancing in the field of what little vision I had. Milliseconds from blackness, my lungs regained their purpose and I heaved like a drowning man, wheezing, coughing, and sputtering like a Model T.

I struggled to a sitting position and watched her strut away, the damp towel clinging to her perfectly shaped posterior like a wet washcloth draped over a bowling ball. Cindy had legs like the women I'd seen in my father's *Playboy* magazines.

My chest felt unusually warm. With my one good eye, I watched blood drip, drip, dripping from my nose onto the front of my white T-shirt.

"George, what on earth happened? You're bleeding. And look at your eye…and your lips. Oh, George, have you been fighting again? What have I told you about fighting, young man?"

I hung my head to avoid eye contact, thinking that Butch Sinclair could use a lecture or two on fighting. "Look at me, George." I looked up, hoping that Mom would misinterpret the terror I was experiencing for shame.

"Let's hear it, young man."

"You should see the other guy," I said, attempting a grin with misshapen lips.

She placed a hand on each hip. "George…"

"I was looking for Buster," I lied. I hate lying to my mother, but I hate the punishment that comes with the truth even more. If she didn't pick up something and flog me, she'd get Pop to do so when he got home. The worst was a flogging from both, then the excruciating ordeal in the Court of Grounding. In my house, once punishment was decided upon, it was almost always maximum sentencing without parole.

I didn't have a choice. Peeping on the next-door neighbor wasn't one of those things that left me in doubt as to the outcome. My parents would kill me on the spot, and maybe invite Mr. Turner over for a round or two. But there was still a chance Cindy might not rat me out. She was a pretty neat girl. She just didn't like being spied on while in the nude.

"How did looking for Buster do that?" Mom asked, breaking open a tray of ice and plunking cubes into a dishtowel. "Weren't you just over cutting Miss Ginn's grass? How'd you find time for a swollen face? Miss Ginn hit you with something, George? I know you two have a running disagreement about your fee and she's mean enough to hit someone, of that I have no doubt."

"I rode uptown after I finished the grass. I thought I saw him when I went past the alley at the discount store. I rode my bike right into the exhaust pipe at the back of the dry cleaners."

She piled a few more ice cubes into the dishtowel, giving me the tight-lipped smile and intense eye contact that was a difficult combination to read. I waited, my heart pounding and my ears ringing. Finally, she spoke. "Oh, George, bless your heart. I know that must hurt like sin."

"Yes, just like sin," I agreed, stifling a sigh of relief.

She wadded the ice into the dishtowel and handed it over. "You get that clumsy nature from my side, you know. Here, press that against your eye. Do your lips too. You're going to have quite the shiner. I know this'll go in one ear and out the other, but you need to be more careful."

"It'll be okay, Mom."

"George?"

It was coming, the "I know you didn't run into the cleaner exhaust" proclamation. "Ma'am?" I said, the word barely audible.

"George, I don't know how to say this, but the worst might have happened to Buster. I'm not trying to upset you. I just want you to understand that sometimes bad things happen."

"I know, Mom. I just don't want to think about it." My Oscar-winning performance was over. Reality brought tears to my un-swollen eye and I looked away.

Mom knelt and hugged me. "I'd bring him back if I could. I'd bring him back this second."

"I know you would." My voice hitched. She let me off the hook the way moms do when they're trying to preserve their son's dignity.

"Run outside with that ice before it starts dripping on the floor."

I went out back and sat on the steps, sans Buster. I stuck the ice poultice to the side of my face, to my nose, my lips, then back to my eye, promising that I wouldn't go near Cindy's oak again for the remainder of my life. As I sat nursing face and feelings, I thought about the best way to approach the Ginn house. If I got close enough to Pug tonight to speak to him, what was I going to say? More to the point, what was *he* going to say?

Around six, I saw Pop walking home from work just like he had every day that the weather permitted—and sometimes when it didn't—for as long as I could remember. He had a comic book in his hand.

"What in the hell happened to your eye?" he asked when he got within earshot.

"I ran my bike into the exhaust pipe at the cleaners," I lied again. If the truth came out, I was going to be in more hot water than a Sunday chicken.

He looked me in the eye. One corner of his mouth tightened. He was about to accuse me of lying, but for some odd reason, he changed his mind and extended the comic. "This yours?"

One of the things I couldn't know about my parents was how transparent I was in their eyes. I didn't know this because keeping it a secret is one of a parent's greatest child-rearing tools. I reached out and took the Superman comic.

"You need to enjoy this while it lasts, youngster," he said, a comment that had become more and more frequent. "I get caught short fairly often down at the station and could use an extra hand. If nothing else, a hand to keep me from going crazy."

"I am, Pop," I said, dreading the day I had to work for a living, but looking forward to decent pocket money, nonetheless.

He disappeared into the house where, in my mind's eye, I watched his routine. He'd stop at the bathroom to wash his hands. Next, he'd walk into the kitchen, hug my mother from behind if she wasn't engaged in some dangerous frying chore, and then he'd grab a beer from the fridge. After two or three greedy swallows, he'd hide in the den before our little black-and-white Zenith, read the paper, and smoke while Walter Cronkite delivered the news.

I kept waiting for the back door to explode off the hinges of Cindy's house as Ralph, her behemoth of a father, rumbled toward my unsuspecting parents, foaming at the mouth and cursing as he tied a length of clothesline into a noose. It didn't happen.

We watched *Gomer Pyle* and *Bewitched*, then I hugged Mom and went to bed. It wasn't long before the television fell silent, and I listened as the two people who formed the center of my universe talked about the things parents talk about before drifting into sleep. The cadence of their voices made me think about my dog. I wanted to grow up, but I didn't want to grow up, because growing up meant losing things, precious things. There was much about Eden to call *fairy tale*. I was vaguely aware of this, but the stones in the cemetery were there to remind me that fairy tales had endings.

At ten after ten, I slipped out of my window into the bright light of a full moon, reminding myself that my skulking form would be visible from a half mile without binoculars. I hoped that Miss Ginn would be engrossed in a TV show.

I used ground cover as best I could, making a beeline for the old oak that served as home for my tree fort. After that, I stayed low until I could hide in a cluster of azaleas in the corner of our yard. From the azaleas to the rear of Miss Ginn's house was open ground. I waited, studying each window, listening to crickets fussing at frogs and dogs speaking dog language. Occasionally, a car passed by. Night air lay cool and damp on my skin. The sweet smell of freshly mown grass hung in the air, reminding me once again of how cheap and manipulative Miss Ginn was. I took a deep breath, then sprinted into the shrubbery that ran the length of the back of her house.

I moved toward the first open window to my right and listened as the Jolly Green Giant sang the 'ho, ho, ho' commercial. Black and white images flashed against the curtain over my head and through the window over the back porch.

Five minutes passed as commercials played, then the movie came back on, and I wondered what in the hell I was doing. Something was wrong with me. I couldn't believe I'd thought spying on Cindy in broad daylight was a good idea. This was a worse idea. A ghost had told me to ask a man who hadn't spoken a word in my lifetime how to find my dog. *Something was wrong with me.*

I rose to see what I could see, and the back of Miss Ginn's well-coiffed head came into view—a mass of sprayed hair that looked like silver cotton candy. She sat in a high-backed chair, a lamp sitting on the table to her right. My eyes widened at the sight of a cigarette smoldering in an ashtray. Next to the ashtray lay her birding binoculars. Pug was nowhere to be seen. I left the window and moved to the next window on the left. Experience had revealed this to be Pug's lair, but there was no Pug, just a very neat, very boring room dimly lit by a bedside lamp.

The next room down belonged to Miss Ginn. It, too, was spic and span and as orderly as a soldier's locker. Nearly out of options, I circled the house. Pug was slumped in his rocking chair on the front porch.

"Shit," I whispered, stopping dead in my tracks. I dropped

to my knees and leaned into the shrubbery. Pug didn't appear to have seen or heard me. I watched him closely, sitting in his Pug world, oblivious to all but whatever it was his mind created for him to see. He held his right hand up in the light and touched the tip of each finger to the tip of his thumb, beginning with his little finger and moving to his index finger. Over and over, he repeated this process, his blue eyes and the gray stubble of his beard reflecting moonlight.

"What do you want, George?" he asked, continuing to hold his hand in the light and count on his fingers.

I didn't answer. I blinked several times instead. This was, as the saying goes, virtually impossible. In my life, Pug had never done anything but grunt, and he rarely did that. He didn't turn to look at me. The door and windows behind him and across the front of the house were closed. I could still hear the television's muted babble, but there wasn't anyone else who could have spoken.

"I'm talking to you, George." This time I saw his lips move. He still didn't look at me, but there was no doubt whatsoever that Pug Ginn had just pronounced a sentence.

I stood from my place in the shrubs and walked closer, crouching down and moving back into the shrubbery when a car turned at the corner and rumbled past. "Are you afraid to be seen out and about?" he asked. His voice was raspy and broken, the way someone might sound with a bad cold.

I left my hiding place. "Someone told me that you could help me," I said.

"That's it? You've been walking and riding your bike by here for years, staring at me as if I were a two-headed Martian, and that's all you have to say?"

"I'm sorry I stared at you," I said, staring for all I was worth. For a second, I entertained the possibility that I might be asleep in my room, dreaming, but it was all too real. Pug's flat-top haircut and the droopy flesh beneath his chin were right before me. He wore a stiff pair of Wrangler blue jeans, a frayed flannel shirt, and a pair of black Converse tennis shoes. He was as real as I was, as real as the night—and the full moon.

"I suppose it's normal," he continued. "Everyone else does it. I see no reason to be angry with you, because you've been a curious boy your entire life, but it's still bad manners, you know. I know that you've been taught better. What happened to your eye?"

"Yes, I should know better," I admitted, cowed by the lecture.

"I can find out what happened to your eye if I want."

I watched him continue to count on his fingers. "Cindy Turner hit me with a basketball," I said, my gut telling me that a lie was a bad idea.

He closed his eyes, but his fingers continued their obsessive rhythm. "You want Buster back," he said. "Dog is God spelled backward. Did you realize that, George?"

"I just did."

"Do you believe in God, George?"

"Of course I do. What kinda crazy question is that?"

"Not nearly so crazy as you might think."

"Do you believe in God?" I asked.

"Of course I do. I do now, at any rate. You want something else, don't you, George?"

"I want to know what happened to you. I heard you were normal a long time ago."

"Normal... Is that what you heard? Do you feel that you own a firm grasp on the concept of normal?"

"Yes, sir, I do."

"What's normal, George?"

"Knowing when to go to the bathroom."

"That's it?"

"No, it's a lot of stuff. Answering the phone when it rings, eating when I'm hungry, knowing not to touch a hot stove burner."

"I like your logic, George. Logic is everything."

"Why did Albert Einstein want to see you?"

"He wanted to ask me a question."

"Why would Albert Einstein come to Eden, South Carolina, to ask you a question?"

"I sent him a paper a long time ago."

"What sort of paper?"

"A paper I wrote on metrics…mathematical metrics as they relate to physics and philosophy."

As with spying on Cindy earlier, it had taken me all of two minutes to get in over my head. I silently repeated *mathematical metrics as they relate to physics and philosophy* while I stared rudely and wondered how long it took him to wear out a pair of tennis shoes.

"What did he ask you?" I asked.

"What did who ask me?"

"Mr. Einstein, what did he want to ask you?"

"He asked me what the key was. Considering his brilliance, it was an incredibly simple question."

Pug was making me pull information like eye teeth. "Well, what did you tell him?"

"I told him that imagination was the key. It's strange, George. I thought everyone already knew that."

"What happened to you?"

"Imagination happened to me. I'd long seen the numbers, the metrics, and the equations. They constantly expressed themselves in my mind. I've always been fascinated by history. As I studied the great works from humanity's past, I realized that I was reading someone or some leadership's version of what had happened. If you're a country and I conquer you, I get to write the history—not you."

"What's that got to do with numbers?"

"Mathematics is how we explain things, how we quantify and determine what is necessary to achieve accurate results. Mathematics is truth. One afternoon I was sitting in our small library. It was autumn, the sun was setting, and the light filtering into the room was magnificent. As imagination is fundamental to progress, light is fundamental to living.

"I sensed that I was drawing nearer and nearer, the formulas growing more and more complex, but at the same time, more and more simplistic. It's like seeing an intricate structure in the distance, and, upon approaching close enough to study the structure in detail, you see that it is comprised solely of small bricks. It's in understanding how the bricks are assembled that brings light.

"Our parents had installed beveled glass in the library windows, and the sunlight was splintering into a rainbow of colors as it refracted through the windows and scattered across the wood floor. I saw the clarity of the formula that I'd been working on literally night and day for years and, when I saw the formula, George, I also saw the fissure."

The word *fissure* gave me the same feeling I get when I spot a water moccasin on the riverbank. "The...the fissure?"

"Yes, an access plane appeared in the room. Have you ever watched gasoline fumes escape from the filler neck of a car in summer? That's what the fissure looked like. If I moved my head to the left or right, the plane closed to a razor-thin line. If I viewed it at just the right angle, it opened to a width and height that I could walk through if I chose to do so. The plane rose from the light on the floor to form a door to another place, a place that whispered my name. I stood from my chair and walked over.

"The closer I got, the more I felt its pull. I could hear what sounded like a motor running on the opposite side. I put my hand up to touch the vaporous surface and a hand, a duplicate of my own, appeared on the opposite side—a hand that matched my every movement, no matter how detailed. The fissure offered no resistance as I pushed past its surface and touched the matching hand, resting my fingertips against the fingertips of the offered hand.

"The popping sound of the running motor grew louder.

Through the contact with its fingers, the hand began to pull at the mechanism that makes one aware of himself as a human being. The pull increased in power, like that of a giant vacuum cleaner, the engine noise growing louder in proportion. The experience gave new meaning to referring to the body as a vessel.

"Part of me was afraid. Terrified might be a better word, but I knew that the equation had opened this access, and I could no more have walked away than you can walk away from trying to find Buster. I allowed the 'other me' to complete the transfer and found myself in another dimension, George. The fissure was a gateway to the past.

"Earlier in the week, I'd been reading about the Wright brothers' first flight at Kitty Hawk. I walked from the modest library in our little house almost into the rotating blade of the Flyer I."

"But I don't understand. Why do you live like this?"

"Like what?"

"You're a vegetable. At least, you have been for my entire life. My mother says that you have been like that for as long as she can remember. How are you talking to me now?"

"For whatever mysterious reason, I can slip back across when the moon is full. The light works for me then, but I can't come back in entirety. I can't figure the equation for coming back as I once was. When the moonlight is gone, then I'm restricted once again to the other side, to the dimension of our immediate past."

He sounded sad when he said this. No matter how wonderful his ability, it had stolen his life. His parents had died. His friends married and had children. Wars had come and gone. His genius had trapped him. "I...I'm sorry, Pug."

"It's not as bad as it seems, George. I've seen many things, been to many places, and acquired much knowledge. It'll be a much better existence when I can slip back and forth through the fissure without losing myself so completely to the other world."

He'd explained the constant figuring on his fingers. He was

trying to formulate an equation that allowed freedom of movement, but he was fast running out of time. "What have you seen?" I asked.

"Much, George. I've seen much, but we'll talk about that some other time. Sister will surely catch you if you remain. When did you last see your dog?"

"Tuesday, May the second."

"You'll have to come back tomorrow night, or sometime while the moon is still full. If you miss me during that time, I'll not be able to speak to you again until the next full moon, and Sister may or may not wheel me out onto the porch. That's bad, but what might happen to your dog in the meantime is unmentionable."

"What if you aren't out here tomorrow night?"

"It's a chance you'll have to take. Otherwise, you'll have to figure a way to get to me inside the house."

"Holy crap," I blurted. It was too much. I blinked a few times, then forced myself to stop. A mental freeze-up was not acceptable. I took a deep breath and slowly exhaled. "Thank you so much, Pug. I'll try not to stare at you anymore."

"Good night, George."

"Pug?"

"Yes?"

"Does your sister know?"

"Does my sister know what?"

"That you come back like this?"

"No, she doesn't. You're the first person I've spoken to in forty years."

"Then why?"

"Why what?"

"Why me?"

"Francois told me you were coming."

I left Pug alone in the moonlight, desperately pursuing a calculation that would allow his permanent return to a body now old and wrinkled. He'd asked me about God. And then I wondered where he'd been—and what he'd seen.

On my way home, I slipped through the ivy in the corner of the fence and rapped out the first part of shave and a haircut over and over but got no response. The downstairs lights were off except for the fluorescent one over the kitchen sink. I looked upstairs. The light slipping through from inside the house looked exactly like moonlight, and the big band music sounded divine.

8

Pop leaned back in his chair, inhaled from his Lucky Strike, blew a few smoke rings to entertain me, and smiled. "What does my little adventurer have on his agenda today?"

He was in a good mood. Boyhood fire still flickered in his blue eyes from time to time. I suspected that he often wished to appear in my life one morning as a boy my age and spend the day wallowing in summer magic with me. We would ride our bikes, play on the railroad trestle, swim naked in the river, steal apples out of Mr. Hubert's orchard, and go to the movies. At day's end, he would hug me and speak of Peter Pan before vanishing into the night.

One of my father's favorite rituals is walking the oak-shrouded streets back and forth to his gas station to do 'bidness' with people he's known his entire life. He stops along the way to chat with neighbors, to pet dogs, to tease preschool children racing about on tricycles, and to watch squirrels play in the gigantic oaks. He lives his life slowly and refuses to let go of the simpler, finer things. He can find more laughter and happiness walking 'up the street' in one morning than many hapless individuals will find roaming city sidewalks for a lifetime.

His love for our small town and my mother had trapped him, and Eden's a better place for it. He'll extend credit to an unfortunate farmer or fellow Edenite when he has none to extend, but there isn't a man within twenty miles of Eden who wouldn't cross the street to shake his hand.

Like Mom, he understands the important things—an easy smile, an easier laugh, ice-cold RC colas, Moon Pies, and a good day down on the river. He's the man who taught me to sit still and watch the sunset whenever possible, a priceless lesson. He also taught me that to see the color of a man's skin before you see the man is one of life's most grievous sins. Long ago I began to suspect that no matter how noble this lesson was in intent, it was one that isn't shared by all.

Pop tapped his cigarette into an ashtray and dug a dollar out of his pocket. "Get a haircut. You look like that sheepdog on the *Bugs Bunny/Road Runner Hour*," he said, tossing the wrinkled buck at me.

I eyed him as I took the dollar. He won't watch the cartoons with me, but I often catch him standing in the doorway, his belly jouncing with stifled laughter. I tucked the dollar into my pants, thinking I could win ten more just like it if he'd tell the truth—that he knew the name of every one of the Looney Tunes characters.

"I might go fishing," I said, instead of making the wager.

"Didn't have much luck the other day, did you?"

"Not too much. I didn't go to Mingo."

"Well, there's fish in the river from one end to the other. You just got to figure out where."

"Maybe we can go together before it gets too hot."

"We'll play hooky from church and go," he said, checking his spouse's reaction from the corner of his eye.

"Always a reason not to go to church," Mom obliged.

"The river *is* church," Pop countered. I smiled because I couldn't agree more.

"Tell that to St. Peter when he slams the pearly gates in your face."

"Pete isn't going to be minding any gate, dear. He's going to be handing out free bait and cold beer at the tackle shop while all you holy rollers are lined up at that gate. I'm thinking God might have my own river waiting for me. One with my very own rope swing hanging from the top of a cypress tree about eighty feet tall. The thing about swinging into the river from a rope swing in heaven is that you can do it all day, maybe for a century or two, and not have to worry about drowning."

"You're as hellbound as your cousin Dink. You'll be praying for a drop of water, let alone a whole river to call your own."

Uncle Dink is a moonshiner—and the one thing my mother would change about our family if she could. He comes to town on Saturdays in the summer with no shirt beneath his overalls and no shoes. He keeps a big chew of tobacco stuck in his jaw and appears proud of the fact that half his teeth are missing. He's woefully short on social graces but has never let this shortcoming keep him from engaging whatever soul might cross his path.

He especially enjoys watching the bluebloods squirm when he stops them on the sidewalk to talk about old times. His target of the day never fails to make it a point at some later date to inform my mother of the fact that he or she "had an unfortunate encounter" with Uncle Dink.

Pop ignored Mom and winked at me. "You remember that rope swing?"

I nodded and laughed, even though I knew it might cause trouble. The thought of having my own river in heaven was nearly enough to make me change my ways.

"I've been asking around about Buster, George," he said, changing the subject, a trick he used when he detected a tad too much strain in Mom's voice.

My breath caught in my throat. Pop's tone had that foreboding note he gets when he's about to punish me for something or tell me that a friend or relative of his has passed away. When I looked up at him, he saw the terror and tears building in my eyes and understood immediately. He raised a hand.

"Whoa, I haven't heard anything bad," he hurried to say. "Theo Williams came by the station Saturday morning and told me that he thought he saw Buster running down an alley over in Bangalang."

My heart sank. This was nearly as bad as a dead loved one. A sighting of my dog in Bangalang had horrific implications. I'd have to venture across the tracks, and in so doing, possibly place my life—or at least my limbs and head—in Butch Sinclair's fat, dirty hands. *Please, God, let Pug help me find Buster on this side of the tracks.*

"What?"

I looked up, my eyes wide with disbelief. Pop was looking at me as if I'd suddenly grown two heads. Had I actually said that out loud? "Nothing," I said, the rest of my face turning as purple as my swollen eye. "I was just thinking out loud."

"Did you say something about Pug?"

"I don't think I did. I can't remember. I'm pretty upset about Buster, Pop." My consternation over Buster worked.

Sweet Jesus, I thought, careful not to speak that out loud too. *I need to be more careful.* "May I be excused?" I asked.

"Go forth and seek adventure, fruit of my loin," my father said with a theatrical wave of his hand. "Bring fish for the table, conquer a foreign land, kidnap a host of beautiful young virgins."

"Lloyd!" my mother yelped.

My father arched his bushy eyebrows and shrugged. "Sorry," he said, with a huge grin.

"Well, at the rate I've been going, it might be easier to bring home virgins," I said, rising to make my exit before I said something else totally stupid.

"I'm going to ground you both," Mom said. "I can't do a thing with you. Neither of you is cutting hooky from church again. It looks to me like you need to go every day the good Lord sends."

I walked out the back door and retrieved Lightning. The moan of the morning train's whistle sounded in the distance. I smiled the smile kids get when they've been set free from the oppression of school for an entire summer. My unruly imagination immediately erased the smile with thoughts of dressing up to go to church every day of the week. Such an arrangement would constitute a fate worse than the hell I was trying to avoid by going to church in the first place. Sunday mornings were bad enough.

It's not that I don't want to go to heaven. I just don't want to have to go to church to get there. Church is stifling, especially in the spring when the river's warming up. It's also a place where the wicked can congregate to hide behind the cross with smiles so false and hearts so black that I sometimes wonder why their heads don't burst into flame.

The sudden appearance of Francois Dulcet completely derailed my thoughts on church and its threat to boyhood, small towns, and Christianity. As he stood staring at me with glowing green eyes, I pushed Lightning out onto the sidewalk and looked to my left, then my right. True to form, there wasn't another living soul in sight. All was quiet save for the lonely wail of an approaching train.

Francois was standing by a four-wheeled contraption resembling a large go-kart. He and his latest invention were smack in the middle of a deserted Main Street. The train whistle came again, much closer.

He'd donned a black jumpsuit made of leather, with custom-tooled, knee-high boots to match. A bright green scarf was looped around his neck. Of course, his goggles and aviator cap were present. He waved at me and grinned, his tooth still missing.

"Bubba!" he yelled. "What you doing, son? I thought you'd be down at the river, pretending you was fishing and chasing after that pretty little colored girl. I know that's what I'd be doing if I was you." He pointed at me with a white-gloved hand, then stopped with his mouth open. "What in the hell happened to your eye?"

"I don't want to talk about my eye. What in the heck are *you* doing?"

"I'm about to set the land speed record right down the Main Street of this little one-horse burg you call home. This town ain't never gonna forget Francois Dulcet," he said, performing a professional salute and bestowing another of his devil-may-care grins.

It was impossible to ignore this guy. His mysterious, flamboyant vehicle ruled out any chance of pretending he wasn't there and, of course, I couldn't resist. I walked over for a closer look. The invention sat low to the ground on what looked like motorcycle tires. Two round cylinders, the kind I'd seen at Mr. Cecil's welding shop—only shorter—rested side by side in a cradle mounted to the frame of the cart just forward of the steering wheel. One of the cylinders was painted red and the other yellow, the colors so bright they hurt my eyes. Another cylinder, this one white with a chrome interior, had its ends machined off, and was mounted to a pedestal that rose to just above the rear of the cart's seat. Tubes and hoses connected the two front cylinders via a manifold to the rear cylinder, which had an array of odd-looking spark plugs placed around its diameter.

A fan, attached to a small gearbox, was fixed in the cylinder's intake behind a screen. A dash with knobs, switches, and gauges was located below the steering wheel. I couldn't put it all together in my head, but I suspected that I was eyeing a bomb on wheels.

"What in the world is this?"

"You mean you don't know? Aren't you a rocket fan, Bubba? This is a genuine rocket-mobile."

I laughed at his pronunciation of *genuine* which came out *gin-u-wine*, and Francois's missing-toothed smile vanished. "What's so funny?"

"There's no such thing as a rocket-mobile."

"What's wrong with you, son? You're standing right in front of one telling me there ain't no such thing. I don't understand people like you."

I gazed into his green eyes and shook my head. "You're kidding me, right?"

"Kidding 'bout what?"

"I'm worried that I'm slipping off my rocker, but you're the one who's crazy as a danged bedbug."

"I ain't never said I wasn't crazy, Bubba, but this rocket-mobile is real as the end of your nose."

I reached up and touched the end of my nose. Francois gave me a thumbs-up, and then flopped into the seat of his outlandish creation. I had to admit, the machine was fascinating. Its spoke wheels glittered in the morning sun, and the gauges, switches, and knobs of the control panel beckoned to the gadget lover in me.

As Francois flipped one of the switches, the fan located in the intake of the cylinder whirred to life—and it was no ordinary fan. Its speed increased rapidly until it emitted a low-pitched howl.

I took a step back but remained unconvinced. "You aren't moving very fast," I said.

"You real funny, Spy Boy," Francois said. "I know what happened to your eye. If that girl's daddy doesn't kill you, yours prolly will. Your momma too. Ain't gonna be nothing left of poor old Bubba but stained and tattered underwear."

I blinked. "Will they?" I asked.

"Will they what?"

"Will they find out?"

"Maybe, maybe not." His green eyes twinkled with merriment. Everything was a source of amusement. He adjusted two knobs until the gauges suited him, then he pressed a button. The odd-looking spark plugs began a rhythmic *pop, pop, pop*.

"How are they doing that?" I asked.

"I used high-voltage power supplies from a couple of televisions. Just call me Einstein," he said, reaching to open a valve on the control panel.

"What's in the tanks?"

"Kerosene and oxygen, Bubba—rocket fuel."

"Francois?"

"Yeah, Bubba?"

"The train's coming."

"Train? What train? I don't care 'bout no stinking train," he answered with a maniacal laugh. He pulled his goggles down and slowly opened the valve. The reaction was immediate and tremendous. A flame closely resembling that of a large torch blasted from the rear of the propulsion cylinder, and a much larger propeller, located in the interior of the cylinder, began to rotate. The spinning rotor quickly increased speed and, in seconds, accelerated from a whine to a loud scream. I was sorry I'd poked fun at his machine.

"Hey, Bubba," Francois yelled at me.

"Yeah?"

"You might better step up on the sidewalk. And, Bubba?"

"Yeah, Francois?"

"Don't forget to see Pug tonight, and don't get too rattled. You ain't gonna have to do it by yourself."

He opened the valve fully and blasted down the center of the street as if he'd just been shot from the muzzle of a howitzer. He hadn't been kidding. He was seated behind the wheel of a gin-u-wine rocket-mobile.

From my house to the railroad track was about a half-mile. The lights down at the crossing beyond the bridge were winking their deadly warning. Before Francois reached the crossing, he had to pass through the intersection of Main and Front Street, right smack in the middle of town.

The leaves and smaller limbs of the oaks forming the tunnel on my street fluttered and flew in the superheated exhaust. Dust and bits of trash billowed in Francois's wake. He miraculously cleared the intersection, but there was no way he was going to beat the train.

He passed over the bridge at the river and collided with the train with such force that the ground shook beneath my feet. A mushroom cloud rose high into the sky. The plate-glass windows across the street in the Piggly Wiggly rattled the way they do when the jets from the Myrtle Beach Air Force Base fly over.

"Holy crap," I said. I jumped on Lightning and took off toward the devastation, peddling for all I was worth. I passed Mr. Andrew, the town patriarch, standing by the sidewalk staring after Francois and his rocket ride.

"George," the deep voice caused me to brake my bike. Mr. Andrew never spoke to me. Heck, he hardly spoke to anyone in town because everyone was afraid to speak to him. I was surprised that he knew my name.

I looked back at him. "Sir?"

"You need to watch who you keep company with, son." He turned and walked back toward his house, unconcerned with a reply. I blinked at his back.

I was about halfway to the crash site when it dawned on me that besides Mr. Andrew, I was the only one in town who noticed anything amiss. Had Mr. Andrew actually seen Francois? What exactly was he trying to say? I was too upset to study on it.

I passed Mrs. Becky Cramer, who was rocking on her porch, enjoying a cup of coffee. She smiled and waved at me, oblivious to the fact that a rocket-mobile had just blown by, and a bomb had gone off smack in the middle of town.

I also passed the Hemingway sisters, arguing over whose turn it was to pull the weeds from the brick walk that led to their still grand but decaying old house. They waved at me as I sped by. When I got to the red light, there was nothing to see but the usual morning activity in a small town. Francois had abused me again, and I'd swallowed the entire event, hook, line, and sinker.

I lowered my head and said a prayer. *Dear God, I'm sorry I don't like going to church. I'm sorry I peeped at Cindy, and I'm sorry that I don't say my prayers every night before I go to sleep, but, God, please, please, don't let me be crazy.* I finished the prayer, looked across the bridge at the passing train clattering by, and, while I was wondering what a straitjacket might feel like, Francois's last words came back.

Don't forget to go see Pug tonight, and don't get too rattled. You ain't gonna have to do it by yourself.

"Do what by myself?" I said.

I shoved my hands in my pockets and felt the dollar Pop had given me. I'd added my recent lawn earnings to keep it company. Three bucks: I was rich. I shrugged Francois's psycho-technics off. No one had been killed, including me. I thought I was beginning to understand the entertaining apparition. He was all about delivering messages and he was definitely connected to Mr. Free, but how and why? I rode up to Mr. Allen's barber shop, determined to make the most of what remained of my day.

"I'll tell you exactly what I think," Mr. Hal Haley said as I walked into the cool of the barber shop. The cowbell over the door clattered, and everyone looked at me. Mr. Hal gave me an odd look, wrinkled his forehead, and wiped his mouth with the back of his hand.

"Spit it out, Hal," Mr. Allen said, holding his head back and peering through thick glasses at the back of Mr. Haley's head. He removed a small pair of scissors from the breast pocket of his white smock and took a few more snips from the problem area. Mr. Allen had told me on numerous occasions that he was a professional with a capital P.

"I think the man's a queer. That's what I think," Mr. Hal said, finishing his sentence.

"A queer," Mr. Allen repeated, shaking his head. He placed his hands on his hips and cocked his head, staring at Mr. Hal in the mirror. "Do tell? Just because he wears those fancy suits doesn't make him a queer, Hal."

"It ain't just the suits. It's that car too. When you ever see a white Caddy with a white interior? And he waters his grass, for God's sake, Allen. Who do you know in this town who waters grass? And have you seen his yard?"

"I hear you can order those Caddies up just about any way you please these days," Mr. Allen said. "If you got the money, that is."

"Oh, he's got money, no doubt about that," Mr. Buddy Davis chimed in. Mr. Allen and Mr. Hal looked over at Mr. Buddy, who was hiding behind the newspaper, his short legs crossed. Mr. Buddy lowered the paper. "Morning, George," he said, nodding in my direction. He looked back at Mr. Allen and Mr. Hal. "I don't know if he's a queer or not, but I think he might do some sort of government work."

"I think he's an assassin for hire," Mr. Pete Doster said, nodding and adding a confident snort.

Mr. Allen's barber shop wasn't normally this crowded on Tuesday morning. I'm usually the only one to show up in the mornings during the workweek. I'd picked out a *Boy's Life* magazine and was trying to hide in the corner, hoping to attract about the same amount of interest as a potted plant. The plan didn't work.

"You live right next door to him, George. What do you think?" Mr. Allen asked.

I lowered the magazine, stared at Mr. Allen, and blinked. He stared back. Mr. Allen was far-sighted. His dark eyes swam like fish in a bowl behind the thick lenses of his glasses. He sometimes gave me the creeps. He was tall, rail thin, and wore his sparse hair in a comb-over. His nose was long and narrow, but false teeth lent him a nice smile, and he went out of his way to give me the impression that he was popular with the ladies.

He was my grandmother's age, and he always asked about her the way some of the older guys in school asked Jerry Baker about his sister, Tish. Tish wore shorter skirts than the rest of the girls in her class, and according to our small town's nasty little rumor mill, she had yet to meet a boy she didn't like.

Mr. Allen made me feel like he knew something about my grandmother that would embarrass the hell out of me if I knew it too. I liked him sometimes, and other times I didn't.

"I don't know what a queer is, Mr. Allen," I said, switching my gaze to Mr. Hal's reflection in the mirror as the lie rolled out, "but I like his Cadillac and his suits. Pop likes his Cadillac too. Says he's gonna get one just like it someday. Pop's tired of his Chevy, but I kinda like it. I think a '57 has class."

The response brought an attentive inspection from Mr. Allen and his customers. Mr. Allen studied Mr. Hal in the mirror again and made a face at him.

Despite my rambling about the Caddy and Pop's Chevy, to a man they were trying to determine whether a word had just been introduced into my life that would require that I seek counsel from my parents. In the South, the first question after a kid inquires about a new cuss word (or as Mom calls them, "grown-up words") is, "Where on earth did you hear *that*?"

Mr. Hal cleared his throat. "Never mind about the queer thing, George. You never heard the word. Have you spoken to your neighbor?"

Mr. Buddy hid behind his newspaper again. This was a point-blank question that needed to be addressed in a point-blank manner. "No, sir," I said, my eyes wide and innocent. "Mom and Pop told me not to go over there."

"Good for them," Mr. Hal said. He turned in his chair to look at Mr. Allen. "What'd I say, Allen?"

"I don't think we need to repeat what you said, Hal," Mr. Allen said, puckering his lips into a tight little wad and staring at Mr. Hal with his large dark eyes. He grabbed his little neck broom and whisked around Mr. Hal's collar.

Mr. Allen was a prissy sort of fellow. He was always squared away, as Pop would say, his hair and moustache neatly trimmed, his shoes shined and his shop in perfect order. He swept up after every haircut and kept the trashcan with the hair in it in the little storeroom with his supplies. He reminded me in many ways of Mr. Free. I couldn't help but wonder if the similarities were why he'd defended Mr. Free's manhood.

"I don't think Mr. Free's an assassin," I volunteered.

"Why not?" Mr. Gordon asked.

"Well, he does a lot of yard work, plants lots of flowers and all. You reckon assassins do lots of yard work?"

Mr. Gordon rubbed his chin-whiskers. He was a farmer by trade, but he was retired. His overalls weren't worn in the places that a working man's overalls get worn. As a matter of fact, his overalls looked practically new. "Well, I can't say as I'd know one way or the other on that one, George," he admitted. "Could be it's part of his cover."

Just like you don't know one way or the other that he might be a queer, I thought, but I was too afraid to say it out loud. "Mr. Gordon?"

"Yeah, George?"

"What's a queer?" I watched him squirm in his seat, then look at Mr. Hal, Mr. Buddy, and Mr. Allen.

"Well, George," he said, a grin tugging unsuccessfully at the corner of his mouth. "I reckon you ought to ask Hal about that. I ain't rightly sure."

"That'll be a dollar, Hal," Mr. Allen said, snatching the barber cloth from Mr. Hal's big belly.

Mr. Hal removed his fat wallet and dug out a dollar for Mr. Allen. He gave Mr. Gordon a sour look, then winked at me. "Ask your daddy, George. If he wants to know where you heard the word, tell him Mr. Gordon said it, and I'll give you a good deal on a used car one of these days. Might find your daddy a nice Caddy while I'm at it." He donned his straw hat and waddled out onto the sidewalk.

"George, why don't you come on up and get your trim next? I don't think these fellahs'll mind," Mr. Allen said. I climbed up in the chair, the clean smells of Mr. Allen's tonics and shampoos wafting in the air around me. "How's your grandmother doing, son?"

I snitched two extra pieces of bubblegum after Mr. Allen asked about my grandmother, then I went to the Dime Store, stood at the plate-glass window, and gazed inside. Mrs. Lucille Thrower was buying hot cashews from Delores Martin. Delores was pretty and spoke with a slow, almost poetic rhythm, pronouncing each word as if it needed special treatment. It took forever for her to tell a story, but she was as sweet as cotton candy.

Mrs. Lucille was chastising Delores for some indiscretion and Delores looked like she was about to cry. I don't like Mrs. Lucille, but she's one of the richest ladies in Eden, so everyone pretends to like her. Whenever avoiding her is impossible, I pretend as well, and I don't like that about myself. Pop once told me that money made some people turn ugly, but he taught me to be polite to my elders whether I wanted to or not, or whether they were rich, or not.

I made a face and turned away, nearly walking into the old

mechanical horse. Every kid in Eden for the past twenty-five or thirty years had rocked on the faithful old mare. I stared into its vacant black eyes and admitted to myself that the only reason I didn't drop a dime in for a ride was because I was ashamed of being seen. Riding the chipped old horse once brought a thrill that could only be had when the circus came to town, or we went to the Myrtle Beach Pavilion on weekends.

A peculiar sadness seized me as I realized that I'd outgrown the longing that walking past the old horse with my mother had once brought. Childhood things were slipping away, and I wondered if I'd miss them until it hurt, or simply shrug and let them fade away.

There's a scale with a mirror in it right by the rocking horse that will tell your weight for a penny. I've never seen anyone use the scale, but it's been there for as long as the horse. Like the horse, its paint is nicked and peeling but it has some sort of mystique, as if it might have been put together by gypsies, or creatures that live underground in the woods. Maybe weighing isn't as much fun for older folk as the horse is for the youngsters, or maybe the mirror says things to grown-ups that it doesn't say to kids.

"Hello, Sixteen," Iris said.

I jumped at the sound of her voice and turned into a smile that brought the river, sunshine, a sweet kiss, and the heady aroma of honeysuckle. She wore bib overalls that were a lot more faded than Mr. Gordon's, and she had a red bandana tied around her head. She was more beautiful than the first time I saw her.

"What in the heck happened to your eye?"

I reached up to touch the blue, swollen place that was once a cheek and tried to think of something totally outrageous to say. "Um, I, uh... Someone hit me with a basketball."

"You're a real athlete, huh?" she asked, grinning, and poking me in the stomach with a stiff index finger. Her amber eyes danced with her smile behind round spectacles. "You gonna ride that horse, or not?"

"I can't ride the horse," I said.

"Why not?"

"I'm too damned old."

"Must you curse?"

"I suppose not. I don't usually make a habit of it. You want to ride?"

Her smile faded, and she shook her head. "I don't think so. I'm not allowed."

It was a response that spoke volumes, but it was a topic for which fourteen-year-old male minds are ill-equipped. Besides, she'd just turned a fine summer day finer, and I saw no need to create clouds. I pointed to the bench near the exit. "Let's sit down."

"Okay." We both sat down together, and I fought the urge to hold her hand.

"I got my hair cut," I announced.

"You should get a special award."

"You're such a smart ass."

"I like to think so."

I dug into my pocket for a piece of bubblegum. "Here, don't chew it yet. I want to buy you an ice cream cone."

"Sixteen, I…I don't know."

She kept looking up and down the sidewalk and inspecting the riders in every car that rolled by. She was fine on the outside, but she wasn't nearly as relaxed as she'd been down at the river. "You aren't used to the big city, are you?" I asked, leaning against her the way she had leaned on me at the river earlier. Her bare arm was soft and warm. She smelled divine. "What's that smell, Iris?"

"It's jasmine. Do you like it?"

"It's wonderful."

"You're always smiling, Sixteen," she said. Her voice was soft, almost a whisper.

"Iris, are you okay?"

"I'm just a little nervous. I didn't know if I'd find you uptown or not, but I wanted to try. Daddy's at the Feed and Seed, talking farming with Mr. Lawrimore. He didn't want me to come up here by myself."

"You don't have to worry, Iris. You'll be just fine here. What flavor of ice cream do you want?"

"What's your favorite?"

"Grape, but chocolate's good too. Pop says God sent chocolate down Himself and that we should eat it every chance we get to show proper appreciation."

"In that case, I'll take chocolate."

"But Dr. Ulmer's favorite is grape."

"I love Dr. Ulmer," Iris crooned.

"I love his hats," I said, "but I hate his tongue depressors. He gags me with those things every time."

"When I was little, I asked him if he got into trouble for delivering colored babies."

"What'd he say?"

"He bent down close so he could look me in the eyes and said, 'Iris, honey, there's no such thing as colored babies. There's just babies.'"

The bell on the Dime Store door clanged, but I paid it no mind. Iris was giving me a smile so sweet I'd decided to swim in it. Suddenly, her expression changed, and she stiffened, her smile replaced by a look of fear.

I looked down to see a pair of polished black pumps. I knew who it was from the way the ankle fat poured over the tight-fitting shoes. I'd seen these ankles in church hundreds of times. Eden's most infamous blueblood was hovering like the Hindenburg. She'd spied us through the glass and dumped a grateful Delores like a cooler of bad fish.

"Excuse me." I gave a respectful expression all the effort I could muster and looked up into the plastic smile of one Mrs. Lucille Thrower.

Mrs. Lucille wasn't really a fat woman, but she was a big woman, the kind who looked like she could cut firewood all day, then work the second shift at the mill without breaking a note. She had what my mother refers to as 'peasant ankles' when we're alone in the house. "Hello, Mrs. Lucille," I said, smiling only because it was a parents' rule of order.

"George, do your mother and father know what you're doing?" she asked, digging in a white bag of hot cashews.

"Yes, ma'am, they sure do," I said in a friendly tone. I indicated Iris with a nod. "Mrs. Lucille, this is my friend—"

"I'm not interested in your friend, George." She was talking to me, but she was doing her best to stare a hole through Iris.

I looked at Iris, who was looking down at her pretty bare feet and gorgeous, slender ankles. Iris knew exactly what was going on with Mrs. Lucille. I could only imagine what she was thinking of me. I suddenly found myself in that place that Mr. Free had referred to as *on the spot*.

"Mrs. Lucille, did I do something to make you mad?" I asked.

The big woman raised herself on her tiptoes and put one hand on a hip. I had no doubt that she could break me in half if she chose. Judging by her expression that's exactly what she wanted to do—after she chewed Iris up and spit her into the rain gutter.

"George?"

"Ma'am?"

She opened her mouth to ask a question, then closed it and glared at me for a few seconds. "What did you do to your eye?"

"I had an accident, Mrs. Lucille. What was it you wanted to ask me?"

"George, what day is it?"

"Why, it's Tuesday, Mrs. Lucille. There's going to be a full moon tonight." *Maybe something will rise up out of the river and eat your head off,* I thought. She glared at me with cold blue eyes. I didn't know what Mrs. Lucille had on her mind, but I could tell from her expression and attitude that it wasn't good.

Lucille Thrower was the real thing. Immersed in the comfort zone of Eden high society, I was certain that when she looked in the mirror, the queen of England gazed back. The bylaws of acceptable social conduct in Eden were written and enforced at the whims of Mrs. Lucille and a handful of her elite followers. The laws were in a constant state of flux as personal convenience dictated. Change was often necessary to create spontaneous rulings designed to exclude undesirables or excommunicate the unruly.

"George, you're aware that Saturday is the day reserved for most rural visitors." She said, "rural visitors" the way Pop sometimes said *Nazi*. Turning to Iris, she added, "Your father should be ashamed of himself, young lady. He would have been much better served to have mated with his own kind." Mrs. Lucille looked at Iris as if she were a large palmetto bug struggling to right itself on her kitchen floor.

I blinked repeatedly by way of an astonished reply. I'd also added a slack jaw. I was no stranger to rudeness, but this was a new benchmark.

"George, did the cat get your tongue?" Mrs. Lucille's disdain made me feel pretty much the way I suspected Iris was feeling.

I kept blinking, but instead of the usual meek response, for some odd reason I said, "No, ma'am, the cat didn't get my tongue. I can see that it hasn't bothered yours either. In fact, I seriously doubt that any self-respecting cat would come anywhere near that nasty thing you call a tongue."

"Oh my God," Iris whispered, concentrating on her toes as if they were the most fascinating things she'd ever seen.

It was Mrs. Lucille's turn to blink. Her cheeks flowered like scarlet rosebuds. "Excuse me?"

"I wish I could think of a good excuse for you, Mrs. Lucille, but don't believe I'd have the time. As Mrs. Patterson says, 'The time or the inclination.'"

"Why, I never—"

"Never what?" I interrupted. "Never stopped for two seconds to think about other human beings, or their feelings? This is a town, not your living room bridge table. You don't reserve days for people to come into town and spend hard-earned money. Which reminds me, Neckbone Rodriguez comes and goes as he pleases. Are you going to ask Mr. Andrew about that?"

I felt my cheeks burning cherry with everyone else's. Never in my fourteen-going-on-fifteen years had I dared talk to an adult this way, let alone our very own version of British royalty. Two thoughts glowed at the center of my consciousness: I was probably going to die for this, and I loved growing a ball sack.

Mrs. Lucille's reaction was a pleasure to behold. Her upper lip began to quiver while she did her best to destroy me with hateful, old-woman eyes. "I'll speak to your father and mother about this, young man," she sputtered. "And don't you ever utter Andrew Thomas's name in my presence again." She looked at Iris, and I was amazed to see that she was capable of even more hatred. "And you need to learn your place, young lady."

"You like my haircut, Mrs. Lucille?" I asked, fascinated by her Andrew Thomas comment but understanding that this was not the time or the place to pursue it.

She glared her death glare again. "What is *wrong* with you, George? Have you lost your mind?"

"No, ma'am, I'm growing a ball sack." I couldn't believe I said it, but since I was probably going to die anyway, I figured I should make the most of the moment.

The queen of Eden society spun on her heel and marched off toward the theatre, her large rear swinging with quick rhythm. I'd never seen an adult so mad, and I'd never seen Mrs. Lucille move so quickly.

"You're in a lot of trouble, Sixteen," Iris whispered. "You don't talk to people like her that way and get away with it." A tear fell from her left eye. I turned in my place on the bench and wiped it away with my thumb. I may have just cut my life short, but it wasn't over yet.

I stood in front of the bench and made an announcement. "Remember what you said down at the river, that I might not be the same person next time you saw me?" She opened her mouth to speak, but I held up an index finger. "Never mind. You stay there. I'll be right back."

Iris shook her head and looked down at her beautiful bare feet again. "I'd better get back to the Feed and Seed."

"Iris, the busybody is gone, and I have a treat for you. Don't you dare leave. I can see you from inside."

"Okay, but just for a minute." She was so subdued my heart ached. Her beautiful fire had been blown out by a hateful old woman: a bitter old woman resentful of everything that her money couldn't buy.

Delores made an extra-heaping double dip of chocolate and grape ice cream cones, excited by what she'd seen but not heard. She kept looking at me and smiling brightly. "George," she said, dragging my name into three syllables with her musically lilted Southern voice. "Mrs. Lucille sure did look mad the way she went huffing down the sidewalk."

"She's just having a bad day, Delores," I said. I tipped Delores a dime for piling the ice cream on and went outside to present her artistry to Iris. "That's almost as pretty as you, isn't it?"

"Stop teasing me." She dug her tongue into the chocolate and an expression of sweet contentment pushed away the pain Lucille Thrower had left in her wake. "Oh my, that is delicious," she said.

"One more thing," I said, standing and walking over to the horse. "You've got to ride the pony."

"I'm too old now, Sixteen. I can't ride the horse."

"If Francois Dulcet can pilot a rocket-mobile down Main Street, you can danged sure ride a mechanical horse."

"Who?"

"Never mind, come on over here and get on the old girl. I'm betting she has one more romp left in her," I insisted.

"Sixteen?"

"Yeah?"

"Did you say 'ball sack' to that woman?"

"Yeah, I think so."

I dropped the dime in the slot, and the mare took off, performing as she had since earliest memory, up and down, squeaking, wheezing, whirring, and clattering—tearing across an imaginary plain with rolling hills and blue sky overhead, hooves thundering and nostrils flaring. As Pug had so accurately observed, all it took was imagination. The expression on Iris's face swept me away. We get few moments brimming with all that's good about living. I believed as I watched her smiling down at me that I had a lot more living to do on this spinning orb, but I didn't believe, not for a second, that I'd ever see a more beautiful girl, or a sweeter, more innocent smile.

9

When I got home, I was relieved to see that Mom wasn't standing at the door with the *look*. You know the one. It's the one mothers across America get when they're trying to figure out how to make an impression on one of their offspring that he or she will never, ever forget. Mrs. Lucille hadn't called Mom and, as far as I knew, she hadn't spoken to my father either. I should've been a nervous wreck from sheer dread, and if it weren't for Francois Dulcet and Pug, I probably would've been. I was certain that peeping at Cindy would weigh in as my most serious wrongdoing, but the one that would haunt my mother and father longest would be the disrespect I'd displayed toward Mrs. Lucille.

I wasn't nearly as worried as I once would have been. The encounters I'd had with Francois and Pug made my social transgressions seem darned near insignificant. Something huge was happening in my life, something inexplicable.

Pop came home in a good mood. He liked my haircut and didn't query me on the day's events after he found out that I'd decided against fishing. Mom made fried chicken, mashed potatoes with thick brown gravy, green beans, and apple pie for dessert. We sat at our little table with glad hearts, and I listened as Pop gave thanks for God's grace and His creatures. Tonight, he mentioned chickens by name—as he did hogs and cows whenever they made an appearance on our table.

Pop once told me that he believed all animals had souls, no matter what the preacher said. All I had to do was think about Buster and the way he cared about me for Pop's thought to make sense. I watched the look of satisfaction on my father's face as he bit into a crispy leg, and I made a decision.

"Pop?"

"Yep?"

"Why aren't the coloreds allowed to come to town during the week?"

He swallowed his food and chased it with iced tea, then he looked at me in the way he does when he knows an answer will be remembered for years to come. "It's not that they aren't allowed, son. It's sort of an unspoken rule."

"Why's it a rule?"

"Because some people in this town are narrow-minded, self-centered, and hateful."

"Lloyd, I swear," Mom said.

"We go to church with a lot of them," he continued, ignoring Mom.

I did my blinking thing.

"They want the colored people in town to spend their money on Saturdays, but they don't want to see them at any other time."

"I want to sit in the balcony at the Anderson theatre with them. That's against the rules, too, isn't it?"

"I'm afraid so," my father said. "I can only imagine what would transpire if they showed up at church right smack dab in the middle of Eden on a Sunday morning. What brings all this on, George?"

This was a critical juncture. I'd been wrestling with my Iris problem since I laid eyes on her. "I have a friend," I said, trying hard to find the right words, "a friend who didn't follow the rules. Mrs. Lucille Thrower is mad at me."

"Oh God, not Lucille," Mom moaned. She put her elbows on the table, closed her eyes, and rested her chin in the fold of her interlaced fingers. Waning sunlight poured into our little kitchen and danced on the gloss of her red fingernails.

"Well, that does it for us," Pop said. "We'll no doubt be asked to leave. Hell, Lucille will probably stand up and ask us to leave town during the service Sunday."

"Honestly, Lloyd," Mom said. She sat back in her chair and crossed her arms. She looked sick. "What exactly did you say to Lucille, George?"

I'd stepped in it. "I don't remember exactly," I lied.

"What did Lucille say to you?" my father asked.

"She asked me what I was doing."

"And what were you doing?"

"Sitting on the bench in front the Dime Store talking to my friend."

"Who is this friend?"

"Her name is Iris."

"Ah, it's a she," my father said.

"Yes, sir."

"I don't like the sound of this one bit," Mom said, "and I don't know any Irises. Iris who, George?"

It occurred to me that I didn't know Iris's last name. "I—I don't know, Mom. She's pretty, and she wears glasses. She's sixteen."

"Iris Green," my father volunteered, winking at me and smiling. "I know her mother." Sunlight played on grease from the chicken on his lips and chin. It was clear that he wasn't the least bit upset, but Mom was slipping into the abyss.

"Sweet Jesus," she whispered. Mom gave Pop a hard look, her lower lip trembling. "Your son is going to get us run out of town on a rail, Lloyd."

"He was *your* son when he wrote about his mother last Mother's Day and *The Weekly Observer* published it."

Mom met his point with silence. She pushed her plate away and closed her eyes again. "The problem with you two is that you don't understand how difficult it can be to live in a town like this," she said.

She sat for an uncomfortably long time with her eyes closed, then rose and began clearing the table with the jerky little movements she uses when she's thinking that throwing something might be a great idea. I thought about Iris never getting to ride the pony while she was growing up and felt like I was getting a pretty good idea how difficult Eden could be, but I didn't dare say. I'd grown enough ball sack for one day.

We watched television in the silence that prevails when people are offended, angry, or both, and then went to bed. I waited longer than I usually wait to sneak out the window because Mom and Pop weren't talking.

10

The moon hung in the night sky like a huge streetlight, threatening to expose the peepers, prowlers, lovers, and one Spy Boy. I turned to inspect Cindy Turner's house, touching my sore cheek as I did so. The swelling had gone down, but I had a very respectable shiner. I wondered what Cindy might be doing within the moonlit confines of her room, but I wasn't about to try and find out. She still hadn't ratted me out, but possible outcomes were hanging on the horizon of my life like a bad storm cloud.

She and Theresa Russell were friends. If Cindy had decided that she didn't want to tell my parents or hers, then she had undoubtedly come to the conclusion that she was capable of doing more harm to me than proper discipline might. If she and Theresa caught me out alone, they'd beat the living crap out of me, ball sack or no ball sack, and I would no more tell on them than I would try and rob the Anderson Brothers bank.

I looked over at Mr. Free's house for something to take my mind off my oppressive prospects. Once again, it appeared that he had his own moon hanging inside the second floor of his house. Silver-white light spilled from every crack and crevice of his window treatments.

My favorite apparition was standing on Mr. Free's roof. He waved at me and grinned. He wore a tight-fitting jumpsuit and opened his arms wide to show wings fitted from his wrists to his ankles. He looked like a giant bat. His round goggles captured and reflected the moon. When he spoke, I heard the words inside my head.

Don't even think about coming up here, Spy Boy.

"Coming up where?" I asked aloud. By way of answer, he spread his arms wide and dove from the roof of Mr. Free's house. I expected an immediate crash into a garbage can that would wake the neighborhood, but Francois glided over Mr. Free's back yard, the fence, and over the roof of Miss Ginn's house like a duck coming in for a lake landing. I grinned and applauded softly, hating him equally for his rocket-mobile and the ability to glide off rooftops.

I ran for Miss Ginn's and, once again, into her shrubbery. A mop bucket sat by the back doorstep, and I picked it up. The living room was empty. I moved down to the end of the house. Through a crack in the Venetian blind, I saw Miss Ginn lying in bed with her eyes closed. Her Bible rested on her chest, rising and falling with a steady rhythm. A cigarette smoldered in an ashtray on her bedside table, possible leverage for lawn fee renegotiation, if I could explain how I found out about it.

I sneaked around to the front of the house, hoping to see Pug, but he wasn't on the porch. "Boo!" said a voice from directly behind me. I spun on my heel, adrenalin racing through my veins. Francois bent double and did his best to stifle the laughter.

"That was *not* funny," I hissed.

Francois stuck his tongue out. "Yes, it was. It was hilarious."

I took a swing at him. He saw it coming and stepped back, but I clipped his chin. There was the barest sensation of resistance as my fist passed through. Sparkling white dust exploded in the air like a miniature Fourth of July fireworks display. I stared at the glistening dust on my fist, then at Francois's chin, which appeared unaffected.

"Holy crap."

"That's the same thing as cussin', Bubba."

"Holy crap," I repeated.

He put an index finger to his lips. "Miss Ginn is going to hear you and call the law or shoot you with that double barrel she keeps underneath her bed," he whispered.

"Miss Ginn has a double-barrel shotgun?" I whispered back.

"Yes. For some strange reason, she has a fear of Peeping Georges."

"Holy crap."

Francois put a gloved hand on each hip. "You're going to have to go inside."

"But you just said that Miss Ginn has a shotgun."

"What does a shotgun have to do with finding your dog?"

I fell to the ground, my legs crossed, my shoulders sagging. Wet grass tickled my thighs and bare feet. I hung my head. "I can't go in the house, Francois. I just can't do that."

"You can and you got to, Bubba. You got some strange guidelines for a Peeping Tom. It's time to sack up, son."

I looked up and saw moonlight reflecting from his round goggles. Francois grinned and gave me the gloved thumbs-up. "He's in that little library he likes so much."

I looked toward the bay window. I'd seen the library before when Miss Ginn let me in for a glass of water. I shook my head.

"I want you to think about something, Bubba. Pug's about to help you out in a big way. Maybe you can do something for him sometime. The front door's unlocked. All you got to do is walk in."

"What in the world could I ever do for Pug?" I asked, turning back to look at Francois. Fireflies winked in the darkness beneath the trees, and a cat ran across the road near the corner of Miss Ginn's yard. Crickets chirped their tunes, and frogs croaked and grunted their rhythms, but there was no Francois. He was gone and I was on my own.

I crept toward the big bay window of the Ginns' library and peeked inside. Light from their television competed with that of the moon, but Pug seemed oblivious. He stared out at the moon, drawing some hieroglyphic that only he could see in the air with the long nail of the index finger of his right hand. Pug's lips moved with silent concentration, and his eyes shimmered with wetness. I stood and waved, but he either couldn't see me, or chose not to.

The front door is unlocked, Bubba. All you got to do is walk in, Francois' voice repeated in my head. I looked at the big front door, and my skin crawled. I have little to no reservation about peeping through a window, but walking into someone else's

home in the night was something that I hadn't entertained for
so much as a second during my near-fifteen years. Not even
Cindy Turner's bedroom was that alluring.

You can and you gotta, Bubba. Ball sack time.

Summer was teaching me things about myself. I walked up
the front doorsteps, crossed the porch, opened the screen door
with ever so much care, and turned the doorknob. I was hoping
that Francois was wrong, that the knob would refuse to obey,
but it turned without hesitation, and the bolt cleared its nest
with a soft snick.

I pushed with only the slightest of pressure, and one of the
hinges answered with an audible little squeak. *Could an old woman
with a double-barrel shotgun hear that?* She was at the other end of
the house and had appeared sound asleep earlier, but the weight
of her Bible, lamplight, or a full bladder could wake her at any
second.

Stop it, I said to myself. *You've got to do this. Francois is right.
It's ball sack time.* For my entire life, no one had been better
at talking me into trouble than me. I pushed the door open,
stepped inside, and let the screen door shut softly, its closer
spring twanging and creaking. I listened for a full minute, then I
pushed the front door almost closed and walked down the hall
and into the library.

"You're a brave young man," Pug whispered, continuing to
draw with his index finger.

"I'm desperate," I whispered back.

"Desperate people aren't always brave people."

I shrugged. There was no point in arguing logic with a man
who invented his own system of math. Besides, he was right.
"I'd love to visit, Pug, but Pop always says there's a time and a
place for everything, and this isn't either."

"I always liked your father. He's different."

I thought about the conversation at breakfast and nodded
agreement.

"Pug, did you find my dog?"

"I most certainly did."

"Is he okay?"

"He's fine, and he'd love to come home, but he can't."

"Oh God, what does that mean?"

"It means that he's being held prisoner."

"Prisoner? I thought he was chasing a woman."

"Women can certainly be trouble, can't they, George?" Pug didn't look at me, but I detected the barest hint of a smile.

"You got that right," I said.

He shifted position slightly, stretching to reach a bit higher, something I'd never seen him do. His fingernail was long and crooked, like the beak of a crow, with concentrated moonlight glowing at its tip. He moved his finger lower, leaving a trace of light about twelve inches long hanging in the air. He continued until he'd drawn a square, then touched the square in the center. Butch Sinclair's rundown clapboard house appeared as if Pug had switched on a television.

"I know that house," I said.

"Yes, I know. I'm sorry."

"Why are you showing me this?"

"It's quite simple. Your dog is underneath that house."

"*What?*"

"Buster loves a treat. You know that better than anyone. Butch tossed a ham bone underneath the house and Buster went right in after it."

I'd seen the fence wire around the bottom of Butch's house in the past, but I'd never thought much about it.

"The gate is in the rear."

"The old hospital is back there," I said, more to myself than to Pug. This was getting worse by the moment. "How many people died in that old hospital, Pug?"

"I wouldn't know. I don't think it's important." As I stared, the floating photo evaporated like steam from a coffee pot.

Ask him, Francois' voice said inside my head. The voice made me jump, and I rubbed my temples. A serious headache was brewing.

"I appreciate you doing this for me, Pug. How can I repay you?"

"What?"

"Is there something I can do for you in return?"

"No, there isn't, George."

I heaved a sigh of relief. Butch was going to be enough for me—and ten others like me.

"But you can do something for someone else. Actually, you can do something for two other people. Each would be a tremendous kindness."

"Excuse me?"

"You could take Hugh McVey fishing."

"What are you talking about? What does Mr. Hugh have to do with any of this?"

"Nothing. He had nothing to do with any of this. You asked if you could help."

"I don't understand."

"Hugh is going to kill himself."

The words stunned me. "Why... Why would he do such a thing?"

"Some people aren't made for this place, George. You can't see it now, but life is a harsh struggle. Some with truly kind hearts and spirits don't make it. Those who tend to think in terms of basic right and wrong can't accept the injustices. It's a habit of coarser folk to refer to them as selfish and weak. I don't share that opinion, but you'll need to come to your own conclusions."

"I didn't think you could see into the future."

"I can't."

"You're too much for me," I said. I was frustrated and full of despair.

"He stopped to talk to you shortly after you lost Buster. I saw him."

"I still don't understand."

"I went looking for Buster and I came upon Hugh McVey and Vance Baker that same day. Vance was digging in the garbage behind Hugh's store. He'd just found a box full of bright red socks, George."

I guess Pug could tell by the look on my face that I was as lost as a blind man in a hurricane. "Hugh told Vance he'd trade him a new winter coat and some matching socks for a pistol," Pug continued.

"Oh," I said. I still didn't understand completely, but I knew that Mr. Hugh wasn't a pistol kind of guy.

"Vance asked Hugh why on earth he'd want a pistol and he said, 'Because I'm tired and I'm lonely.'"

"But he has a wife," I mumbled, overcome by the enormity of the task being assigned because of looking for my dog.

"Yes, he has a wife—a depressed, alcoholic wife. Perhaps he could use a true, honest friend as well, and he likes to fish."

"Why do you care what happens to Mr. Hugh?"

"He was a friend of mine, a good friend. There are few things more satisfying and rewarding than a man you can call a devoted friend."

"What's the other favor?"

Pug drew another sheet of moonlight in the air and began filling it with symbols, letters, and numbers. He might as well have been drawing Egyptian hieroglyphics. "Pay close attention, George. You're going to need to remember this."

"You've got to be kidding, Pug," I whispered, stifling an impulse to laugh. "I'm still struggling with long division."

"Come over here," he said, motioning to me. I walked over to his side, and he took my hand. "Touch the script." I hesitated only inches away from the glowing formula, but a deal was a deal, so I did as I was told. The moonlight equation vanished before my eyes, flashed inside my head like a camera bulb, and then disappeared.

"Pug—Pug, is someone here? Are you *talking*, Pug?" Miss Ginn's bewildered voice sounded from the darkness at the end of the hall. "I have a shotgun, whoever you are. You leave my Pug alone and get out of my house this instant."

"You should go," Pug whispered.

"Really?" I said, the snapping breech of the shotgun making the hairs on my neck bristle like needles. Pug smiled and pointed toward the door. Miss Ginn's bedroom slippers slid across the wood floor of the hall, closer and closer.

I raced across the back yard and through the ivy-covered access at the corner of the Great Wall, stopping to catch my breath and collect my thoughts. I couldn't bear the thought of Mr. Hugh killing himself.

Then I made my way across Mr. Free's back yard, studying the light in his upper rooms as I walked. Bats flitted to and fro in the moonlight, but Francois seemed to have disappeared until next time. When I prepared to give the secret knock, I noticed the door was ajar. The light was on over the sink, and I could see past the French doors into the dining room, but there was no Mr. Free. From somewhere within the depths came the sound of music from a long time ago—big band music.

I stepped inside. "Mr. Free?" I waited for a minute or two. For the second time in one night, I was in a house without consent. I thought about the German pistol. I hadn't asked if it was loaded.

I pushed my way through the French doors into the dining room. The music was louder, but when I reached the entrance to the study, I saw that the old record player was quietly waiting for its next performance. I stood for a moment, feeling the house of shadow tease me with mystery and secrets. The lamps that Mr. Free had placed so well were extinguished. I felt that I'd entered a world just out of reach from the daytime existence people call life, a world beyond a door or veil that I couldn't see, much like my friend Pug.

I walked into the study. A mantel clock marked the passage of the night, one pronounced tick at a time. Books watched me in stern silence. The room, with its collection of artifacts and treasures dusted with the residue of danger and excitement from Mr. Free's past, pulled at me, but the thrill of playing sleuth lacked the powerful allure of the music.

I moved toward the den, my heart pounding, my eyes adjust-

ing to moonlight slanting through floor-length windows. I padded across the expensive carpet and past fine furnishings, the
musk of old things lingering just beneath the mingled aroma
of cleanser and floor wax. Turning left, I walked to the foyer to
gaze up the wide staircase. It was dark at the top of the stairs,
but somewhere in that darkness, somewhere in the cavernous
second floor of Mr. Free's house, a big band was swinging with
the rhythm of a heavy brass pendulum. I mounted the first riser
and a hand fell hard on my shoulder, a hand with a grip like a
warrior.

"Don't even think about going up there," Mr. Free said. His
words pulled me back from a place I hadn't realized I'd gone. I
didn't jump with shock the way I normally would have. I turned
to look at him with the nonchalance of a drunken sailor being
addressed by a superior, the ether of another world swirling in
my head.

"Why not? Sounds great to me. Sounds fantastic, to tell you
the truth. Where's your pistol?"

"You might not come back, Spy Boy," Mr. Free said, his eyes
soft but serious.

My head was fuzzy, the way it felt when I kissed Iris the
first time. I'd become unmoored from the dimension in which I
lived my life. "What are you talking about?" I asked. The music
stopped and I looked longingly into the darkness at the top of
the stairs.

"I think you, more than anyone in this town at the moment,
realize that sometimes you can get stuck in places that seem
beautiful at first glance." Mr. Free's words chased the last of the
magic away.

I opened my mouth, but he stopped me with a raised hand.
"What on earth are you doing over here at this time of night?
A fellow could get shot, you know."

He turned and strolled toward the library. He wore a smartly
cut, black pin-striped suit topped with a black Fedora sporting
a silver ribbon. I'd never seen a fellow who looked so good
dressed up. I'd also never seen men walk around in the middle

of the night dressed as if they were about to leave for the party of the year. I followed like an obedient puppy.

"You're wearing a hat in the house," I said.

"I was going out until an intruder interrupted me. Take a seat," he said, pointing toward the wingbacks. I did as I was told, wondering where on earth anyone would be going in Eden at this hour. He walked through the French doors into the kitchen and in a few minutes returned with his tray, hatless. He performed his ritual, opening my little Coke and handing it over, then mixing his adult libation.

"To imagination," he said, raising his glass.

"To imagination," I repeated with a smile.

"Mind if I ask what happened to your eye?"

I looked at the models hanging from the ceiling and sipped my Coke by way of reply.

"I see," he said, fitting a Gauloise into his holder and lighting it.

I rose to wander the room, too excited to sit still. I walked over to a large book lying on a shelf. The word *Yesterday* flashed at me in faded gilt letters from its cracked leather cover.

Moments of people and places were frozen in black-and-white stills and held captive between clear covers. Yellowed newspaper clippings held clues for my curious eye. Ladies in dresses with wide shoulders and mid-calf hemlines strolled along cobblestoned sidewalks as Model As chugged by. Children frolicked on a beach somewhere with tall cypress trees; a lighted Ferris wheel stood against the night sky. One of the children looked familiar. I held the book up so that Mr. Free could see.

"Who are these children, Mr. Free?"

"Spy Boy, do you come to visit me, or do you come to visit my house?"

"I'd have to say a bit of both," I admitted, closing the scrapbook and returning it to its place, feeling its pull like that of the music. Like the room, the album was filled with the mystery man's past, and it was all I could do to release it.

He gave me one of his pleasant chuckles and tapped his cigarette into a brass ashtray. An interesting artifact, it looked like the end of a bombshell, with foreign coins curved to hold the smoke of one's choice. The coins were soldered around the shell's circumference at the twelve, three, six, and nine o'clock positions. "Do your parents know where you are?"

"Of course not."

"What are you doing wandering about at this hour?"

"I...um...I was bored."

"You're aware that a mind easily bored is fertile territory for trouble, and I mean trouble in a way you've never before considered, I assure you."

I ignored the implied threat. I was almost certain that wandering about "at this hour" was no more dangerous than whatever it was lurking in the upper floor of his house. "An idle mind is the devil's workshop," I said.

"Something like that. Do you not agree that it's a bit strange for a respectable young man to be wandering around town in the middle of the night? I mean, if you were to get caught, it would take only minutes for one—or both—of your parents to get curious about your excursions. Parents are like that, you know."

"Brother, do I know." He was using the oldest trick in the book, lecturing in an effort to change the subject. I didn't want to play. "I'd hardly refer to myself as a respectable young man," I said. The instant his lips cracked into a smile I added, "What's at the top of the stairs?"

His smile vanished. "Aren't you the wily one?" he asked, and took a puff from his holder. I said nothing and he smoked a bit more before relenting. "The second floor, a place I'm going to ask you to avoid, boredom or no boredom. You can and may come over here anytime you please, anytime at all. However, you must promise that you'll not go up those stairs, especially during a full moon. Do you promise?"

I thought about making promises, and the near-irresistible fascination created by being told not to do a certain thing during a full moon in the summer, or any other season, for that matter. I didn't like to make ordinary promises: promises to look both ways, promises not to swim in the deep part of the river, promises not to climb the water tower, or jump off the Black River Bridge structure. I'd kept the bridge promise. The bridge structure had haunted me for years and the thought of jumping from it, like most of the boys my age had already done, made me sick to my stomach. I'd kept the bridge promise because not keeping it terrified me, but this promise was going to be damned near impossible to keep.

"George, promise that as long as I live in this house you won't go up those stairs," Mr. Free insisted.

"Okay."

"Okay what?"

"Okay, I promise," I said, my voice dripping with resentment...and my fingers crossed. Lovecraft's words came to mind: *No new horror can be more terrible than the daily torture of the commonplace.*

11

Most of Eden's merchants close up shop on Wednesday afternoon because they work either a half or entire day on Saturdays, depending on what time of year it is. If I was going to ask Mr. Hugh to go fishing, today would be the perfect day for it. That is, assuming I survived my upcoming attempt to rescue Buster.

Pop was already in the kitchen, enjoying the newspaper, a smoke, and a cup of coffee. "Good afternoon, George," he said without looking up.

"Pop, it's eight o'clock."

"I've been up since dawn, son. I did my exercises, read the Bible twice, and meditated. Now I'm waiting for my squaw to kill and prepare the morning feast."

"Honestly, Lloyd, you're so full of it, I'm surprised you can walk," Mom said, shaking her head.

"You like me like this, heap big woman. Admit it," Pop said in a deep voice. He rolled up his paper and leaned back to swat my mother on the rear.

"Don't do that in your son's presence," Mom fussed.

"You forget he's chasing Iris, Nancy. I'm afraid that he already has a mind of his own, and it probably hasn't spent much time on rolled-up newspapers."

I cringed and looked at Mom. She was standing at the sink with her back turned, but I could tell by the way her shoulders slumped that Iris was a sore subject.

"I think I might ask Mr. Hugh if he wants to go fishing today," I blurted.

"What?" Mom and Pop said in unison. Pop looked at me as if he suspected I might have a fever.

"Why on earth do you want to go fishing with Hugh McVey?"

I hadn't expected such a strange reaction. I stared at my father and blinked.

"George, your father asked you a question." Mom was good at injecting two cents when I didn't need even one. "Answer him."

I had no idea how to explain why I planned to go fishing with Mr. Hugh. Moments like this called for careful planning and, true to my nature, I had nothing.

I decided to try something that rarely worked, probably because I rarely tried it. "Because he's lonely. Because he doesn't have any friends. Because his wife is depressed, and I think he wishes he had a kid." I'd done it. I'd told the truth with no frills.

Last year during school, Ben Tanner had returned from a weekend visit to his uncle on Bull Street in Columbia with wide eyes and stories of straitjackets, padded cells, and hypodermic needles. If I told my parents that I'd sneaked out of my room and gone over to have a midnight chat with Pug, I'd be enjoying Bull Street hospitality of the same variety.

"Why, George, that's Christian of you," my mother said, her face beaming with pride and approval.

My father continued to frown. "You aren't sick, are you?" he asked.

"No, I'm not sick. He stopped one day on the way to work to ask about Buster. He always asks about the fishing. He's a nice man, and I think he's sad."

"Don't show him our favorite spots," Pop said.

"Lloyd, I swear, I don't know what I'm going to do with you."

"Honey, going fishing is pleasure enough. There's no reason for George to give up our best spots because he feels sorry for Hugh."

"It wouldn't hurt a bit for you to be a tad more generous in spirit, Lloyd."

"We're talking about fishing here, Nancy, not feeding the poor. There are rules." He looked at me, his eyebrows arched. "Isn't that right, George?"

"Yes, sir."

"George, you don't have to agree with everything your father says," Mom said.

"He agreed with me because I'm right, Nancy, not because I'm his father. Isn't that right, George?"

"Yes, sir."

"You two are ganging up on me," Mom said, her lower lip protruding in a pout.

"No, I'm not, Mom," I said.

"Leave the boy out of it," Pop said.

Mom put her hands on her hips, her pout disappearing in a flash. "*I* didn't bring the boy into it, Lloyd Parker," she huffed.

"May I be excused?" I asked.

"You certainly may, young man, and I want you to think long and hard about all this fishing conspiracy nonsense," Mom said.

I sat on the front porch steps and thought about Buster and the fact that he was locked underneath Butch Sinclair's house enduring God only knew what torment.

Imagination is a terrible thing when you're wondering what the school bully might be doing to your dog. For all I knew, Buster's eyes had been poked out with a stick. I studied on how gutless I was and why the thought of climbing onto Lightning and heading toward Bangalang was making me sick to my stomach. Facing Butch was going to be nothing at all like facing Mrs. Lucille. Butch Sinclair would kick my ass.

It's because you have no ball sack, my little voice said.

"Oh God, not you again," I mumbled.

"Who you talking to, son?" a strange voice asked.

I looked up to see a big boy—make that a *huge* boy, who looked about my age standing on the sidewalk. "Who are you?"

"You ain't supposed to answer a question with a question, but since I'm new in these parts, I guess I'll play by your rules," the big boy said with a grin. "Name's Lee Roy. Lee Roy McAlister."

He grinned, exposing a gap between his front teeth large enough to pull nails. His sparkling deep brown eyes drilled into mine, and I accepted with an intuition that rarely fails me the suspicion that this boy had something that I did not—a ball sack, a permanent one, not one that came and went like a summer breeze.

He also had about forty pounds of muscle on me. His arms and legs rippled when he moved like the farm boys who came to town on Saturday afternoons. Pop would no doubt make his "good stock" observation with this one.

Lee Roy's light brown hair bordered on blond from the sun and was trimmed crewcut style; he had a smattering of freckles across the bridge of his nose and cheeks, and his ears protruded from his head like tea-set saucers. He wore cut-off jeans and a raggedy T-shirt. Even though he looked as if he might be capable of kicking Pop's ass, I didn't feel the least bit intimidated by him.

"Mine's George, Lee Roy. George Parker." I stood and walked down the porch with my hand extended. He took my hand and squeezed. I felt strength in his grip but more importantly, I felt the restraint of a gentle man.

"Nice to meet you, George. I'm glad I ran into you. I don't know a soul around these parts. I was getting ready to amble on up the street and see if I couldn't meet me a friend or two. This here's a mighty fancy town, but a fellah needs a friend no matter where he finds himself, far as I can see."

"You aren't from around here, are you?" I asked, unable to stifle a grin. He was about as country as I'd ever seen, but I was pleased that his hand hadn't disintegrated when I shook it.

"I'm from the Pleasant Hill neck of the woods. My uncle and aunt moved in a few houses down. We had some tough times in my family here of late, and Momma sent me into town to live with Uncle Bill for the summer. I might go back home when school starts, but I don't know for sure. Things are kinda up in the air, as my momma says." He said this last bit in a much softer tone of voice and looked down at his big bare feet.

It'd been a long time since my internal compass pointed so directly to a boy my age with real hope. Mark Vaxton had been my last real friend, but being a preacher's kid, Mark didn't stay in Eden long. This kid looked and sounded like he might be worth a try.

"Well, my mom is always telling me that I need to have a friend other than my dog. I reckon we can give it a shot."

"You reckon?" he said, raising his head to show me a grateful grin.

"Yeah, I reckon."

"What happened to your eye?"

"I fell out of a tree."

He squinted at me for a few seconds while he thought on my explanation, then he nodded. "Any good fishing around these parts?"

"Fishing's pretty good around here. I'd love to take you, but I got something I have to do today, something right important."

"You need any help?"

I surveyed him again. He looked like a small tank, his chest already taking on that barrel shape that men of brawn possess. *Don't forget to go see Pug tonight, and don't get too rattled. You ain't gonna have to do it by yourself.* Francois' words appeared in my head out of the blue, and I smiled.

"Well, I got a job to do, and it might get a bit dangerous," I said, my smile fading.

His gap-toothed smile morphed into laughter, and he slapped his thigh with a big hand. "I can't see this place being that dangerous, Mr. George," he said, looking around. "You ever tried to cut a boar hog after you waited a bit longer than you should?"

My mouth dropped open. "What do you mean, 'cut'?"

"I mean cut their balls out, that's what I mean. Neuter—castrate 'em."

"Okay, I got it. I got it," I said, shaking my head. "Can't say that I've neutered many hogs, Lee Roy."

"Well, it ain't a Sunday church social," he said with more laughter.

"You got a bicycle?"

He lowered his head again, the way he had when he spoke about leaving the country to come live in town. "No, I ain't got no bicycle. Wasn't a whole lotta extra cash lying around where I come from."

"Well, it isn't a big thing. We can walk. Probably should walk now that I come to think of it."

"You sure?" he asked. He had a look that waffled between gratitude and expectation. My compass was right; there was a lot to like about this kid.

"Sure, I'm sure." I headed up the street, and he fell into step beside me, his grin firmly in place.

As we walked beneath the oaks toward the red light, Lee Roy's gaze was locked on the stately branches above us. "These are some evermore fine trees right here, Mr. George. Ain't nothing in the world like a fine climbing tree."

"I agree with that one hundred percent," I said. "One of my favorites is that big magnolia in the Piggly Wiggly parking lot. I like to climb it first thing in the morning and watch the people come and go. They never know you're up there. If you want to hear some interesting conversation between the ladies in Eden, you ought to climb that tree sometime and be quiet. Women will say just about anything in the grocery store parking lot."

"That's called eavesdropping where I come from. Momma would skin my hide for that."

I laughed. He was nowhere near as menacing as he looked, but I was counting on Butch to take a little while to figure that out. Butch *was* every bit as menacing as he looked.

"Is it okay if we stop by the department store?" I asked.

"Yeah, that'd be great. I love to go in stores."

The bells over the side door at McVey's announced our arrival. There was a water fountain just inside the door to the right that produced the coldest water in Eden. I stopped and hit the button, gulping until my teeth hurt, and Lee Roy followed suit.

While Lee Roy drank, I inhaled the store. I love the way McVey's smells. As soon as you enter, the shoe department is on the left, and the scent of fresh leather mingles with new dungarees, suits on the rack, and dress shirts. There's always a faint trace of perfume riding in there somewhere as well. It's one of the best aromas in the world.

"This place smells like going back to school," Lee Roy said, wiping his mouth with the back of his hand.

"Why, hello, George," Mr. Hugh said. "Who's your friend?"

"Hiya, Mr. Hugh. This is Lee Roy. His uncle lives in the house just down from me. They're the ones you saw moving in the other day."

Mr. Hugh gave Lee Roy a big smile and extended his hand. "You're right, young man, this place does smell like going back to school." Lee Roy's cheeks reddened.

"Where on earth did you get the shiner, George?"

"I just woke up and there it was," I said.

Mr. Hugh didn't miss a beat. "Well, people get black eyes for all sorts of reasons they don't want to talk about, George. What brings you in during summer vacation? You need church clothes?"

"No, sir, I don't need any clothes," I said, uneasy about his response to my smart aleck answer about my eye. He probably knew more than I wanted him to know, and that meant the rest of the town did too. "Lee Roy was just asking me about the fishing, and I thought I'd stop by and see if you'd like to go with us this afternoon."

Mr. Hugh looked from me to Lee Roy, then gave a response I recognized immediately. He blinked at me a few times, his great big Adam's apple bobbling up and down in his throat. "Why, George, I'd love to go fishing with you fellahs," he said, looking at his watch. "I usually close up at one. Is that too late? If it is, I might try sneaking out a little early for a fishing trip."

I thought about how pleased Pug would be with Mr. Hugh's excitement and shook my head. "Nope, one o'clock'll be just perfect. Lee Roy and I got a little job to do. If we survive that, we'll meet you out front, okay?"

"That'd be great, George, just great," he said. There was a

glistening film over his eyes that looked a great deal like tears in the making. I turned away and headed for the door with Lee Roy hot on my heels.

"Okay," I said over my shoulder. "We'll see you then."

"Nice to meet you, Lee Roy."

"You, too, Mr. Hugh."

"He's a right nice fellah, George," Lee Roy said when we were back out on the street, "but he looks kinda sad."

I looked at my new friend. More than once, I've listened to Pop exchange words at the gas pump with an old man who would go unnoticed all day on the streets of Eden by the average citizen. When the man would drive off, Pop would say, "George, that's good people right there." I think he'd say the same thing about Lee Roy McAlister.

We crossed Front Street, the bridge, and then the railroad track that announced entry into No Man's Land. I guess No Kid's Land would be more appropriate. At least, it was land that didn't belong to kids on the east side of the tracks. We walked two blocks, then took a right down a row of houses that had served a long time ago as nurses' quarters for the old Johnson hospital.

Bangalang hadn't always been called Bangalang. Years before, Dr. Timothy Johnson, gifted with vision unlike most small-town doctors, took a look around and decided that Eden would make a wonderful location for a hospital.

For a time, people came from all around to seek medical treatment at Dr. Johnson's hospital. Eden had a railroad depot, a bus station, a small industrial park, and a telephone system, all a result of Dr. Johnson's vision. Unfortunately for Eden, he was unable to predict the consequence that long hours and much hard work would bring to a genetically deprived heart muscle.

He fell dead at the age of fifty, leaving unfinished work and unpaid bills. The hospital never recovered from the loss, slipping further and further with each passing year until only a barely recognizable skeleton of Dr. Johnson's dream existed.

With the hospital's demise came the collapse of the small community that had grown up around it and the influx of families like Butch's.

"Damn, that thing's just about scary, ain't it?" Lee Roy said. During its heyday, the hospital had been a bright, inviting white, but its once-gleaming façade was streaked gray with tar residue that had seeped from its roof during years of rain and the stucco cracking and breaking off in chunks. Many of the windows were broken—no doubt by Butch and his unsavory cronies' predecessors.

Paint peeled and flaked from the awnings over the windows. Other awnings dangled by a thread, and some had fallen into the unkempt shrubbery. The big double doors at the top of the steps stood agape, inviting anyone with more ball sack than brains to enter. I wouldn't have gone into the place in broad daylight, let alone at night. No wonder Butch was so mean. He was living right down the street from a structure filled with the ghosts of people that medicine and prayers couldn't save. I stopped two houses down from the hospital and stared at Butch's residence as if it were an abandoned asylum.

"What we doing here, Mr. George? This don't look like the friendliest part of town."

"Is it worse than neutering hogs?"

"Not yet, but something's telling me that we're getting there fast."

I studied the fencing that served as the underpinning for the house. "Buster is under there," I said.

"Who in the hell is Buster?"

"My dog."

"What's he doing under that house?"

"I don't have a clue." Much to my surprise, and totally to my chagrin, Butch Sinclair strolled from around the corner of his falling-down clapboard house with a flat shovel in one of his fat, dirty hands. He saw me standing in the street and waved, positively glowing from the good fortune of finding one of his favorite whipping boys standing in his front yard.

"Ain't life grand?" he commented as he strolled through his litter-strewn yard. He jerked his big head back and to the side to shake untrimmed bangs from his eyes, his droopy chin jostling like Jell-O.

"Looky, looky," Lee Roy said under his breath. I chanced a look at my new friend to see if he was anywhere near as terrified as I was. Lee Roy wore a relaxed, easy grin.

Butch walked to within inches of us and stopped. "Well, if it ain't my favorite snob. Who's the big ape, little George?" He'd slung the shovel over his shoulder like a shotgun as he approached. Fresh dirt clung to the shiny underside of the blade.

"My name's Lee Roy. Lee Roy McAlister," Lee Roy said, ignoring the big ape comment. He extended his hand and smiled. "I'm right pleased to meet you."

Butch didn't acknowledge Lee Roy's extended hand or his friendly greeting. Instead, he stared at me with his dull blue eyes and grinned. His teeth were yellow, his blond hair lank and stringy with oil. He smelled as if he hadn't had a bath since school let out.

"What the hell you doing in Bangalang territory, bed-wetter?" he hissed.

I opened my mouth to respond, but Lee Roy beat me to it. "You ain't got very good manners, son."

This observation got Butch's attention. "You ain't got very much brains, boy," he said with a pained expression.

I had to admit one thing about Butch: he owned more ball sack than twenty of me. If he had Lee Roy's superior size and build to worry about, there wasn't a clue to indicate it. No doubt he'd taken stock of Lee Roy and decided that bowing down in his own yard wasn't an option.

I watched with grudging admiration as Butch bent slightly forward and spat on Lee Roy's dirty, bare left foot. He grinned at the big country boy and winked at me as he wiped his mouth with the back of a filthy hand, pleased as punch with his strategy and bravado.

"Shit, I reckon," Lee Roy said, staring down at his foot. He looked up at Butch as if the fat bully had suddenly sprouted a cabbage from his greasy forehead.

I wanted to laugh but didn't dare. I'd never heard anyone say 'shit, I reckon' before. I stood quivering in my place like a little girl, trying unsuccessfully to will my ball sack into place—a feat that Mr. Free had assured me was possible.

Butch shoved me hard in the chest and I stumbled backward at least two steps. He was big, fat, and strong as a small stud bull. "What're you doing with that shovel?" I asked, my voice trembling. The sound of my voice made my face redden with shame. To my ears, I sounded exactly like a little girl bed-wetter.

"I might be burying stray dogs with it," Butch said and spat again, this time on the street. "Seems a pack of curs come through a week or so back, tearing washing off the line. I killed some directly and saved some to kill later. Been buryin' a few 'cause of the smell." I wished with all my heart that his fat, oily head would explode.

"Ain't nuthin' better than killin' stray dogs." He pressed a finger against one nostril and bent to his left, blowing snot all over the place and leaving a shiny tendril on his upper lip. "What happened to your eye, Nancy?"

"Shit, I reckon," Lee Roy repeated in awe. "You ain't got a dab of manners."

I didn't have to resist laughter this time because Butch's ominous statement was revolving in my head like a lighthouse beacon. *I might be buryin' stray dogs with it.*

A hot fire started in my belly, erupting in a cloud of dark, crimson hatred behind my eyes. The longed-for ball sack appeared like seed bursting from a flower pod, and I slammed my right fist into Butch's snotty nose.

Butch's head snapped back. He used the shovel to regain his balance, grabbed his nose with his left hand, and stared at me in amazement, his eyes watering. Blood dripped from between his fingers. Instead of the retreat I expected, Butch let go of the shovel, wiped his bloody hand on ragged jeans, and grinned with yellow teeth. The game was on.

He grabbed the front of my shirt with his left hand and hit me on my fading shiner with a beefy right, rocking my head back and blurring my vision. Pain radiated throughout my skull, and tears spewed forth instantly. Butch laughed with glee and pushed me to the street with a tremendous shove.

I skinned the palms of my hands and my elbows in a futile effort to break the fall. The sting of the wounds was suppressed by the realization that I was about to leave this life for another, and I hadn't saved Buster.

The big bully fell on me like a tree, smelling of rotten garbage and fouled underwear, his fat rear on my stomach, his knees pinning my arms. Somehow, just before the pummeling started, I freed my right arm and stuck my index finger in his left eye as hard as I could. Butch let go with a howl that could have come from a wounded coon dog, but he remained undeterred.

Butch Sinclair was a playground scrapper from way back. He had begun the fight by hitting me on an already sore eye and cheekbone. He knew most of the tricks, but he didn't know them all, for what Butch needed at the moment was the ability to see out of the back of his head.

I'm not sure why the Bangalang bully had chosen to pretend that Lee Roy didn't exist. Maybe he was just plain over-confident. East-side kids unfortunate enough to get caught on the west side of the tracks didn't fight back, not even when they showed up with friends. We usually endured our beatings with humility and then fast-tracked it home to lick our wounds.

Butch cocked a beefy fist and grinned at me, his bloodshot eye swelling and running tears. To his amazement, I smiled back. My grin caused a second of hesitation. In his good eye I saw the glimmer of suspicion that something might not be quite right. He turned his head slightly to the left to locate Lee Roy, but it was too late.

Sunlight glittered off the shovel as it arced through the air. A dull, metallic echo rang up and down the littered street, courtesy of Butch's large, thick skull. His left eyelid began to tremor, and his right eye rolled up and back into his head, revealing a yellow-tainted eyeball. He fell over like a bowling pin, releasing a whistling sigh as he settled on his back in his weed-infested yard.

"Shit, I reckon," I said, sitting up and staring over at Butch. "You s'pose he's dead?"

"That's one rude fat-ass right there, Mr. George," Lee Roy said, smiling down at me.

"He's gonna be a whole lot ruder when he wakes up, Lee Roy. You reckon he's dead?" I asked again. "I hope he's dead."

The big country boy rubbed his chin. "I don't think he's dead and it don't make no difference how rude he is if we ain't here when he wakes up."

Lee Roy helped me to my feet, and I stood over Butch, staring down at the miserable kid who'd made my life a living hell for so long I couldn't remember. I spat squarely onto his forehead and unzipped my pants.

"Whatcha doing, Mr. George?"

"I'm getting ready to anoint this fat bastard," I said.

"Damn, and I thought fatty there was rude."

"Probably not, but believe me, Lee Roy, I've earned this."

"No, no, you ain't earned nothing. You ain't gonna piss on the man while he's down like that."

"Yes, I am."

"No, you *ain't*. I'm needin' a friend real bad, George, but you ain't gonna be him if you do this."

I hesitated. "Gimme a break, Lee Roy," I whined.

He pointed down at Butch. "Give that boy a break. Look at his clothes. Look at his house. Look where he lives. I ain't making no excuses for him 'cause they ain't none for behaving the way he does, but by the looks of things, there's some damn good reasons."

I looked at Butch, *really* looked at him. He wasn't nearly as menacing with his bloody nose and swollen eye. I heaved a re-luctant sigh and zipped up my fly, realizing with a bit of shame that Lee Roy McAlister was as large in character as he was in stature. My mother, if she'd witnessed this exchange, would no doubt label him a saint before banishing me to my room without supper for the remainder of the summer, perhaps forever. I was disgusted with the turn of events. It was just my luck to get stymied in the commission of what would have been until now the greatest achievement of my life, pissing all over Butch Sinclair's swollen, fat head.

"You're a good guy, Lee Roy," I said, my disgust evident. "You just haven't walked a mile in my shoes. You reckon we could get my dog?"

"Sure can," Lee Roy said, slapping me on the back. I led the way to the rear of Butch's house and, just like Pug had shown me, found Buster penned beneath the house.

"How'd you know he was here?" Lee Roy whispered.

"A friend of mine saw him and told me about it."

Buster heard my voice and raced from the darkness of his prison. He stood at the gate with his nose pressed against the fence wire, his tongue hanging out of one side of his mouth and his eyes wide with fear, emitting the most pathetic bout of whimpering and whining I'd ever heard. I opened the gate and he knocked me onto my backside, then straddled me and tried to lick my cheeks off.

"What in the hell is you boys doing down there?" a gruff voice asked from above. The three of us froze and stared up into the unshaven, tubby face of Dex Sinclair, weaving back and forth like a damaged top trying to find center.

In my world, the only thing scarier than Butch Sinclair and water moccasins was his father. Dex's hair, blond like Butch's, hung down in his eyes. He weighed in at near three hundred pounds and wore a pair of faded blue jeans with no shirt. His face was sweaty, and his unfocused eyes had the deranged look common to binge drinkers who are one or two hangovers from the abyss. I would have bet a body part that Dex Sinclair didn't know what day of the week it was.

He took a swig of cloudy brown liquid from a quart Mason jar and swayed back and forth some more. His lips parted into what was supposed to be a grin, but the absence of front teeth made the expression anything but pleasant. For a second, I honestly felt sorry for Butch. Lee Roy and I stared at Dex and played the role of deaf-mutes.

He waved the jar of moonshine around. "You boys can't talk? I asked you a question. What the hell y'all doing in my *yard?*"

Lee Roy found his voice first. "We came to get our dog."

"That ain't your damn dog. That's Butch's damn old cur."

"What's he doing locked under the house like this?" Lee Roy asked.

Dex leered at Lee Roy. "He was tearing clothes off the line," he said and took another swig from his jar. "Somebody's gonna have to pay for those clothes."

"I don't see no clothesline," Lee Roy said, scanning the back yard.

Dex looked at Lee Roy as if he had two heads, then squinted at me, rubbing his oily, whiskered face. "Say, don't I know you?"

"I…I don't think so," I stammered.

"Maybe not. My memory ain't what it used to be, but you look a lot like old Dink Parker. Me and him went to grade school together till I quit. Say, where in the hell is Butch anyway?"

"He's out front," Lee Roy said.

"I don't like strangers in my yard," Dex said. I stared at the drunken man, marveling at how much Butch already looked like him. Butch already smoked. I wondered if he was drinking too.

Dex pointed a crooked finger at us. "Y'all rich brats stay right where you at. I'm coming down there."

"I ain't staying anywhere," Lee Roy mumbled.

"Me either," I said. Lee Roy broke first with Buster and me in hot pursuit. We made a run for it, leaving Dex to his rant.

The exhilaration of leaving a nightmare behind was short-lived. When we made the turn at the corner of the house, we came face to face with what my father calls a rock and a hard place. Butch was being helped to his feet by a shabby congregation of Bangalang warriors.

Wordless, he pointed a shaky, accusing finger at us. The beleaguered bunch looked like snarling wolf pups. We'd invaded their territory and humiliated Bangalang royalty in the process. Poverty is horrible, but in the eyes of a Bangalanger, it won't hold a candle to humiliation at the hands of an outsider. Behind us, we could hear Dex hitting another gear in his tirade of fury.

"Shit, I reckon," Lee Roy said, pulling up so abruptly that I slammed into him. Buster whimpered support. Lee Roy was big and strong, but he wasn't that big and strong. I looked around Lee Roy and took stock of the situation. I'd been here before and knew there was only one way out. We had to run for it. I pulled hard on his shirt.

"This way," I yelled and turned toward the back of the house.

"How 'bout the old man?"

"Never mind him."

We blew by Dex like a summer storm. I headed straight for the old hospital with the Bangalang gang in hot pursuit.

"We ain't going in there, are we?" Lee Roy yelled. I didn't answer and didn't break a note until I was standing on the terrace of the old hospital. I turned to look down on the pursuing gang of ruffians. "Well, unless you think you can take them all by yourself," I answered between gasps.

"What you gonna be doing?"

"Watching and praying," I said backing through the big double doors with Buster by my side. Lee Roy watched with wrinkled brow and shook his head, but he followed me inside.

"Y'all think it was gonna be bad out here," Butch yelled from below. "You and your bumpkin friend is gonna die in there for sure. Then we'll eat your stupid dog." Something in Butch's voice made my skin crawl.

"How's your head, fat boy?" Lee Roy yelled back.

"Better than yours is going to be, hick," Butch answered.

"Yeah, hick," one of Butch's cohorts yelled. A rock flew past my head and clattered in the shadows behind us.

"Butch, Butch, don't you boys dare go in there," I heard Dex warn. His drunken slur was gone. Big Daddy was scared. It was what I'd heard in Butch's voice.

Butch shook his head. "We ain't going in, Pa," he said.

"Why don't y'all come on in and join us?" Lee Roy yelled. "Maybe we can dance or something."

"No way in hell we going in there, country boy," Butch shot back. "Tell you what's funny, though. Probably ain't no way in hell y'all are coming out. I bet we don't even get to eat the dog."

Buster whimpered again, and Lee Roy looked at me. "George, what in the world is he talking about?"

I shrugged and tried to look innocent. "Well, you know," I said.

"No, I don't think I do know."

"The place is…uh…um… It's supposed to be haunted."

"Shit, I reckon," Lee Roy said again, licking his lips. Standing in the shadows the way we were, his eyes looked a bit like Dex Porter's, wild and slightly crazed.

"Don't tell me you're afraid of ghosts," I said.

He grinned, but it wasn't an amused grin. "Don't tell me you ain't. How we gonna get out of here?"

"I don't know, but we gotta think of something. We have to meet Mr. Hugh."

"Mr. Hugh might have to go fishing all by his lonesome, George."

"That won't work. That wasn't part of the deal."

"What deal?"

I opened my mouth, then slammed it shut, returning Lee Roy's steady gaze and licking my lips. "I'll tell you about it later."

Despite obvious courage, the old hospital was getting the better of Lee Roy. I looked past the double doors at the bright, ghost-killing sunlight and the safety it would bring.

"Why don't we see if we can find some old sheets," I whispered, hoping that my voice sounded more convincing than I felt.

"Why in the hell do we need old sheets?"

"They obviously think the place is haunted. They think we're going to die at the hands of whatever's in here. Let's dress up like a ghost, or like crazy doctors with masks on, or like any-

thing that might fool those idiots. We can chase them from here
to the river if we find the right get-up."

Lee Roy shook his head. "I don't think they're that stupid,
and you sound kinda desperate. Why don't we just go around
those stairs and sneak out the back?" he asked, jerking a thumb
at the giant set of stairs in the center of the lobby.

There was a large parking lot in the rear of the hospital and
an access road that ran back out to Main Street. The problem
was that Lee Roy was right about the brains situation. The Bangalang bunch was poor, but a few of them were smarter than
Willis Ford, who was the smartest kid I knew on our side of
the tracks—the difference being that the Bangalang kids didn't
waste much time with their noses stuck between the covers of
schoolbooks.

"They'll be waiting for us," I said.

"Then we'll put both our plans together. We dress up, and
we sneak out the back. Let's split up and look for whatever we
think might get us out of this. I'll go down this hall and you go
down that one. If you find something that looks like it'll work,
yell for me. I'll do the same."

"Come on, Buster," I said.

"How come you get to take the dog?"

"'Cause he's my dog," I said and made tracks faster to avoid
argument.

Medical literature was scattered about. Gurneys and old
wheelchairs lay on their sides. Baby brochures and blank birth
certificates and open filing cabinets reminded me that new life
once graced this spooky old place. Most of the rooms on the
ground floor were for examinations, supplies, and clerical work,
but when I got to the end of the hall, I discovered large double
doors with frosted glass panels marked *Surgery*.

I pushed through the doors to find a stainless-steel operating table with a large dome-shaped light hanging over it like a
dead moon. The table was fixed in the middle of a light green
tile floor littered with plaster, rat droppings, bits and pieces of
tattered yellow gauze, and an assortment of the tools of the

trade: scalpels and needles, scissors, forceps, and something that looked like a small carpenter's saw.

The saw brought horrible visions to my fertile imagination. I picked it up and turned the fine teeth in the light, wondering how many bones they'd worked their way through. What suddenly bothered me more than the surgical tools was the fact that they were still here. No doubt, the implements scattered about the operating room floor would be viewed by the Bangalang kids as treasure. Yet, here they lay, free for the picking. The children of Bangalang, the toughest, scrappiest kids on earth, were terrified of this place—and so were their parents.

The room was eerily quiet except for Buster's breathing and the occasional scrape of a breeze-pushed tree limb outside one of the frosted-glass windows. "Don't forget about our father," came a tiny voice from behind me. I stiffened.

I'd been doing quite well, facing Butch and his cronies without screaming in terror or throwing up. But a timid voice in the still of an old operating room was more than I could take. I wet my pants.

I turned slowly. Two little girls stood holding hands just inside the double doors. The oldest appeared to be about my age, the younger not far behind.

The girls shared pale skin and silken black hair with eyes as black as their manes. They wore white dresses embroidered with pink and yellow lace, matching socks, and black, patent leather shoes. In the South, outfits like these are worn on Easter Sunday.

The girls looked familiar, and they were deader than Carl Pope's grandmother, Trudy, whom I'd seen down at Morris's funeral home just last winter.

"You promised you'd take him fishing," the smaller girl said. "He's a good man, George. Please don't let him down. He's been let down enough. We need to speak to him."

They look like Hugh McVey, my little voice volunteered. To my dismay, Buster was gazing at the girls with his tail tucked between his legs up to his belly. He cocked his big head to the left, then to the right.

"Holy crap," I said as I turned and slammed through the big doors with Buster hot on my heels. The girls reappeared in the hall, but I had too much momentum to brake. They turned to vapor as I ran through them, and I felt a chill to my bones.

"Lee Roy!" I yelled as I hurtled toward the lobby, picking my way through the maze of derelict medical equipment at max speed. Buster emitted a terrified wail as he slipped and slid on the tile floor behind me.

Lee Roy emerged from the shadows of his hallway, running toward me at about the same speed, his eyes nearly as wide as his mouth. We turned toward the rear of the hospital and ran down the center corridor, our bare feet slapping on the dusty tile.

Lee Roy began to edge me ever so slightly as we approached the doors. Unlike the front, the back doors were closed. We hit them with a prayer at full speed and they gave freely, exploding outward with a loud concussion only to reveal four of the Bangalang warriors standing in wait at the foot of the stairs.

We stood at the top of the stairs, heaving like thoroughbreds, Buster panting between us with his head low, his hair bristling along his spine. Lee Roy was fiddling with something in his right hand.

"Y'all ain't so smart after all, is you," Shorty Broward drawled, his broken grin revealing crooked, neglected teeth.

I couldn't respond and Lee Roy didn't attempt to. Instead, he raced down the stairs, stopping inches from Shorty and raising an enormous hypodermic needle high into the air, where sunlight raced its length as if it were a battle sword.

Shorty let go with a horrified yelp when he caught sight of the needle. "To hell with that dog," Ruck Goddard said, looking from Lee Roy's hypodermic to the saw in my hand. "I don't want nothing else to do with this crap. These two are crazy, and Butch is big enough to fight his own battles." Ruck gave me a strange salute and took off, the remainder of the Bangalang pack in his wake.

"I'm gonna stick this needle up your asses," Lee Roy yelled after them. "I swear to God, I will. Then, I'll stick it up your mommas' and daddies' asses," he added for good measure. He looked at me when it appeared we were in the clear. I was staring down at the saw in my hand, which I'd completely forgotten. We didn't stop running until we crossed the tracks and hit the bridge, where we lost the needle and saw over the side.

"George," he said, wheezing like an old man.

"Yeah?" I wheezed back.

"George, I saw my granddaddy in there."

I didn't say anything. I couldn't catch my breath and didn't want to. I walked back to the bridge entrance and made my way down a secluded path that led to a small beach at the river's edge. I walked into the cool black water to my waist as Lee Roy watched.

"Whatcha doing, Mr. George?"

I didn't want to admit to washing piss from my underwear and shorts. "I'm cooling my feet. I think we broke some sort of land speed record."

Lee Roy came down and waded in beside me, his head lowered. "Well, I didn't want to say anything, but I wet my pants in that damned hospital. They ought to tear a thing like that down." It was at that moment that I realized I wanted to call him a friend. I was pretty sure that Lee Roy hadn't wet his pants in the hospital.

Our waist-deep venture turned into a full-fledged swimming romp until Lee Roy looked at me and said, "Ain't we supposed to be going fishing?"

Mr. Hugh was standing by his truck when we reached the department store, grinning like a kid on Christmas morning. "I took off a few minutes early and went to the house to get my truck," he said, slapping a rusty fender. The truck was a beat-up old '49 Ford that'd seen better days.

"I got poles, bait, and plenty of tackle—and bologna

sandwiches, George. We don't have to stop for anything." He opened his mouth to say something else and stopped, a look of concern growing on his face. "Your eye looked a lot better this morning, George. What happened?"

"I ran into an old friend."

"Some friend," Mr. Hugh said, shaking his head. "Hey, take a look at this." We walked to the rear of the truck and looked into the bed. An old Western Flyer bicycle lay on its side, waiting to be rescued.

"Had it for a long time, but I don't ride anymore. Probably won't ever ride it again with my knee the way it is. You reckon you fellows could find someone interested in fixing it up?"

"I reckon we could," I said. Lee Roy was staring at the bike as if it were a brand-new Corvette. I slapped him on the back and teased Buster into the bed of the truck.

"Did you guys stop for a swim, that why you late?" he asked, shaking his head and grinning.

"Oh," Lee Roy said, patting his wet shorts. "We can ride in the back, Mr. Hugh."

Mr. Hugh laughed. "It doesn't matter to Betsy. She couldn't care less about wet pants as long as y'all don't. I'll be glad to take you home to change."

"No point in that," I said, climbing into the cab first. The weary flathead V8 ran like a fine old sewing machine. We bounced and creaked over the tracks back toward the way Lee Roy, Buster, and I had just come, through the forbidden territory of Bangalang.

As we rolled past, Lee Roy and I stole glances down Butch's lane at the old hospital. I couldn't resist a small shiver, but Lee Roy looked at me and grinned. Bangalang was a lot less stressful from this angle.

The landing at Mingo is located near the bridge at the end of a steep length of dirt road. We could see the cars and trucks parked beneath the trees when we made the turn. You can always tell if the fish are biting by the crowd at Mingo Landing, as well as the yellow butterflies.

We walked along the bank beneath river birches and cypress trees, a woodpecker banging out a rhythm deep in the woods, the rich, wet earth heavy in our nostrils. Mr. Hugh and Lee Roy chose a place jutting out into the river near a large honeysuckle bush, while Buster and I went down a few yards farther and picked a spot that looked fish friendly.

An old colored man wearing a pair of overalls about two sizes too large sat nearby. I knew with a glance at him that I'd chosen well. I also knew better than to ask if this was a good spot, because he'd lie like a rug.

"May I sit here?" I asked.

He looked at me and shrugged. "Just don't tangle us up," he said, looking directly at me. His black eyes were rimmed with a ring of blue.

"Yes, sir," I said, sitting to bait my hook. Buster leaned into me and pressed his head against my chest. "I missed you too," I said, hugging him tight.

"You is a well-mannered young man. Who's your daddy and his daddy?"

"Lloyd Parker's my dad. George is my grandfather. I was named after him."

"Nice to meet you, George. I know your daddy and that pretty momma of yours. Doc's your other grandaddy," he said with a grin. Sunlight flashed off his gold-capped front teeth. "My name's Amos, Amos Mention. You know, Doc once swam 'cross this creek buck naked in the dead of winter."

I'd heard this story a half-dozen times and hadn't believed it since I was ten. "You don't believe that, do you?" I asked, returning his smile.

"Course I b'lieve it. I watched him do it. Lost five dollars to my best friend 'cause I didn't think Doc could make it both ways." Amos let go with a belly laugh.

"I got too old to believe that story," I admitted.

"He's quite the storyteller. Well, used to be back in the day. I ain't seen him in a month of Sundays. He doin' all right?"

"He's doing well, Mr. Amos. Still embellishing the truth to make it more interesting, as he says. I'll tell him that I ran into you."

"You do that, son. You do that."

I hooked a fat bream and watched the fish dance on the water's surface, sunlight splashing off its red breast and painting the waterdrops amber. Amos clapped with delight, and soon added one of his own to his stringer.

About an hour passed as water bugs traced delicate wakes across the creek's surface and dragonflies devoured tiny flies that glowed with sun-haloes, while Amos recalled old times, hard work, and good people he'd known. His large hands baited his hook with the deftness of a surgeon, and he caught another tiny bream as soon as the hook hit the water. To my disappointment, he kept the little fish.

"Mr. Amos, why would you keep one so small?"

"Well, I know he's little, but this creek is chock full of fish, George, and I got a frying secret."

"A frying secret?"

"You can fry these little fellows just right without doing anything but dropping them in the grease. Let them sizzle till they float, then slide they crispy little selves 'tween two slices of light bread. Eat them head and all."

I gave him a direct, challenging stare, and he laughed. "You been around your granddaddy too long, son," he said.

Mr. Hugh walked up with a grape Nehi and a bologna sandwich. "Hello, Amos. I haven't seen you in a while. You doing okay? I heard you've been under the weather."

"A man fishing on a day like this can't be doing nothing but good, Mr. Hugh."

Mr. Hugh looked at me. "George, it's a fine day on the creek. Lee Roy and I have already caught our limit. How're you doing?"

"I got three big ones and a small one, Mr. Hugh."

"Well, fish on for a little while and eat your sandwich. Lee

Roy and I are going to eat and relax. Amos, come see me next time you're in town. Looks like you might need some new overalls. We'll work something out."

"I'll do that, Mr. Hugh," Amos said, the gold of his teeth shimmering in the sunlight.

Mr. Hugh left and I gave my sandwich and grape Nehi to Amos. "I didn't have the heart to tell Mr. Hugh that I already ate," I said. "You want these two large bream, Mr. Amos? I need to keep the smaller one. I got a need for him."

"I ain't no charity case, son," Amos said, shaking his head.

"Didn't say you were, Mr. Amos. You told me you were a friend of Doc's. That makes you my friend, too, if you'll have me."

He smiled again and took the sandwich, the drink, and the fish. "Make sure to say hello to Doc for me." He extended his giant hand. The hand was calloused and, despite his recent illness, strong but gentle, like the man himself.

"I sure will. It was a pleasure to meet you."

"You too, son." He winked at me again and I compared the feeling this gave me to the one I get whenever I meet an old friend of my father's, a man who loves me simply because I'm the son of a man he loves.

"I don't understand why you kept the one small fish," Mr. Hugh said.

"Me neither," Lee Roy piped in. "You city boys are a strange breed."

I looked at Mr. Hugh and smiled. "I'll show you later."

Mr. Hugh let Lee Roy and me off at my house. "Thanks for everything. It was great," I said.

"Yeah, thanks a lot," Lee Roy said.

"I had a lot of fun, George. I've been a bit down in the dumps lately," Mr. Hugh said.

My stomach knotted with the effort to say what I needed to say. "Mr. Hugh, your daughters loved you very much." It was a dangerous thing to say. I had no idea what sort of reaction I'd get. A man who's been contemplating suicide is a man I don't know how to read. As a matter of fact, I can't read adults at all.

Hugh McVey didn't flinch. He didn't ask how I knew about his daughters, and he didn't tell me to mind my own business. "I loved them, too, George. Thank you for saying that and thank you for this fine day. Maybe we can do it again soon."

"Sooner than you think," I said and slammed the door of the old truck.

He stuck his head out the window and looked back. "Don't forget the bike. I wish one of you would take it, but if neither one of you needs it, find someone who does."

Lee Roy grabbed the bike, a huge grin on his face, and we watched Mr. Hugh rattle away.

"That there is a fine, man, Mr. George, and I had a damn fine day. I was a mite worried about living in this city by myself. I got me two new friends and a brand-new bicycle in one day. It don't get no better than that."

"Thanks for everything you did to help me today, Lee Roy," I said.

"Well, I can't say that I hope every day in my new hometown will be this exciting. You reckon you'd like some of my catch, George? That's a tiny fish you kept."

"Well, you know what they say, Lee Roy."

"I don't reckon I do."

"Little fish make big fish." I turned toward my house with my dog. "I'll see you later," I said over my shoulder as I walked around to the back. Pop had built an outdoor table with a sink for fish cleaning. I cleaned the fish, cut it into chunks, and put it in the fridge in the kitchen. Buster followed me every step I took, happier than a pig in slop to be home.

"Well, where are all the fish?" Pop asked when I sat down to a big platter of Mom's fried pork chops. "That doesn't look a whole lot like fish right there," he said, looking from the platter to me. "And what happened to your eye—yet again?"

I touched my battered eye and winced. "Butch Sinclair hit me when I went to get Buster."

"You got Buster back? Where in the heck is he?" Pop jumped up and ran to the back door. "Buster, you fat old rascal. Get your cur ass in this house." He stood holding the door open until Buster came slinking in. Buster knew that he was no house dog, but he wasn't about to pass up the invitation, especially with the smell of fried pork chops in the air.

My father was happier than I was about Buster's return. In one of those moments of insight called 'growing up,' I saw a different man. His stoic handling of Buster's disappearance had been for my benefit, and I loved him all the more for it. He sat back down at the table, pointed at the platter of pork chops with his fork, and gave me a questioning look.

"No fish today," I said. "I gave them away."

"You did what?"

"I gave them to Amos Mention."

"I'll be damned. I thought Amos was dead."

"He looks like he might be headed that way."

"That's not a very nice thing to say, George," my mother said. "But it was nice to give him your fish," she said, slipping Buster a whole chop under the table.

I smiled and pretended I didn't see her. "I gave him my lunch too."

"Aren't you turning into quite the young gentleman," she said.

"A starving gentleman," I added.

"I believe that your grandfather and Amos Mention were good friends growing up," my mother said.

"Yes, they were. That's why I gave him my fish…and my lunch."

After supper, we repeated a ritual that innocence and blissful ignorance had led me to believe would never end. Mom knitted, peering occasionally over her half-glasses at the television and chuckling over Gilligan's antics as Pop read the paper. I continued with *The Mysterious Island* while the Skipper yelled, and Ginger and Mary Ann made young men all over America think about anything but a television sitcom. Buster was curled on the couch at my feet, sleeping the sleep of the dead.

At nine, we went to bed, listening to the approaching train's whistle and to the clattering and rumbling of steel wheels. As the mighty engine's powerful rhythm faded, the hushed voices of my parents floated through my door. I read about Nemo and his strange island until the parent talk waned, then stopped. I turned out my light and lay quietly, wondering where the train had come from and where it was going.

Tonight, I couldn't exit through my window. I reached into my drawer and removed the little bag that Iris had given me, along with a roll of fishing line. Buster had taken his rare place at the foot of my bed. I scratched his ears, told him to rest up, and tiptoed to the kitchen in the dark, avoiding the squeaking board in the hallway. Then I retrieved my fish from the fridge and let myself out the back.

I was banging at Mr. Hugh's door about three minutes later. He answered my knock, dressed in his pajamas and rubbing sleep from his eyes. "George," he said through a yawn. "What on earth are you doing?"

"I'm here to take you fishing twice in one day," I said, but it didn't sound right. Before Mr. Hugh could say anything, I corrected myself. "Okay, you took me fishing. I'm here to repay the favor already."

He looked at his watch and stifled another yawn. "But it's almost midnight."

"I know that, Mr. Hugh."

"Do your parents know where you are?"

"Of course not. Are you going to tell? If you tell, it might be the end of our fishing expeditions."

He grimaced at me. "That's just awful, George. They call it *blackmail* in a court of law."

"Mr. Hugh, I'm fourteen, going on fifteen hard. You want to go fishing, or not?"

His frown morphed into a great big smile. "Heck yeah, I want to go fishing. Come on in. I have to change." I walked into his den, and he motioned toward a chair.

"You can turn on the television, George, but keep it low. Gladys is asleep."

"Yes, sir," I whispered. I took a seat but left the TV alone. Instead, I closed my eyes against the silence of the well-kept house and felt for the joy that ought to be in a house where children lived, searching for the essence that would betray the existence of a cocoon like my own. I felt nothing but loneliness and opened my eyes. Two little girls smiled at me from the confines of a silver frame atop the silent TV. I recognized them immediately.

We walked beneath the oaks in silence, enjoying the quiet of Eden at night and the moon's way of scattering itself through the overhead canopy of limbs and leaves. Silver lily pads floated on the road's surface. A shiver of delight traced down my spine. This would be a perfect time for Francois to appear.

"George?"

"Yes, sir?"

"What's in the bag?"

"Bait."

"We don't have any poles."

"We aren't going to need any poles. At least, I was told that we wouldn't. I've never actually fished like this before, Mr. Hugh, and I got to tell you, we aren't going to catch any fish tonight."

"Then why are we going?"

"Well, we got to set lines."

"That's not mystery fishing, George. You're talking about a cat line."

"Yes, sir, but this is gonna be a bit different. I promise."

We went downtown, past the red light, and across the bridge. When we reached the path leading to where Lee Roy and I swam earlier, we walked down to the water. Beneath the full moon, I poured the two hooks into my hand, where they glowed as if they were creating light of their own.

The hook's a secret, Sixteen. You can't tell anyone, okay? The words were so clear that I glanced back up the path.

"What's wrong, George?" Mr. Hugh asked. I looked at him. His dark eyes glittered in the moonlight.

"Mr. Hugh, you got to promise you won't tell anyone about these hooks. They're a secret."

"Those are strange-looking hooks for river fishing, George."

"Yeah, like I said, they're a secret." I looked at him, waiting before I did anything else.

"Okay," he said with a smile. "I promise."

I tied the hooks to my line, baited them, and waded out to a low-hanging river birch limb. I threw the hooks out and looked back at Mr. Hugh, but he had his back turned. We weren't two fishermen alone on a moonlit night anymore. My ghost girls had followed us.

The girls walked slowly toward Mr. Hugh. I waited for him to scream, to turn toward me and accuse me of the most heartless atrocity imaginable, or, at the very least, for him to tear out across the river in a blind panic. Instead, he opened his arms, spread them wide, and fell to his knees in the wet sand.

"You were the finest father ever," the oldest girl said, as they walked into his embrace.

"Yes, Daddy, the very bestest," the younger girl chimed in. As in the hospital, they were beautiful in their Easter finery. The little one fixed me with her coal-black eyes and smiled.

The moment will be burned into my mind forever. I watched Mr. Hugh's shoulders shudder with silent sobbing. "Why?" he was finally able to say.

"We can't tell you why," the oldest said. "All we can tell you is that we've always loved you, and we'll love you when next we see you."

They stepped away together and looked at me. "Thank you so much, George," they said in unison, and with these words, they vanished.

Mr. Hugh rose and turned toward me. I was still standing waist deep in the river. I couldn't stop the tears. I'd never seen anything so beautiful.

12

I rose before dawn the next morning, pulled my old Radio Flyer wagon from beneath the back porch, and rinsed it out. Dew was heavy on the ground, birds were singing, and flowers scented the air. Buster and I walked beneath the oaks toward the river, my Flyer squeaking every time the right rear wheel made a revolution. I've oiled the wheel on and off since the beat-up little wagon was a bright and glossy red. Sometimes it works, and sometimes it doesn't. No matter: I had my dog back, and all was right with the world.

Set the hooks before dark and check them early the next morning. It's cruel not to check them early.

We hadn't set the hooks before dark, but I was certain they'd work. Buster and I negotiated the incline with the Flyer, and I pulled it across the strip of beach to the water's edge. I waded out and pulled the first line, which was tighter than a guitar string. I gave it a tremendous tug, worried that I was about to lose Iris's hook on the first trip out.

Getting a better purchase on the river bottom, I put my weight into it. The line gave slowly, loosened, and then tightened again. It wasn't hung on a submerged log or a stump. The tug of war continued for about ten minutes, and when the cat's head finally emerged, I was glad I'd thought to bring the Flyer.

As I pulled it from the water and onto the riverbank, Buster showed his true colors, running up the path about halfway, then turning around and barking his head off. The fat fish filled the wagon from one end to the other. I guessed that it would weigh in at somewhere around forty pounds. To my pleasure, the second catfish was about ten pounds larger.

"Damn, those are some fine fishes right there, Bubba," said a voice from above. I looked in the top of a cypress and, sure enough, there was one Francois Dulcet, dressed like a peacock in some sort of bright yellow circus leotard with red flames leaping up the legs. As usual, he wore the aviator cap and goggles.

"Where do you get those clothes, Francois?"

"At the gettin' place, Bubba."

"Where do you come from?"

"Ain't we full of questions this morning?"

"You certainly ain't full of answers," I retorted. "If I tell anyone about you, they'll take me to the padded room for sure."

"I don't know 'bout that, Bubba. There's some people hereabouts who wouldn't allow them to cart you to the loony bin."

"Who might that be?"

"Just think about it, George. It'll come to you."

I studied the skinny boy with the red hair and wondered about the summers to come. Surely, none would compete with this one.

"And, Bubba?"

"Yes, Francois?"

"Pug is a mite pleased with you." With this announcement, he spread his arms and performed a beautiful swan dive, barely rippling the river's surface.

I waited several minutes for Francois to pop up, but he never did. "Thanks for helping me get my dog back," I said softly.

Pulling the Flyer up the hill was a job. Its contents were almost too much for the thin wheels and sandy path. When we reached town, Buster strutted before me as if he'd caught the huge cats himself, his head high and his tail whipping proudly. The show was to no avail, because there was no one to appreciate our tiny parade. It was early, and most of Eden was fast asleep.

"My God, those are the biggest catfish I've ever seen, George," Mr. Hugh exclaimed.

I extended my hand for a shake, but he bent and grabbed me in a huge bear hug. "George, I don't know how you knew to do what you did when you did it, but trust me, it worked." Mr. Hugh gazed directly into my eyes, rubbed his chin, and shook his head. "You're a fine fishing partner, George Parker."

"So are you, Mr. Hugh. You want the big one or the bigger one?"

I rolled my wagon back up the street and stopped at the Cindy tree. I touched my sore eye, wondering why on earth I did some of the things I did and if being grown up would make me stop. Buster and I squeaked our way to the rear of the house. It was time for Pop to be doing Pop things in preparation for work: enjoying his after-breakfast smoke, reading the newspaper, and sipping a third cup of coffee.

"Morning, Pop," I said, grinning like a possum eating briars. "You think you might step out back for a sec? I'm gonna need a hand with this thing."

"You're up and at 'em early," he said, glancing at his watch. "A hand with what thing?" he asked, eyeing me. He followed me out to the back. "George, I'm already running a little late— damn! That's a whopper of a catfish, son." He laughed and slapped me on the back. "Oooweee, that's a fine one. Let me get my filleting knife."

"That's the little one. Buster and I caught two," I said.

"What'd you do with the other one?" he asked while honing the knife on his favorite stone.

"I gave it to Mr. Hugh. He helped me set the hooks."

Pop grinned and fell to work, forgetting about his station duties. Some things are simply more important than a job.

"We'll have catfish steaks Friday night for sure. Hell, we'll have catfish steaks the rest of the summer, and fried nuggets too. How'd you learn to fish like that, son?"

I hesitated, but it was time I stopped dancing around such a huge issue in my life. "Iris taught me," I said, and waited for the eruption.

"Don't tell your mother," Pop said, without missing a beat. I gazed at him in surprise. He shrugged and plucked his cigarette from a glass ashtray with bloodstained fingers. "You know, son, there are things a man says to his son sometimes that he probably shouldn't—just because of timing. But, when a fellow starts to dwell on timing, what he ought to consider more important than the exact right moment to say a thing is the fact that trucks hit people all the time. People fall dead with heart attacks or strokes. Hell, Pete Ross got hit by the damned train."

I gave him a couple of blinks to indicate that I was completely lost.

"So, I gotta tell you, that little Green girl is about the finest thing I've ever seen, and I've seen enough to know what I'm talking about. She reminds me of your mother at that age."

"People won't approve, Pop."

"What do you care? The only person who needs to approve of what's going on in your life is you, George. My house, my rules, but outside of that, George's life is George's to run. It damned sure ain't for Lucille Thrower to say." He took a drag and slowly exhaled.

I wasn't sure what to make of his pronouncement. Something had happened to me when Iris kissed me, and again when she told me that she never got to ride the dime store horse.

Pop squinted through the exhaled smoke. "And if you tell your mother I said that, well, you and me are gonna have to sit down for a come-to-Jesus meeting. You understand?"

I looked him straight in the eye and nodded. "Hell, yeah, I understand."

He put the smoke back in the ashtray and extended his hand. As my father looked into my eyes and squeezed, I realized that I'd just left another piece of my parents' little George behind.

"I gotta go to work, son. Bag this up and put it in the freezer. Try to stay out of trouble today, okay?"

"Okay, Pop."

I walked back into the house, as pleased with myself as I'd ever been. Mom was waiting, and in a tizzy. "Congratulations on the catfish, George. You know how your father loves fried catfish. Looks like we're stocked up," she said, reaching for a box of freezer bags and placing them on the counter.

Before I could say anything, she waved a pair of white gloves at me. Mom loves her white gloves. "I'm on my way to the beauty shop. I have to have my hair done today. We have supper club at Jeffery and Cynthia's Saturday night. I need you to behave, and try to keep up with your dog. What are the chances, George?" she asked, her painted-red lips pursed firmly together. It was her don't-talk-nonsense look.

"The chances are good, Mother," I answered with proper humility, sending a silent prayer that she hadn't asked how I learned to catch such large catfish.

"Pray tell, where did you learn to fish like that, George?"

I blinked, but only twice. "My new buddy, Lee Roy, taught me," I said, adding two more blinks. She studied, her mom radar whirling behind her eyes with such intensity I thought I heard it buzzing. She knew the blinks weren't good, but I hadn't given the accustomed number, plus, I'd thrown her off her game.

"Who is Lee Roy?" she asked.

"He's the new kid who moved in on the other side of Cindy. I like him, Mom."

"I'm thrilled to death that you have a friend, but why couldn't you have chosen one you grew up with?"

A knock came at the screen door, saving me from the consequences of a nasty retort about my friends being my own business. We looked toward the door in unison. A caller at this time of morning was odd. I followed Mom into the living room.

"Good morning, madame," said Mr. Free through the screen door. He performed a flourishing bow, extending a white fedora in one hand as he did so. In the other hand his index finger curled through the handle of a cup. He looked like he'd just escaped from the leading role in a silent movie and, as my father is fond of saying, a million bucks. I swallowed hard.

Mr. Free stood upright and flashed a smile that reminded me of a handsome shark. He wore his purple suit with the black shirt and yellow tie, along with the red carnation in its usual place of honor.

"Oh my," was all my mother could manage as she fussed a bit with her hair and then of all things, bit at a freshly painted nail. She realized this faux pas instantly and jerked her finger away. I was embarrassed for her.

"I certainly hope that I'm not intruding."

"Intruding?" Mom muttered, this time wringing her hands nervously.

"I wouldn't want to interfere with plans," Mr. Free said, his voice as smooth as a baby's cheek. I rolled my eyes and made a face at him from the cover of Mom's back.

Mom, horrified that she'd put her finger in her mouth, lowered her hands and inspected her nails. Mr. Free winked at me.

"I'd suggest something in an oxblood. Your skin is fair and, if I may be so bold, quite striking." I looked at him again, squinting as if through a rifle scope. He ignored me.

"Understated tones suit beautiful women nicely. If I may, you require very little makeup at all."

I rolled my eyes again and stuck my index finger down my throat. The brazen compliment made Mom giggle. My cheeks burned.

"You're our next-door neighbor, aren't you?" Mom asked. It was a ridiculous question, and she knew it. I finally realized where my blinking habit originated.

"That would be me," Mr. Free obliged. "I believe you once baked an apple pie for me. Or would it be more accurate to say that you baked an apple pie for one of my rocking chairs?"

"The one with the big white Cadillac," Mother added, ignoring the apple pie comment. She sounded like a schoolgirl.

Mr. Free decided on a change of subject. "I see that you're a proud mother," he said, inclining his head toward me.

Mom continued to be as flummoxed as a seventh grader suddenly finding herself face to face with one of the Beatles. There's no doubt that Mom loves Pop with all her heart, but Mr. Free was an animal unlike any she'd encountered in the jungles of Eden. He dripped sophistication and confidence, not for the sake of impression, but because he owned the traits the way a tiger owns its stripes.

"I...I'm sorry I haven't welcomed you to the neighborhood properly, Mr. Free. It would seem that I've been busier than a bee as of late."

It wasn't the whole truth, but it was enough to please Mr. Free. She could've feigned shock and disgust over his big bad wolf introduction and slammed the door in his face, but she'd not done so. If anything, her reaction was flattering. What she'd chosen to do was be nice. Beautiful and nice are difficult to beat.

"Not at all, madame, not at all."

"It's Nancy, Nancy Parker, Mr. Free," Mom said as she pushed the screen door open, "and this is my son, George."

Mr. Free removed his hat and stepped into our house. "What a pleasure, what a genuine pleasure to make the acquaintance of each of you." He displayed his shark grin. "I believe that I've seen this young man before."

I eyed him warily.

"You race about town on your bicycle with a dog in tow."

"Yes, sir, that's Buster," I said meekly. "It's a pleasure to meet you, Mr. Free."

"Likewise, I'm sure." Mr. Free winked as we shook hands.

He smiled at my mother again and I thought of Little Red Riding Hood. "Nancy," he said, raising the cup. "I wonder if I might trouble you for some sugar. I realize that the store is just across the street, but they've yet to open, and I'm in mid-recipe."

Mom led the way into the kitchen and, just like that, the big bad wolf was seated at our table, where Mom nervously poured him a cup of coffee. He'd taken Pop's place and began to exercise his skill as a first-rate raconteur—entertaining Mom with tales of military exploits, travels abroad, and a colorful New Orleans childhood. I sat and pretended to be interested because it was easy. I was as enthralled as my mother.

"So, you see, Miss Nancy, I'm most certainly *not* a Yankee. I chose to spend time there for the sake of commerce, an enjoyable form of reverse-carpetbagging, if you please."

"Would you like more coffee?" Mom asked, spellbound.

"Of course, you brew an excellent cup." I glared at him

when Mom rose to fetch the pot. He glared back and stroked his immaculate mustache.

"What have you been up to this summer, Spuh…uh… George?" he asked. "I'll wager a small town can be rather boring for a young man."

"Fishing," I said, my tone flat.

"Well, there's more to life than fishing. My dear old mother once told me that there's adventure right around the corner, if you know which corner to look around."

"I believe that's true, Mr. Free," my mother said.

I almost succeeded in not making an about-to-gag face. Mom would've agreed to eat chocolate-covered chicken shit with her pinky extended if Mr. Free had suggested it. I was about to remind her of her appointment when Mr. Free looked at his watch.

"Oh dear, Nancy. This has been wonderful, but as I said, I'm in mid-recipe, and I've an appointment later. Would you mind terribly if I borrow and run?"

"Oh no, of course not," she said, her eyes wide. "I have an appointment at the beauty parlor myself. I'd completely forgotten." She gave Mr. Free a beautiful smile. "You're quite the distraction, Gerard."

"Gerard?" I said.

They looked at me as if I'd suddenly appeared from nowhere. "Sorry," I mumbled and walked out the back door.

I sat on the steps with Buster and hugged him tight. Mr. Free was after my mother, and there wasn't a thing she was going to be able to do about it. I was going to have to kill him. I'd already begun a plan when she interrupted.

"George," Mom said from behind me. I turned, an accusation of betrayal in my eyes.

"Do *not* look at me like that, young man. I didn't do anything wrong. I'm ashamed of myself for not having welcomed him earlier."

"Well, you certainly made up for it. If we had ticker tape and a nurse's uniform, it would have been perfect," I said, the famous *Life* photo flashing in my mind. "I thought for a minute there that you two were going to crawl into his big white Cadillac and take off for the Crescent City."

"The what?"

I gulped and tried not to blink. "Nothing," I quipped and turned my back. I put my arm around Buster. "I'm telling Pop," I said softly.

"George, are you jealous of your neighbor? For heaven's sake, he's such a...a *strange* man."

Strange and handsome as hell, I thought. Going for the guilt was a dirty trick, but she deserved it. I knew she was silently repeating Crescent City, wondering where it was and how I knew about it. She was going to ask me; I could feel it in my gut. "Well, maybe just a little," I muttered with a touch of calculated sadness.

She stepped down off the porch and sat with us. "George, Mr. Free is an attractive, interesting gentleman, but I'll never love anyone but your father." She put her arm around me and leaned in. Buster leaned in from the other side. I smiled.

"Okay, Mom." Mr. Free had made her as breathless as a sophomore cheerleader but there was no point in belaboring the point.

As soon as she pulled out of the driveway, I bee-lined it to Mr. Free's. I bypassed the secret knock and walked straight to the library. He was working on his painting and looked as content as a fat old tomcat with a full belly.

"What in the hell was *that* all about?" I asked.

"It's nice to see you, too, young man. Why don't you fetch us a libation?"

I returned with ice, glasses, Cokes, and, of course, the poison *du jour.*

"Please, George, do the honors. You know how I take it. And, George?"

"Sir?"

"This is the only woman I'll ever love," he said, adding a brushstroke to a barely concealed breast. The woman's body was beautiful beyond description and he was nearly finished. I couldn't wait to see her face. "I'm certain after my little visit that Nancy feels the same way about your father."

"Why are you such a flirt?"

"Because women enjoy it."

"What do you mean? The girls at school hate it."

"No, they don't. They just don't enjoy it to the fullest yet. At least, not like they'll enjoy it once they discover the power."

"The power?"

He looked at me, tilted his head slightly to one side, then the other, and narrowed his eyes. "Never mind about the power. That's one for you and dear old dad."

"I thought you were going to eat her."

"Oh, please. What did I just tell you?" he asked, indicating Jolie.

I looked down at my Coke. "I guess."

"I'd never do anything to upset the fragile equilibrium of your peaceful little world. You are, above all else, my friend."

"Mr. Free?" I said, taking a seat in my wingback.

"Yes?"

"What happened to Jolie?"

"She was killed beneath a full moon in the wee hours by a drunk driver, Spy Boy."

Words he'd spoken upon our first meeting came back. *I told you, Jolie is the love of my life. I believe that she'll soon return.*

"Mr. Free?"

"Yes?"

"I saw the light."

"As in Christ's message? That's a most singular experience, young man. I'm happy for you." He took a seat in the other wingback, crossed his legs, and relaxed.

"No, the light that comes from the second floor during a full moon."

"It's your imagination, Spy Boy. Or perhaps I should say that it's *my* imagination."

"What's that supposed to mean?"

"It's the moon, of course, a play of light." He looked directly at me, but this time, the serious eye contact didn't work. Something deep inside told me that he was lying, and I questioned my trust in him. He'd just completely manipulated my mother. *She's coming, Spy Boy. She's coming any moon now.* He didn't remember saying this—too many adult libations, too many late nights, too much wandering lost and alone in his large, beautiful house.

"I don't think so," I said. "I've heard music too. Big band music… The night I came over and you caught me at the foot of the stairs."

"I play it all the time, George."

"You don't play it upstairs."

He took a long drag from his holder and exhaled slowly, his brow furrowed in thought. "This house is filled with strange and wonderful things, Spy Boy. You've seen them yourself—artifacts from my past, music, paintings, and portraits, and of course, magic and light from the moon. Why don't we just say that it's about to talk and leave it at that?"

"What's about to talk?"

"Why, the moon, of course."

"What's going to happen when the moon talks?"

"Real magic will happen. Not this silly stuff you've been dabbling around with all summer." He sighed and dismissed further talk with a wave of his hand. "Play us some music, young sleuth, and stop being so contrary."

"Me? You want *me* to play the music?" He had thus far refused to allow me near the records or player. The concession was deflection, another attempt at derailing my curiosity. We both knew it wasn't going to work, but I let it go.

"What do you want to hear?" I asked.

"Look for Benny Goodman with Helen Forrest."

"What are we going to listen to?"

"I'm talking to the moon, Spy Boy, but the moon won't talk."

13

Mr. Hugh, Lee Roy, and I continued to fish on Wednesday afternoons. Lee Roy and I went to the movies at the Anderson Theater on Saturdays. The westerns were my favorite, but Lee Roy liked zombie movies. I wouldn't tell him, but the zombie movies scared the bejesus out of me. I couldn't sleep nights after watching them, and I roasted because I was afraid to leave my window open.

Lee Roy cleaned and polished Mr. Hugh's bike until it looked better than Lightning, and he was as proud of the old Flyer as if it had been delivered fresh-painted off the assembly line. We rode our bikes to places I'd never been before, down dirt roads that led to mysterious old houses long abandoned beneath giant trees, their broken windows, like soulless eyes, daring us to venture inside to seek the dark secrets of antebellum days.

Though we hadn't talked about it, Lee Roy was coming to grips with the reality that there was something about Eden that wasn't normal, something just beneath her surface that could chill a kid to his bones on hot summer days. We explored every nook and cranny in these places: searching for ghosts, the scattered, broken bones of skeletons, treasure maps—or hidden compartments, passageways, and attics where treasure might hide.

On one adventure, we discovered a family burial plot surrounded by rusty wrought-iron pikes hidden beneath the jade of several magnificent magnolia trees. A crypt rose at the shaded center of the burial ground with the name *Broussard* etched into marble the color of storm clouds.

No amount of prodding and coaxing at our reserves of courage or stupidity would move either of us to open the gate. The crypt emitted a vibration, a subtle aura that felt too much like the inside of Eden's old hospital. We left the tomb with its rusted iron door and discolored marble exactly the way we found it. For weeks afterward, remnants of the foreboding certainty that I'd been in the presence of true evil lingered in my mind.

We camped in my treehouse one Saturday night. While rambling, we saw Andrew Thomas and Vance Baker, the town drunk, standing in the cemetery at the Methodist church. Andrew's white suit glowed in the moonlight as he conversed with someone unseen while Vance tottered about with a fifth of whiskey in his hand and a wild look in his eyes.

The two old men and their crazy behavior sent us speeding to my back yard where we kindled a fire. "Damn, George, those two old guys are as creepy as it gets," Lee Roy said, licking roasted marshmallow from his fingers. "What's wrong with people in this town?"

"There's three of them," I said. "Neckbone's part of that trio, and no one that I know ever gives any of them any flack, not even Lucille Thrower. I think all three of them might be a little off in the head."

"Who's Neckbone?"

"All three of them are like brothers, only Neckbone is colored. It's too weird."

"Anyone named Neckbone is likely to be a little crazy," Lee Roy said. He looked at me for a long time. He had something on his mind. "My daddy's crazy," he said.

Then Lee Roy told me about his father and growing up on the farm. He explained hog neutering in such graphic detail that I lost my appetite for the s'mores we'd been making. After apologizing for the unpleasant dinner conversation, he told me that he lived with his aunt and uncle because his father had lost their farm.

"I love him, George, but he's bad to drink, and he don't do right when he's on a bender. He stills his own liquor and sells it when he can. He's gonna go to jail, ain't a doubt in my mind. I don't know what happened, but he ain't the man my momma married. Least, that's what she's always saying. He ain't got no education, but he's one of the smartest men I ever knew."

Lee Roy's sudden tears tore the lid from what had been simmering in my heart for some time. I couldn't tell him I loved him, but I reached over and squeezed his big shoulder and smiled.

"My granddaddy would say that your daddy is trapped by his heart and his brain," I said.

"What?" Lee Roy said, wiping at his tears.

"Doc says some folk just aren't supposed to be where they are."

"That don't make no sense."

"Well, I used to think that a lot of stuff Doc told me didn't make any sense, but that's because I was trying too hard. Most of it sort of comes to me as time passes. Your daddy might be an artist, or a brain surgeon, or an engineer. Instead, he's plowing corn and neutering hogs."

Lee Roy stared at the fire and tried to digest my grandfather's take on things. "Well, if making sense of that'll come in a few days and make me feel better, I'm all for it."

"It's my turn, Lee Roy."

"Your turn for what?"

"I have something I need to tell, something I should have told you already." He raised his eyes into mine and I told him everything there was to tell about Iris, except the kissing. Pop has told me a thousand times to never kiss and tell. *Gentlemen don't do it.* As I suspected, there wasn't an ounce of judgment or reservation in Lee Roy.

We covered the pros and cons that Iris and I had tackled at length. In the middle of preparing another s'more, Lee Roy looked at me. "George, I've seen Iris uptown. She's the most beautiful girl I've ever laid eyes on. I'm green. When do I get to meet her?"

"Soon, Lee Roy, real soon, but first, I have someone else I want you to meet."

At one a.m. we stood at Mr. Free's backdoor. Lee Roy shifted his weight from one foot to the other as he watched me bang out the secret knock.

"George, you're going to get us killed," he whispered.

"Don't be such a weenie," I said with a grin. Calling the kid who'd knocked Butch Sinclair out with a shovel a weenie was hysterical.

"I've heard he kills people for a living," Lee Roy blurted as the door opened and there stood my magnificent friend, his smoking jacket gleaming in diffused light, cigarette smoldering in ebony holder, and champagne in hand. "Mr. Free, this is my best buddy, Lee Roy," I said. "Lee Roy, Mr. Gerard Free."

Mr. Free smiled and performed one of his gracious bows. He clenched the cigarette holder between his teeth and extended his hand. "Murder for hire, at your service," he said in a deep voice.

Lee Roy struggled to swallow as he stared at Mr. Free's extended hand. He turned wide eyes to me with a *help* expression on his face. Mr. Free enjoyed the moment for several seconds. I made a mental note to speak to him about torturing potential friends, especially the younger ones.

"Calm down, big man. It's an honor and a pleasure to meet the best friend of my best friend."

Lee Roy straightened, took the hired killer's hand, and we followed him inside where, just like me on my first visit, my best friend was swept away. Mr. Free prepared Cokes and allowed Lee Roy time to gawk in wonder as he led us on a short tour. When we returned to the library Mr. Free fetched a third chair, and slipped comfortably into the uniform of world-class raconteur.

As Lee Roy gazed open-mouthed about the room, he was treated to tales of war, long nights in the brothels, bars, and hotels of New Orleans, and voluptuous women with mystery in their eyes and fire in their bellies who called the bayou home.

I marveled at the magic Mr. Free could weave when given the opportunity, and I thought about the second floor of his house as Lee Roy's fears and worries vanished—at least for a night.

Thursday was my day, the day I met Iris. We always rendez-voused where we met originally, at the clearing on the river near the place where I'd first met Francois.

My explanation for alone time on Thursdays was usually that I wanted time by myself for fishing, reading, and thinking. Sometimes, I'd take comics.

On occasion, I got Iris to break from her uppity literary penchants for a good dose of Spider-Man or the Hulk, but most of the time, she read to me from her beloved Fitzgerald or Faulkner, with an occasional foray into Hemingway. As much as I loved her, I couldn't help my whiteness and how being white made me view Iris. I found it strange as hell that she loved the writers she chose to love.

"Where do you get those books?"

"Where did you really get that amazing black eye?"

"It's a long story. Can I tell you about it later? I want to know about the books."

"That's called being evasive, Sixteen," Iris said. My shoulders slumped and I looked down at the ground, shaking my head.

"Okay, don't pout. My granny trades goods for them at the store."

"How does that work?"

"People in Eden throw even the best books out with the trash. The maids will snag one if they think Granny might be interested. This one…" —he held up *Gatsby*—"…probably cost a loaf of bread and some canned goods."

"Are there no colored writers?" I asked.

"Of course, there are. Charles Chesnutt is one of my favorites. He wrote wonderful short stories, but he isn't read much in Eden," she said with a laugh. "Granny got him from a colored traveling salesman a few years ago. She looks after me like that. She wants me to go to college someday. That's funny, isn't it, George? Me in a college?"

I saw the yearning in her eyes and thought about Lee Roy's daddy and being trapped by brain and heart. "It's not funny at all. It's one of those things that has to happen," I said, a surge of fear sweeping through me at the thought of such a beauty going off to college while I stayed behind to chew my nails. Despite the fear, I wanted the dream for her.

Iris had a beautiful, lilting voice that soothed me the way my mother's does when I'm sick. When she tired of reading, she sang folk tunes and lullabies her folks used to comfort babies until the Sandman took them, her voice calming me like the pain shot Dr. Ulmer gave me the time I pulled my shoulder out of joint.

I loved spending time with Lee Roy, but he wasn't a reader. Before Iris, I hadn't realized how starved I was for conversation, or that I didn't actually know what real conversation was. Doc had told me on many occasions that when two people are together, a conversation is when each gets to talk. Otherwise, one is simply listening.

We traded ideas and thoughts on authors and books and confessed a mutual longing to one day write them ourselves, a dream I'd never verbalized to anyone. Iris was a writer in her soul, and she was trapped in the rural South.

Our hearts and minds were engaged in a beautiful summer dance, and the rhythm of easy conversation drew us closer and closer, but I was awakened to the fact that I was in love with a girl who had to be set free. A deeper sense of trust was developing, and, in the excitement of a moment, I told her about my secret friendship with Mr. Free.

"You mean the strange guy with the suits and the big white Caddy? That man is *so* handsome."

"Oh God, not you too," I said.

Iris gave me a woman smile, a knowing smile. "What's that supposed to mean?"

I ignored the unsettling look and question. "Yes, I mean the strange guy with the suits and the big white Caddy. Just remember, it's a secret."

She made a cross over her pert breasts. "Cross my heart and hope to die."

Iris liked to kiss, and so did I. Over the weeks the kisses
had become more and more intense. I felt as if I were riding
a roller coaster that hung in the clouds. She stirred things with
her tongue over which I had little control. It was like the town
drunk, Vance Baker, and his bottle. I didn't care what happened
in the end. I wanted more and didn't want the ride to stop.

I kept going back every Thursday, even when it rained, lying
to my mother that I didn't believe fish wouldn't bite in the rain.

Being the insecure male teen that I was, it bothered me that
Iris was so good at making me feel the way she did. She laughed
at the way my young manhood pressed at my shorts and teased
me with a maturity that amazed me.

"I was born with it, Sixteen. The boys have been chasing me
for a long time," she explained.

"Do they catch you?"

She shrugged and gave me a shrewd look. "Sometimes,
when I feel like being caught." My face colored purple. "Although none have caught me lately but the one I'm lookin' at,"
she added. She was a lot like Mr. Free. She knew what to say
and when to say it.

On particularly hot days, we'd wade naked into the river to
our necks and spend hours kissing and exploring one another. I
was learning things that most fourteen-year-old boys don't get
to learn, and I floated from one hot summer day to the next in
an exotic euphoria of lust and love.

One Thursday, I came right out with it. "I love you," I said
while holding her close. She broke the embrace and stepped
away.

"No, you don't *love* me. You're *attracted* to me. The animal in
you is attracted to me."

"I'm not an animal, Iris. I love you." I said this but didn't
truly believe it myself. Iris made me feel so much like an animal
that at times I was embarrassed.

She rolled her eyes and sighed. "All men are animals, Sixteen,
even young men. You only meet me here, out in the woods,
where no one can see, where it's safe. You don't have to worry

about me telling your mom or dad about Mr. Free. I'm never going to meet your mom and dad."

"That isn't fair, Iris."

"What isn't fair about it?"

"It's your idea to meet here, not mine. I've asked you to the movies. I've asked you out for ice cream time and again. I've asked you to go to the park with me on Sundays after church. You always come up with an excuse."

She was sitting on a log in the sun with her legs outstretched, as beautiful as any flower I'd ever seen with the sun playing in her thick honey-blond hair. She took her glasses off, looked down at her pretty feet, and shook her head. I couldn't see her face, but I saw a tear glisten like crystal in the sunlight when it dropped to a brown thigh.

"I'm sorry, Iris."

"No, *I'm* sorry, George. You don't need to be sorry. This is my fault. I should've let you alone. The first day I saw you and you smiled at me, I loved you. I don't know why it had to be you. There's no shortage of men to love in these swamps and woods, and I know that you're only fourteen. I found out soon after we met, but by then I didn't care."

"Why do you refuse it?" I asked, frustrated that she spoke to me as if she was twenty-five years old and I was a child.

"Refuse what?"

"Refuse what we are to one another. I know you're older, but I've never had anything like this. I don't think people get to have a chance at this over and over. You're trying to make it where I'll look over my shoulder at this summer for the remainder of my life. I think—I know—that this is special."

"Oh, George, it *is* special, but it won't work. It won't work *because* it's so special. People hate for others to have things like this. They hate that they settled for safe, mundane lives. They'll never let us be together here because they've learned that one of the most important tools they have is hypocrisy, and they know how to use it well. We might as well be from different

planets. Have you imagined what it would be like at family reunions? We'd be a two-person leper colony."

I couldn't help myself. I burst into laughter.

"This isn't funny, George Parker."

"You know what?" I asked, forcing the laughter and smile
away.

"What?"

"The only person in life who matters more than loved ones
and friends is your partner, your mate, the person you love with
all your heart. The only thing you can't do with your partner
or mate is die, and even then, the other will be there to the last
breath. It's the way with true partners. Life is only about them.
Everything is done as a team for the betterment of both." I
thought about my parents, Mr. Free, and the love of his life,
Jolie.

"The people who would no longer speak to us because they
don't understand or approve of us don't count. They aren't
worthy of knowing you or me, let alone judging us. The people
who stick by us, those who refuse to judge someone they love,
will be there no matter what."

"It's not that simple, and you know it," Iris said.

"Yes, it is. It completely is." I walked over, sat on the log by
her, and put my arm around her shoulders. She was cool and
clean from the river. I buried my face in her hair and breathed
deeply. "We could always run away. People do it all the time. I
know a special place," I whispered into her hair.

"A special place?"

"Yes, it's called the Crescent City. You can be with anyone
you want there."

"How do you know that?"

"Because Mr. Free told me. Mr. Free once had a partner
almost as beautiful as you, Iris, and he had her in the Crescent
City. We ought to go to Mr. Free's sometime and listen to big
band brass. He'd know how to help us too."

"What?"

"It's too much, isn't it? I'm throwing too much at you at

once. Big band brass," I said, pantomiming a trombone for her amusement. Her smile indicated success. "The secrets of the Crescent City," I added, doing a short rendition of the jitterbug for her that Mr. Free, of course, had taught me. "We ought to go drink some little Cokes, listen to some Artie Shaw, and see what he thinks about all this complicated stuff."

"He won't like me in his house, George."

"What do you want to bet?"

"I'll bet anything you like. He's too refined, too polished to associate with my kind."

"Well, I think he's too refined to associate with Eden, but I'll bet you a night in a sleeping bag naked that he isn't too refined for Iris Green."

"How could you lose a bet like that?" she said, laughing.

"I *can't* lose."

We met the next night at the huge magnolia in the parking lot at the Piggly Wiggly. Iris wasn't there when I sneaked out of my room and across the street. At least, I didn't think she was. I heard her giggling from the shadows above me and climbed up. I could see her amber eyes in the streetlight and her full lips. Her hair was piled up on her head, and her slender neck beckoned for my mouth.

"Stop it, Sixteen. We'll fall out of the damned tree," she scolded.

"I'm good at that," I said. "What are you doing up here?"

"Reading."

"Reading what?" She held a paperback copy of *The Old Man and the Sea*, a flashlight in her hand.

"You and Hemingway," I said in a huff.

"Me and Hemingway, I wish. Young Sixteen would be on to bigger and better things if Ernest gave me a buzz," she said with a giggle.

"Isn't he dead?"

"Lucky for you, huh?"

"Let's go see Mr. Free, Iris. You're getting on my nerves."

"You're getting on your own nerves."

"I'm good at that too," I agreed.

The door opened before I could finish the secret knock. Mr. Free was ready. It didn't matter to him how old a woman was, only that she was a woman. One of Mr. Free's credos was to always please the feminine of the species, no matter their place in life, the physical attributes, or their attitude. If the woman was young and beautiful, achieving the goal was all the more enjoyable.

"Spy Boy was right," he said, extending his hand. "You are beyond compare. Is it true that you're as intelligent as you are beautiful?" he asked as he kissed the back of Iris's hand.

For the first time since I'd known her, Iris was speechless. She looked at me with her mouth open. "He's gorgeous," she whispered. My face reddened. She was behaving exactly like my mother. "And *so* charming."

"Gorgeous is good," Mr. Free said, extending his hand for me to shake. "Mr. Spy Boy, as always, the pleasure is mine. Please, show Miss Iris to the library. I shall be along once beverages are prepared."

"Did he call you Spy Boy?" Iris asked as we passed through the French doors.

"Never mind that," I said as I led the way.

Mr. Free soon returned with his tray, and I had to admit that Iris was right—he *was* gorgeous. He was wearing a cream-colored three-piece suit with a yellow shirt and a burgundy tie that perfectly matched his carnation. His two-toned wing tips were polished to a brilliant sheen. He'd prepared as if the queen were arriving, and it pleased me that he'd done so for my girl and me.

"Mr. Free, please don't eat my girlfriend," I said, as Iris plucked her glass from the tray.

"I only have one love, Spy Boy. You know that."

"That doesn't have a thing to do with eating my girlfriend."

He arched his eyebrows by way of response, but his smile held all manners of worrisome messages. "I shall see the two of you in a moment," he said and turned toward the kitchen.

Iris looked around the room and emitted *oohs* and *aahs* in all the appropriate places.

"This is unbelievable," she said. "Look at all the books—just *look* at them."

"He's almost as old as Hemingway," I said.

Iris giggled and kissed me on the cheek. "But he only has one love. Didn't you hear him?"

"I hear him, and I see him. A shark fin sprouts immediately between his shoulder blades when a female shows up. I recently thought he was going to eat my mother for sure."

Iris walked over to the portrait. Mr. Free still hadn't finished Jolie's head. "Is this the love of his life, Sixteen?"

"That's her." I paused for a moment, then said, "You can call me Fourteen now, I suppose."

"No," she replied. "You'll always be Sixteen to me—even when you're sixty."

"That'll work," I said with a smile, and then we looked back at Jolie's portrait.

"She's put together quite nicely. I wonder how much is reality and how much is fantasy."

"According to Mr. Free, he can't do her proper justice no matter how hard he tries."

Iris left the portrait and lost herself much as I had the first time I visited. Despite the number of times I'd sat with Mr. Free and explored the bottom floor of his house as he painted or read, I still found his home fascinating. The place was having the same effect on Iris. She looked like Alice waking up in Wonderland.

"You can escape in here pretty much the same way you can escape into a book, can't you, Sixteen?"

"I suppose so."

"Mr. Free is like a character in a book."

"What do you mean?"

"I mean he's larger than life. That's why the people in Eden don't care for him."

Iris had pegged in minutes what it had taken me weeks to

unravel. I was growing a bit nervous about bringing her. Mr. Free was going to love her. I suspected that he already did, and I knew why.

He swept into the room in the manner that Iris had just described, larger than life and every bit as suave and debonair. He plucked his rum and Coke from the tray and raised it high. "To Spy Boy and the woman he loves."

"Aw, Mr. Free," I said. Iris cradled her Coke in both hands and looked down at her feet.

"Don't you, 'aw Mr. Free' me, young man. It's obvious from across the room, and I think it's wonderful, absolutely wonderful," he added with his movie star smile. He turned to Iris and asked, "Do you like my home?"

"I...I don't have words for it, Mr. Free. It's amazing, and so clean. How do you keep it like this?"

"I wish I could take credit for all of it, but I met a lady one morning in the Piggly Wiggly named Dodie Paisley. I asked if she'd help me choose a cantaloupe, and we struck up a conversation. She's completely responsible for the cleanliness. She's honest to a fault, a bit too straightforward with her opinions regarding alcohol, and reliable beyond compare."

"I know Dodie. Sometimes she trades books at my grandmother's store. Granny is sort of a country librarian, I guess you'd say."

"Excellent. That is most excellent. No books, no life," Mr. Free said, bringing a smile to Iris's pretty face. "Your grandmother has an inventive way of spreading knowledge."

Iris gave Mr. Free a strange look, one that I hoped didn't lead to one of her incredibly independent and sometimes crass remarks. She could be nasty about the difficulties involved in obtaining proper knowledge. Instead, she rose from her place, walked over to a nearby shelf, and indicated a large tooth. My worry was unfounded.

I'd asked about many of the artifacts in the library but hadn't made it around to the tooth. "I bet this has a story," she said, looking back at Mr. Free with an expression that I preferred she save for me. I wondered how many women Mr. Free had cast under his spell throughout the years. I also wondered about Iris's abilities to fend off his magic.

"How do you do that?" I blurted.

"Do what?" Mr. Free asked. His expression could have rivaled the baby Jesus for innocence.

"Never mind," I said, embarrassed by myself yet again. Mr. Free looked at Iris and let me off the hook.

"It came from an exceptionally large black leopard, my dear, one that supposedly ate over one hundred people: men, women, and children. I shot it myself with a revolver at point blank range, right between the eyes." He used his index finger as a barrel and his thumb as a trigger, then pointed the imaginary gun at Iris. "Pow, just like that." The master raconteur had entered the room.

"Are you serious?" Iris said. I could see her waffling the same way I often did when Mr. Free told a story from his past. And, just like me, I saw acceptance settle into her eyes. One couldn't actually do anything *but* believe him.

"I waited in the village at the well. The leopard is the only large cat that has no fear of man," he continued, fitting a cigarette into his holder and extending it full length. He was having fun. I suspected there'd been a day when he'd held court for his friends on a regular basis. I was the closest he got these days to entertaining guests. He lit the cigarette with his dented Zippo and gave me a little nod. There were times when I expected the man of mind reading.

"I knew when darkness fell that the animal would prowl the village in quest of forbidden fruit. The big cat had committed the ultimate sin; it had tasted human flesh, and it wanted more. I suspect that it'd been awakened to the truth as well, that man is the ultimate enemy of this wonderful planet and the life it supports. The cat knew what I'd known for some time. The more of the creature known as man it could destroy, the safer its home would be.

"Of course, wisdom like this in a dangerous animal can't be

tolerated, and it's sad, because it is but one animal fighting an unwinnable war. I had the utmost respect for the cat and was moved to meet it with minimal firepower, and to meet it when it had the advantage—at night. I chose the pistol of which George is so fond—the Walther, and the khukuri over there in the corner." He motioned toward the fearsome knife with his cigarette holder. "A true warrior would have only chosen the khukuri.

"I stood by the well in the center of the village beneath a full moon and waited—smoking, sweating, and trembling with tiny spasms of fear that I knew would wreak havoc with my aim. My human stench rode a soft breeze into the darkness of the surrounding jungle.

"I imagined every sort of creature lurking in the shadows, their eyes focused on me, their minds tuned to the frequency of the great cat. 'The man is here, Dark Prince, standing by the well.'"

Mr. Free leaned toward Iris and gazed into her eyes. "The great cat's thoughts came to me as clearly as if it were speaking. 'We must kill all who walk upright.' Then I saw the cat when it slipped from the woods, a darker shadow among shadow, death on four enormous paws. Young lady, starlight is enough light if you're hunting to save your own hide."

He took a long drag on his holder, his words hanging in the smoke-laden air. He studied Iris's face. I knew he was weighing the girlfriend of his best friend, comparing her to Jolie, analyzing her character. Iris didn't wilt from his gaze. Mr. Free's expression softened a bit as I watched him decide that he liked my girl as much as he liked me.

"Imagine if you will, Miss Iris, all the creatures of the world deciding at once that they have tolerated man's arrogance long enough."

"I sometimes feel as if I've tolerated enough of it, Mr. Free," Iris said.

Mr. Free nodded and tendered a half-smile. "I'm still a hero in that village," he said wistfully, his gaze far away, as it had been when he listened to the big bands. When Iris applauded, he bowed his head slightly.

"Please, not quite so much admiration. I was actually trying to kill myself but hadn't yet developed the nerve. I've heard men say that killing oneself is cowardly. I would humbly submit for reflection that choosing not to kill oneself when it's deserved is far more cowardly."

"Why on earth would you want to kill yourself?" Iris asked.

"Because I've committed horrible sins. I've killed many men and one woman."

For the most part, Mr. Free had lost the ability to shock me, but this admission bowled me over. I wondered who the one woman was, but I wasn't about to ask.

Iris glanced at the nearly completed portrait. "There is no good reason to kill oneself, Mr. Free," she said softly.

"So I've been told," he conceded with a grin. "This moment is proof of that."

"What do you mean?"

"Had I killed myself, I would have missed this superb opportunity."

"You're such a flirt," Iris said and winked at me. The wink made me feel better.

"I wasn't speaking of you alone, Miss Iris. I was speaking of the wonderful opportunity of seeing the two of you together. It's the next best thing, if you catch my drift. You should see George's eyes when he speaks of you, when he tells me of your opinions on literature, on people, on living."

"You don't see George and me as a problem, Mr. Free?"

"The only problem you have is not understanding what you are and how incredibly rare it is. I've already told George that all he needs is courage."

"We need a whole lot more than courage, Mr. Free. We need acceptance, and we have no idea how to go about asking for it." Her voice carried a note of anger, of what my mother would call righteous indignation.

Mr. Free raised his right index finger to beg a moment. Iris smiled and nodded. Their chemistry was undeniable, and I thanked the Lord for whatever strange reason that Mr. Free was still clinging to the memory of the love of his life. I stood and walked over to the scrapbook. Instead of beginning at the beginning, something I almost always do with any book I pick up, I flipped the big scrapbook open to the middle and got the surprise of my life. Staring at me from a yellowed newspaper clipping nearly as large as the scrapbook page, was one Francois Dulcet, complete with goggles, aviator cap, and devil-may-care grin. He was waving to the photographer from the cockpit of what looked like a rocket of some sort. The publication date was July 4th, 1938.

The headline was typical Francois. *Local Daredevil Killed During Self-Directed Science Experiment.* I turned to Mr. Free to ask what on earth Francois Dulcet was doing in a scrapbook from his childhood, but he was deeply involved in making a point, a point that I wanted and needed to hear.

"I would like for you to consider, Miss Iris, that you forget *asking* anyone for what is yours by birth. You take it. I don't mean take as in steal; I mean take as in claiming what is yours so loudly and with such force that no man or woman can or will deny you. Do so with courtesy, do so with respect, but by all means...do so.

"It's the business of no one how you live your life as long as you harm no one living it. When you wrong someone—and believe you me, you will wrong someone at some point—whether it's intentional or not, make damned sure that the wrong is unavoidable, an incident that you can look back on and know in your heart that it was a wrong of necessity. This is as close as you can come to claiming a properly lived life."

"What are you telling us to do, Mr. Free?" I asked, still staring down at the scrapbook. Everything that he and Iris had said made sense; I just couldn't find an answer in any of it. I was prone to moments like these, and I hated them. The answer was no doubt there, painted with colors as vibrant as Mr. Free could muster, but I was unable to see.

"I'm saying to do what you do best, Spy Boy—use your imagination." I closed the scrapbook. It could wait for another day.

Summer plodded slowly into the stifling oppression of August when steam replaces air, a thick, hazy soup that clings to the skin like warm, wet gauze. August taunts with the promise that no end to the humid hell is in sight—even in sleep.

Another full moon came and went. I stood, sweat-drenched and awe-struck, at the corner of the Great Wall and listened as the golden notes of big band precision rode hazy moonbeams toward the heavens. Something else rode with the music, an exotic whisper that made me think of islands with palm trees and scantily clad girls gyrating around bonfires, passion flashing in their dark eyes like the fire they worshipped.

I felt the way I imagined Mr. Free must feel when he's had one too many and that soon I'd float away and leave Mom and Pop to their small-town lives. I wanted to fly through the summer night to Iris's window, and together, we'd ride our own moonbeam to a place where we could be us.

14

What on earth is wrong with you?" I asked. I hadn't seen Lee Roy so down since the night he told me about his dad.

"School's gonna be starting soon," he said with a sigh.

"I thought you liked having friends. There'll be lots of friends to meet when school starts."

"You talking about all the rich kids who live in the big houses around here, the ones we haven't seen all summer because they're off at camp or traveling Europe?" His twinkling brown eyes drilled into mine. Lee Roy was like a lawyer. He already had a half-dozen answers lined up for this question, and I'd spent enough time with him over the summer to realize it.

He was right. We hadn't seen any of the rich kids all summer, and most of the kids we could've befriended had been working to earn back-to-school money. Lee Roy hadn't been able to get a job, and I hadn't wanted one.

"No, I'm talking about kids from all over. Just because they don't flock over here to visit, doesn't mean they won't like you, Lee Roy. Heck, I can almost guarantee that you'll find someone you like better than me right off the bat."

"How in the world can you say something like that? You don't have a very high opinion of me, do you?"

"I reckon it's me that I don't have the high opinion of," I admitted. "I just have that effect on people. Don't ask me to explain it because I can't. I guess I'm just plain boring."

"I like you a lot, George, and you're anything but boring. Matter of fact, you ought to think sometimes about how smart you are."

"What?"

"Never mind. Maybe you just read too many books. A fellah can read too many books, you know."

I made a mental note to mention this to Iris. "It doesn't matter," I said. "I'll always like you a lot. When summer started, I never dreamed in a million years that Butch Sinclair and his cronies would walk to the opposite side of the street to avoid me. I'll never be able to pay you back for that."

"You ain't gotta pay me back for nothing. It don't take a whole lotta effort to hit a fellow on the back of the head with a shovel when he ain't looking."

Lee Roy had captured me with statements like these. He didn't do drama. He spoke what was in his heart, and he did it plainly and without shame.

"Haven't you had fun this summer?" I asked. "Dang, we caught more fish than you can shake a stick at. We explored haunted houses. I gave you a ton of old comic books to read, and we saw more zombie movies than I'd like to think about," I added, trying to cheer him up.

A smile played at the corners of his mouth but didn't materialize. "I ain't got nothing to wear to school, George, and I ain't got no money. I didn't worry about it for most of the summer because I thought I was going home, but that ain't gonna happen. Momma called. Daddy ain't doing no better. I don't know if I'll ever go home again."

The only person I'd met with more courage than Lee Roy McAlister was Gerard Free, yet here he was, afraid of showing up at school looking like a hobo. I'd be terrified of the same situation, but that was me. Lee Roy had beefier gears running his character.

I looked down at my feet. I wasn't about to tell him that everything would be all right, because it wasn't going to be all right. I'd turned fifteen for real in August. Tenth grade was coming up. I'd seen how some of my classmates could take advantage of disadvantage. It was one of the many reasons I'd preferred Buster's company for so many years. Kids are just plain ruthless. There was no doubt in my mind that Lee Roy could maim pretty much the entire high school, but that wouldn't do a thing to improve his future.

"A fellow can't show up at school every day wearing his Sunday go-to-meeting duds," Lee Roy continued. He threw a rock at the metal dome of the streetlamp on the corner and whacked it soundly. I would've knocked the light out.

Sunday go to meeting. The words stuck in my head, and I watched them go round and round. Sunday go to meeting: I'd heard the phrase my entire life. In the South, you wore your best clothes to church on Sunday, and if there was a meeting of your peers that you felt warranted your best appearance, or a funeral, you dragged out the Sunday clothes. I watched the words whirl in a slow orbit, and as I watched, more words joined, Mr. Free's words. *I'm saying to do what you do best, Spy Boy—use your imagination.*

"George, what's wrong? You look like Pug Ginn," Lee Roy said. I'd been staring at him with my mouth open.

"Nothing's wrong. I'm using my imagination."

He narrowed his eyes. "What are you using it for?"

"To solve problems. To take what's mine without asking for it."

"I don't know what you're talking about, and I don't think I'm going to school."

"You know what my father says about kids who quit school?"

"I bet it ain't good."

"He says kids who quit school won't ever amount to shit. It isn't because they're bad kids. It's because they're quitters. You can't quit, Lee Roy, no matter what. Pop says that quitting isn't an option...ever."

"Looks like it might be more of an option than your daddy realizes. I don't know if I can take it."

"You're fretting for nothing. We've been fishing all summer with the man who can fix this little problem."

"You talking about Mr. Hugh?"

"Yes, sir."

"I ain't no charity case, George, and this ain't no little problem. At the moment, it looks like one of the biggest problems

I ever had. Me and Daddy could always work our way out of a problem until the liquor stole him."

"You'll be a charity case if you quit school. Just look around you. Think about it. How many people with no school do you see trying to scrape by around here? You just need a little help. It's probably all your daddy needed. You're here for a reason. I'm here for a reason. Being too proud to ask for a little help is almost the same thing as being too stupid to ask for it." I held my breath. I was on thin ice, and I didn't want any broken bones.

"My dad is fond of a few sayings himself. If you're born a McAlister in these parts, you're born to fail."

"Oh, horseshit," I blurted. "Your daddy has his life to live, and you have yours." Lee Roy looked away and we grew silent. It occurred to me that I might be making too light of his trouble. I had problems of my own, big problems that I felt far outweighed the plight of having no school clothes, and that was selfish. Leaving childhood behind was becoming more difficult than I'd imagined.

I watched Lee Roy walk back toward his house with his head down. It hurt to see the big boy in such despair. I *was* being selfish, callous, and inconsiderate, all the things I hated seeing in someone else. There are few things worse in a small town than not having decent clothes to wear on the first day of school. I watched as Lee Roy disappeared into his house and decided to take things into my own hands.

When he heard me straddle Lightning, Buster emerged from beneath the porch and followed me at a trot into town, where he waited by the side door at the department store. Mr. Hugh was in the ladies' section talking to, of all people, Lucille Thrower. I stopped and took a long drink from the water fountain, hoping that my new and powerful enemy would disappear into thin air as I drank.

She was still there when I had my fill, so I walked over to the shoe section and took a seat. I closed my eyes, deeply inhaling the aroma of new shoes and suits. I thought about school starting and frowned. I hated the first day of school.

When I looked over at Mr. Hugh again, he and Mrs. Lucille were glaring in my direction. Actually, only Mrs. Lucille was glaring. She pointed a fat index finger at me and said something that her expression told me was bad, maybe even worse than bad.

Mr. Hugh leaned slightly toward her and replied with something that caused her to spin her huge frame on what was no doubt a sturdy shoe heel. I watched her huff toward the front of the store with her head thrust back and her rouged cheeks redder than normal. She turned and gave me one last glare just before the door closed shut and the bells rang.

Mr. Hugh made a beeline to the seat next to mine. "My goodness," he said, slouching into the chair. "Sometimes this job is more than a fellow can stand."

"I reckon you get a customer who rubs you the wrong way from time to time, huh, Mr. Hugh?" I tried not to grin when he peered over his half-glasses at me, but I couldn't help myself. We burst into laughter together.

"Lucille says she refuses to shop in a store that allows juvenile delinquents. Are you a juvenile delinquent, George?"

"That's the way they do it, isn't it, Mr. Hugh?"

He frowned. "The way they do what?"

"That's how they keep things the way they want them, the way they make people do what they want them to do. We both know she's in every social club in Eden, and we know she's rich and that she and her friends shop here. You've been warned, haven't you? It's not that I'm a juvenile delinquent. It's that I smarted off at her when she was rude to Iris. She won't stop until she runs me completely in the ground, as well as my poor parents and now you."

He nodded agreement. "It certainly doesn't pay to offend the grand dames in small Southern towns, George. Who's Iris?"

I looked away. What a blunder. Silence bloomed between us like a drop of burnt oil on a mud puddle. Mr. Hugh sat in his quiet, dignified way, giving me time to make up a suitable lie if I chose to go that route. If he was like most grown-ups, he already knew more than he was going to tell.

I thought about Iris and how she had accused me of only wanting to see her way out in the woods so that I could feel her up and kiss her until I thought I was going to overdose on euphoria. I thought about why I hadn't trusted my best friend enough to tell him about my girl, and here I was, sitting with a man who had befriended me and treated me kindly all summer, about to tell another lie.

I decided to try something that I'd watched Lee Roy do over and over. I looked Hugh McVey right in the eyes. "Do you love me, Mr. Hugh?"

One of his cheeks twitched but he returned the steady gaze. "George, I... George... Love is a powerful word. You're not asking me if I love chocolate ice cream."

"I know what I'm asking you."

Mr. Hugh looked down at his long fingers. He kept his nails well-trimmed and his hands were soft, but he wasn't the sissy that many men in Eden suspected. I'd watched him wrangle with our big cats all summer and stomp through undergrowth like a small bull to get to a new fishing spot. He was well-groomed because he was a professional, and doing his work properly required that he dress the part. After a moment, he looked from his hands into my eyes. "Of course, I love you. I think you know that. But why do you ask such a question?"

"Because I'm different, Mr. Hugh. I'm going to do something that'll cause a lot of people in Eden not to like me anymore. I'm probably going to be ostracized, ex-communicated, banished. I'm thinking that it won't be much different than how I've lived most of my life, but there are a few people I don't want to lose, and one of them is you. You know what my granddaddy says?"

"God only knows," Mr. Hugh said, his serious expression morphing into laughter.

"He says a fellow can't always do what's popular, and when he doesn't, sometimes there's hell to pay."

"I'm with him on that one, George. I just told Mrs. Thrower to take her money and her gossip somewhere else. By the way, I think Iris Green is beautiful, just beautiful. I'd buy her an ice cream any day."

I liked this direct approach. "Lee Roy doesn't have any school clothes and no way to buy any," I said.

"Well, George, that isn't exactly a surprise. He's been wearing the same two pairs of shorts all summer. You could probably read the newspaper through them. I tell you what, though; Lee Roy McAlister doesn't strike me as one who would ask for much by way of a handout."

"I think he'd starve first," I agreed, "but I bet he's a hard worker."

Mr. Hugh gazed out across the store, his bulging Adam's apple working up and down as he figured on the direction of our conversation. It was a large store, and today, as was often the case, he was in it by himself. "I bet he's a hard worker, but he doesn't have any clothes that are suitable for work in a department store, George. You just said so yourself."

It was time to be silent. I watched the gentle fisherman with no children rub his clean-shaven chin and move his pursed lips about. "You think Lee Roy might be willing to work off a fall wardrobe, maybe on Saturdays, and a couple of afternoons a week after school?"

"He looks like a football player to me, Mr. Hugh. Betcha Coach Sutton is gonna ask him about that."

"Well, howzabout Saturdays, then? I could probably cut him a pretty good deal on some of my older stock."

"How about a dress, Mr. Hugh, a nice dress for me?"

"That's a little too much information about you, George," he said with a laugh. "What size do you think you might wear?"

"I think it would be about the same size that Cindy Turner wears."

"Ah yes, Miss Turner and her mother were just in here. Her mother excused herself to go to the restroom while we were looking at shoes, and you know what, George? Cindy said she'd seen the three of us on our fishing trips, and that she gave you that black eye for not minding your own business. Is that true?"

"Yeah, it's true," I said, looking down at my feet. "Can we look at the dresses, please?"

I followed Mr. Hugh over to the teen section. He picked out five, then told me to choose my favorite.

"Excellent choice, George, excellent: understated but beautiful. I think you'll look great in it." We chose shoes and a faux pearl necklace with bracelet to match. Mr. Hugh looked off into space, his brow slightly wrinkled, then he gave me a nod and a wink. "How about a hat? Would you like a hat?"

While he placed the outfit and accessories in a box, I dug in my pocket and pulled out a small piece of folded paper. Mr. Hugh slid the box across the counter, and I slid the paper across to him.

I watched as he carefully unwrapped the gift, a mixture of surprise, pleasure, and wonder painted his face that would have pleased any gift-giver on earth.

"Where'd you get a gold one, George?" he asked, holding the circle hook up to the light.

"It's gold in the daytime, Mr. Hugh, silver in the moonlight."

"George, I can't take this."

"Is it enough, Mr. Hugh? I have money from doing Miss Ginn's yard work if that isn't enough."

"It's more than enough. I'll put some of it toward Lee Roy's bill," he said, his eyes watering.

Pop had called Mr. Hugh "good people" on more than one occasion. I looked into his brimming brown eyes and wished it hadn't taken so long to understand what my father meant. Doc was right; it takes too long to get smart.

I was struggling to tie the package to my handlebars with some string that Mr. Hugh gave me when Francois nearly made me jump out of my skin.

"What's in the box, Bubba?"

"You bastard," I muttered beneath my breath. "Don't you know that already?" I asked.

He pulled the goggles down around his neck, and the anger I'd hoped would fuel the upper hand vanished. He moved in close as his green cat-eyes bored into mine, showing me his missing tooth. "I reckon you got me good on that one, didn't you, Bubba? That pretty little girl's gonna knock 'em out in that dress."

He wore a much different outfit today, and he held the stock of what appeared to be a huge gun against his right hip. For a change, his aviator cap was gone. In its place was an infantryman's steel helmet. The helmet was too large and looked ridiculous. His army uniform was also too large, but the bandolier belt across his shoulder fitted with glass tubes filled with liquids in varying shades of gold, pink, and orange was impressive indeed.

"You have better outfits," I observed and nodded toward the gun. "What the heck is that thing?"

"Ain't you ever seen one of these before? It's a moon gun."

"What in the hell is a moon gun?"

"Exactly what it says it is. You shoot moons with it, Mr. Genius."

I studied the contraption, but as with so many of Francois's gadgets, I could make no sense of it. The large barrel was polished steel, with small hoses and lengths of tubing running from different points to a cylinder at the base of the barrel located just before the stock. The cylinder was making a humming sound, and about every ten seconds or so it emitted a series of whirs and clicks. This contraption made me nervous, but I did my best not to let it show.

Francois walked out into the middle of the street; there was a similar but smaller gun strapped to his back. Mr. Rudy Cox was watching me through the plate-glass window of his service station. He couldn't see Francois, but he could darned sure see me. He was looking at me and my big white box and wondering who in the hell I was talking to. I waved. He waved back and then turned to answer the phone.

Francois braced himself properly and hefted the huge gun

to his shoulder. The cylinder began a growl that increased in pitch until a deafening explosion rocked the earth around us. Francois was big into explosions.

A white ball burst from the barrel of the gun. Rocketing toward the stratosphere, it grew larger and larger until it hung white and full in the daytime sky, an exact replica of a full moon.

"Holy crap," I said.

"Bookworms ought to be a little more creative," Francois said, dropping the larger gun in the street and opting for the smaller one. "Let's see, next full moon should be about this color," he said, pulling one of the pale-orange vials from the bandolier. He fitted the vial beneath the cylinder of the gun, turned a knob, and the pale fluid disappeared.

He blessed me with his missing-tooth grin. "Watch this, Bubba," he said as he aimed and squeezed the trigger. A beam, the same color as the liquid, exited the muzzle of the gun. I waited for the moon he'd created with his magic gun to explode in an incredible display of Francois's pyrotechnic genius. Instead, the beam entered the moon's surface and began to spread like an ink dot on a napkin, turning the sphere the pale orange hue of an autumn moon.

"Pay attention now, Bubba," Francois said. The moon began to grow a face, a serene, beautiful face with a smile like da Vinci's *Mona Lisa*.

"It's almost time, Spy Boy," the moon said, then vanished.

"Holy crap."

"That's much better, Bubba. You'll make a helluva writer someday."

"What did it mean?"

"I don't know."

I rolled my eyes. "Don't hand me that shit."

"Well, maybe I do know, but telling isn't an option."

"Why are you in Mr. Free's scrapbook?"

"Maybe you should ask Mr. Free."

"Why are you here, in my life, at this very second. Why?"

"To show you."

"To show me what?"

"That there's more than this, and you can have it." He made a sweeping gesture with his arm, encompassing Eden.

This made sense. If nothing else, Francois had shown me the power of what might be if I set my mind to thinking about it. "But...why me, Francois?"

"Because you've befriended a friend." His smile was gone. He refitted his goggles. "I need a favor."

The mirrored lenses were unsettling. I had the suspicion that when he was looking at me like this, he could see everything there was to see—things that I didn't like to see or admit to myself. I certainly didn't want anyone else looking at them. I gazed back the best I could and pointed toward the sky.

"Look what you just did. What could I possibly do for you?"

He walked over and dug a folded piece of paper out of his shirt pocket. He unfolded the paper gently, an old brittle page, tattered around the edges and the color of weak coffee. Numbers and symbols completely foreign to my math-challenged mind were scrawled all over the paper.

"What the hell is that?"

"Don't you know nothing, Bubba?" Francois asked. "This here is what them in the know call a mathematical equation. I believe a fellow with the right sort of eye and head would use the word *quantum*, but for you and me, equation ought to work just fine."

My brow furrowed in what I knew would amount to useless concentration. Pug had given me an invisible sheet with figures much like these. I'm better at self-powered flight than math. "What am I supposed to do with this?"

"Give it to Pug."

"Why can't you do it?"

"That's hard to explain, Bubba. You reckon you could do it for me? I'd surely appreciate it."

"When should I give it to him?"

Francois smiled again. "I think you know the answer to that."

Francois Dulcet was without doubt the most mischievous

being I'd ever known. I viewed him much like I would a water moccasin on the opposite side of the river. As long as he stayed on his side, we'd be fine.

I reached for the paper, unable to keep the tremor out of my hand. As soon as my fingers touched it, the parchment crumbled into copper-colored dust and vanished.

I gazed, open-mouthed, at my hand, holding it before me as if it'd just spoken my name, then went stone blind. I could see nothing but white light. My stomach rolled and lurched. I bent at the waist, prepared to lose my breakfast, and saw the symbols and numbers in gilded gold begin to appear against the light.

It was most definitely an equation, and for just an instant, for a flicker so brief that I wasn't totally sure I'd seen it, the intricate inner workings of a clock powered by a tiny sun appeared. It all made sense. I felt the power of dawning understanding and then it was gone, vanishing as quickly as it had come.

I squeezed my eyes shut and rubbed them. When I opened them, the world was back and Pug's moon-paper was hovering in the air before my eyes. Francois grabbed the paper, gave me a salute, and vanished.

My eyesight hadn't come back in time to quell my uneasy stomach. I turned to one side, threw up, and remained bent over for a full minute, spitting bile and listening to Buster's whimper.

I don't know why, but I suddenly remembered Mr. Rudy. He held the phone in his hand and was staring at me the way someone does when he isn't sure if an ambulance is needed or not.

I waved at him and grinned. He raised his hand slowly and waved back. I wanted a drink of water, but instead, I grabbed the box, climbed onto Lightning, and raced Buster back to Mr. Free's.

I rinsed my mouth from the spigot by the back door, and before I could finish the secret knock, Mr. Free opened up. "It's always such a pleasure to see you, Spy Boy," he said, grinning with great happiness, his eyes as glassy as a piece of his fine crystal. He wobbled to his right, over-corrected, then decided to lean on the door jamb. Mr. Free was quite the drinker, but this was the first time I'd seen him physically impaired.

He pointed to the big box. "Is that for me? You shouldn't have."

"You'd look better in it than me, but it's for Iris. Would you keep it for me?"

"You know I will. Won't you come in?"

I followed him into the house. "Mr. Free?"

"Yes?"

"It's a mite early to be drunk, isn't it?"

"Spy Boy, one day you and I shall sit and discuss the horrors of sobriety. In the meantime, please join me in celebration."

"What are we celebrating?"

"I've completed the portrait of the love of my life, and Tante Evangeline is dying."

This wasn't particularly good news. Francois, his talking moon, and his disappearing mathematics had left me with a heavy sense of foreboding, not to mention the fact that I had to sneak into Pug Ginn's house again. As if these weren't enough, I had no idea who Tante Evangeline was.

I stopped at the fridge. "You want a little Coke, Mr. Free?"

"I'm trying to quit, Spy Boy. Friends are concerned about excessive consumption," he said, pushing through the French doors.

I left the box on the dining room table and walked into his study. Mr. Free stood before the portrait, wobbling slightly from side to side, a full drink in his hand, and a freshly lit Gauloise in his holder. He was in a great mood, and I could see why. I'd never seen a more beautiful woman.

"Holy crap."

Mr. Free turned toward me. "That all you got?"

"She's the most beautiful woman in the world."

"That's better."

My hungry eyes roved over Mr. Free's depiction of the love of his life, from the tips of her perfectly formed toes all the way to the auburn hair bundled atop her pretty head. Her eyes were dark and smoldering. Her face was slightly rounded with a firm jaw line, and her lips were the kind that made a man fantasize about kissing, full and turned up slightly at the corners, as if she were always thinking about something that amused her. There was a small mole on her right cheek. Everything about her made me think things I shouldn't be thinking about the love of another man's life.

"I'm not sure I like the look in your eye, Spy Boy. Is it necessary for me to retrieve a handgun?"

"No, sir," I said, swallowing hard and trying not to look at the portrait. "I...I just can't help myself."

Mr. Free laughed uproariously. "Neither could I, Spy Boy, neither could I."

"Mr. Free?"

"Yes, Spy Boy?"

"Francois Dulcet is in your scrapbook."

"Of course, he is."

"You know Francois Dulcet?"

"Yes, in a manner of speaking."

"I know him too."

Mr. Free inhaled his cigarette and inspected my face as he sipped his drink. The ecstasy of celebration drained from his clear blue eyes.

"Have you had a nice summer, George?"

This was a strange question, but I'd come to expect strange questions and behavior from Mr. Free. He didn't participate in life the way I, or anyone I'd grown up with, participated. Mr. Free made his own rules, and when it didn't suit him, he didn't follow those either. "Yes, it's been a wonderful summer."

"You haven't been bored at all, have you?"

"No, sir, but there have been a few times when I wished I was."

"An interesting life is not always an easily controlled life, Spy Boy."

"Mr. Free, I want... I *need* to know about Francois."

Mr. Free unbuttoned his vest, then his shirt. He pulled the

shirt open and pointed to a shiny round scar in the center of his chest that was much pinker than the surrounding flesh. I was surprised by how muscular he was.

"Did a bullet do that?" I asked in awe.

"Yes, a bullet most certainly did do it. Spy Boy, I can't tell you all about Francois, but I can tell you what I know."

He buttoned his shirt back and motioned toward the wing chairs. "Let's sit. This may take a little while."

15

Mr. Free and Francois Dulcet grew up in the Gentilly section of New Orleans. Francois and his younger brother, Bret, lived across the street from Gerard in a neat little frame house.

Francois's father, Justin Dulcet, owned a bar on Elysian Fields Avenue called Lottie Pearl's. The best blues and jazz ever performed rolled into the streets from its dark, smoky, wood-paneled interior.

The music and cheap whiskey brought women looking for a good time—a good time that might, if the cards fell right, lead to a good man. Lottie Pearl's was geared to coax hard-earned dollars from the pockets of frugal men longing for respite from the weight the Depression had left on their troubled hearts and weary shoulders.

Five years separated the boys, and though completely different people, Francois loved his younger brother dearly. He looked out for Bret whenever he was aware of trouble, but it wasn't an easy job. Bret readily shared laughter, but a sensitive heart and the destructive behavior it bred were guarded topics. Bret's silent emotional hieroglyphic was one that Francois had made many frustrating attempts to decipher.

Due to sharing the same age, Francois and Gerard enjoyed more of a typical brotherly relationship. They played, worked, and learned lessons of life in a world adorned with brass bands, card sharks, con men, and kids as tough as whip leather.

New Orleans' mysterious personality was perfect for the women, as beautiful as magnolias, as strong as wrought-iron balustrades, and as sweet as mint julep. It was with certain women of New Orleans that the true power of darkness resided, darkness that made the loan sharks and con men look like altar boys.

Mr. Free told of a jungle populated with beauty and pleasure. Beneath the scented flowers, jade fronds, and ancient oaks
writhed serpents cloaked in intricately woven allure and decep-
tion. Every species of lowlife and street player known to man
schemed for easy money, prowling the shadows, alleys, brothels,
and dimly lit bars.

Mr. Free described Francois's talent for mathematics, a
near-unlimited imagination, and a flair for outrageous inventions—a few of which proved quite dangerous. Francois was
aiming for immortality through reckless genius, an accomplish-
ment that would stand him toe to toe with Edison and Tesla. As
I listened to Mr. Free recall days gone by, I gained true appreciation for the ghost that had spiced my summer with personality
and pyrotechnics.

Francois worked on his projects in a small room at the rear
of his father's bar, because access to Lake Pontchartrain was
just across the street. After a disastrous attempt at what the
world would soon know as the helicopter, Francois attracted
the attention of Big Jim Bradley, a huge man with an oily smile
and an eye for opportunity.

Though brave beyond the point of survival, Francois wasn't
devoid of a heart. After the helicopter incident, to appease his
frantic mother, he set his flying goals aside to concentrate on
less-dangerous pursuits. One such project centered on Albert
Baldwin and his quest to reclaim land from fever-infested
swamps.

Baldwin had been trying for years to perfect a reliable pump
that could be used to drain the swamps and hold the waters
at bay during storms, dike breaches, and the rainy season.
Frustrated, he placed an ad in the *Times-Picayune* in search of
engineering help.

Francois's inventions had always been expensive to produce.
If one believed in an honest, sin-free living, there wasn't much
money to be had in the thirties in New Orleans. Francois was
in constant need of gears and pulleys, of sheet metal and fas-
teners, of tools and newfangled vacuum tubes, gauges, and

electrical components, not to mention the occasional stint in the hospital.

Big Jim had always been there with an open wallet, and his generosity paid off when Albert placed his ad. Francois's pump design would change New Orleans forever. With the pump's success, Big Jim's true colors flew. He wanted more than in; he wanted it all. He readily agreed that the blood, sweat, tears, and brains were Francois's and Albert's, but agreed more readily that the money to make everything possible was his, and so he produced a piece of paper that a cash-strapped Francois had willingly signed years before.

Jim approached Albert one day, demanding the drawings and the patent rights to the pump design—or else. The 'or else' was aimed at Albert's wife and six-year-old daughter.

Albert, blessed with far more brains than backbone, agreed immediately, but a wrench was thrown into the gearing when he opened his safe to find the drawings missing. To make matters worse, the prototype pump was missing as well. Big Jim went looking for Francois.

Mr. Free stopped to collect his thoughts. He sipped his drink and looked at me, his ice-blue eyes as clear as water.

"What happened, Mr. Free? What did Francois do with the plans and pump?"

"He hid the plans in the attic of Big Jim's house and the pump in his garage."

"Francois hid what Big Jim wanted in his own house?"

"Brilliant, wasn't it?"

I shook my head in disbelief. "Things didn't end well, did they?"

"Big Jim showed up one night while Francois, Bret, and I were hanging out on Francois' gallery. I was in the house fetching beers. I walked out onto the gallery, and there was Big Jim, with a gun pointed at Bret. I don't know what made me do it, but I walked in front of Bret, just as Big Jim pulled the trigger."

"And you didn't die?" The question was so stupid my cheeks flushed with color. I looked at my feet.

Mr. Free laughed. "I almost did. I woke up six weeks later in the hospital. My father told me that Francois had come by each day to talk me out of the coma, and to pray for me. That afternoon, when he stopped by as usual, I gave him the thumbs-up and asked what had happened. Bret was dead and buried. My heroics had only slowed the bullet."

"Why didn't Jim kill everyone then and there?"

"I'm sure he would have, but the instant the gun fired, Francois leapt onto Big Jim and stuck a switchblade into his eye, all the way to his wicked brain."

"Francois was just as crazy then as he is now, wasn't he? He wasn't afraid of the devil."

"That's an interesting way of putting it, Spy Boy," Mr. Free said with a smile. "That day in the hospital, he promised to look out for me for the remainder of my life—a well-intended but unfulfilled promise."

"What do you mean by that?"

"Francois was dead a year later."

I was still caught up in the horror of Bret's murder and Francois's fatal attack on Big Jim. "How did he die? Did someone whack him for killing Big Jim?"

"No, Spy Boy, he did himself in, so to speak—killed by the last in a string of outrageous inventions intended to make his name immortal. I assumed I would never see him again. Don't you think it's logical to assume that you'll never again see someone who has blown himself to smithereens?"

I blinked. Logic had taken a back seat since the day he'd pressed the cigarette lighter to the back of my head.

"Spy Boy, don't you think?"

I became aware of the fact that my thigh was damp, and that my little Coke was losing its cold to the warmth of my hand. I blinked a couple more times and nodded.

"Yes, I think it's logical. I just don't know what logic has to do with anything anymore."

He smiled and chuckled but didn't look at me. "It's all about math and imagination, Spy Boy," he said as he gazed into the dead fireplace.

A small mantel clock ticked the seconds away as I pondered *math and imagination* and thought of Pug rocking the days away with his bib and his brilliant, trapped mind.

Mr. Free broke the silence. "I met Jolie in the hospital, Spy Boy."

"Was she a candy striper?"

"No, she came into my room by mistake. Her grandmother was on the same floor, but in the next room over. She apologized with a beautiful smile, backing toward the door. Without hesitation, I asked her not to leave me. I can't describe how the world shifted as we gazed into one another's eyes.

"Jolie walked over to my bed, and I extended my hand. She took it without reservation and her smile intensified. I said, 'I'm in love with you.' She laughed and said, 'You're delirious with fever.'"

"Maybe you were," I said. "After all, you'd been hit with a bullet the size of a golf ball."

Mr. Free laughed and retrieved his Zippo. "Maybe you're right, Spy Boy, but this was a different type of fever." He inserted another cigarette into his holder and held it up for inspection. "Anyway, from that day forward, Jolie, Francois, and I were inseparable. I heard my first big band with Jolie and Francois by my side. Rap Roppolo and the New Orleans Rhythm Kings left us in a state of euphoria. Spy Boy, I was addicted, and I was in love—deeply in love."

"But I don't understand how all this fits into what's happening in Eden, Mr. Free."

He rose from his seat, weaved over to the record player, and dropped Earl Bostic onto the platter. As Earl and his boys filled the room Mr. Free motioned to the painting. "She was more beautiful than this, George," he said over his shoulder. "I tried to do her justice, but I couldn't."

"What happened to her?"

"She was taken by a woman known as Tante Evangeline, a woman who knew how to practice powerful black magic and trade it for favors. That's how all this fits into Eden, George. That's why you chose to spy on me."

My forehead wrinkled and my heart quickened. "I don't understand."

"You're here because you're supposed to be here, George."

It was obviously riddle day. I wasn't going to leave Mr. Free's house with a clear understanding of what was going on, and I knew it. I sipped my warm Coke.

"Evangeline died a short while ago," Mr. Free said. "It would appear that fortunes are about to take a turn for the better. I do want you to know that it's been a pleasure knowing you, George Parker."

These words had a ring of finality that upset me. Mr. Free was quite drunk, and I'd had enough darkness for one night. I'd grown to see him as much more than a friend. I loved him, and he was scaring me.

"It's been a pleasure knowing you, too, Mr. Free. I've had the greatest summer of my life."

"Better summers will come, Spy Boy. I can promise you that." He walked over until he stood beneath the fighters hanging from the ceiling. "The one on the left is a Mustang, a P51D, an amazing aircraft that will stand the tests of history and legend. It was powered by an engine known as Merlin. The one on the right is a Messerschmitt Me 262, equally amazing. Notice the missing propeller. It was powered by an engine previously unknown to the world, the first jet. The invention proved an issue for me late one frosty night over Germany."

He took a thoughtful drag from his holder. Earl played on and visions of being chased through a freezing sky by a monster caused me to shiver.

"That's as close as I've ever come to dying, the only time I knew that nothing I owned by way of skill was going to save me. As the saying goes, I was outgunned…in more ways than one."

He lit the room with his handsome Hollywood smile. "Death was on my trail. By some miracle, I'd avoided the three 262s twice. They attacked the same way the U-boats attacked. The Germans called them the wolf pack of the sky. I'd been hearing rumors of the jets and knew that their flight time was short, but that night it wasn't going to be short enough.

"My cockpit windows began to glow first, then the instruments, the switches, the stick, all awash in shimmering, concentrated moonlight. A voice spoke in my mind, 'Let me have this, Gerard. Let me have this magnificent warbird. You can't handle this one, Bubba.' Of course, I recognized Francois instantly. 'How can this be?' I asked. 'How can you be here?'"

"'Georg-Peter Eder has your machine in his sights, Gerard. You are a dead man in seconds if you don't let go. Let go, now,' Francois insisted."

Mr. Free looked at me and shrugged. "I did as I was told. I closed my eyes, let go, and Francois came into me, occupied me—became me. We did things in the Mustang that night that should have been impossible and I lived, when by any measure, I was destined to become yet another statistic of the madness we know as war.

"Before Francois left, he said, 'Gerard, Jolie has traded her most valuable possession for this night. We must fix this.'"

"Fix what?" I asked, more fascinated by his storytelling than ever before.

"Fix the deal she made, Spy Boy," he said, walking to his glass and raising it in my direction. "To promises."

Mom was frying bologna and slicing a huge onion when I walked into the kitchen the next day.

"Just in time for some lunch, sweetie," she said, pecking me on the cheek and smiling. "School starts soon. Are you excited?"

"No, ma'am."

Her shoulders slumped. "Oh, George, not again. This is going to be your year to shine. You've changed over the summer, grown up a great deal, if I do say so myself. You and Lee Roy had a wonderful time together. You'll have to introduce him to everyone you missed over the summer. Want mayo on your sandwich?"

"Yes, ma'am. Got to have the Duke's," I said in an attempt to sidetrack the conversation. I hated to think about being stuck inside the prison of those hot, muggy rooms, pretending that I gave a shit about learning anything that might help me live a life of dignity and promise.

If I told her what I thought, I'd lose my "grown up a great deal" accolade quicker than she could spread mayo on a slice of bread. Mr. Free's tales of adventure and danger over the course of the summer had done nothing at all to endear formal education to me.

I checked the kitchen calendar while Mom made my sandwich and fried green tomatoes in her cast-iron skillet, noting that a full moon would light the sky on Monday, the eighteenth. Mr. Free's words repeated themselves in my head. *Better summers will come, Spy Boy. I can promise you that.*

"Mom?"

"Yes, George?"

"What sort of man do you think Reverend Paul is?"

She gave me one of those "where on earth did that come from" looks. "Well, he's a minister, George."

"That isn't the best of answers."

"Why not?"

"Because men are ministers, human beings are ministers. Jesus has forgiven them and probably appreciates their efforts, but they're still people, just like you and me. Some of them have backbones and principles, and some don't."

My mother looked from me to the ceiling. "Give me strength," she said and looked back at me. "You sound too much like your father."

"Pop makes a lot of sense when he talks about this stuff."

"Yes, and that's what's so scary about it," she said, slathering mayo on a slice of bread as if she were in a race. I could always tell when Mom was upset because she got into pre-throwing-something mode. She might not throw anything within the next few minutes, but she was preparing, just in case.

"Well?"

"Well, what?"

"Do you think he's a good man?"

"I don't know, George. He preaches a fine sermon. He hasn't been here all that long. Maybe Maynard and Ellen Cribb haven't neutered him yet." She looked at the ceiling again. "Oh my God, I'm channeling your father. Did I actually *say* that?" she whispered.

"Yes, you said it," I confirmed. Her little burst of honesty was reassuring.

Her cheeks flushed red, and her eyes flashed. She looked at the mayonnaise jar. I felt safe; the jar still had too much mayo in it to sacrifice as a projectile.

"I've been watching the church folk for a long time, Mom. So, what do you think? Is Reverend Paul a good man, or a crappy man who talks about Jesus while he hides behind the cross?"

She jumped up and down in her spot by the counter like a little girl. "I'm going to kill your father."

"Mom?" I prodded.

She looked me in the eyes and sighed again. "I think he's a good man, George, an exceptional man."

16

I don't think you're being fair," I said. I was in new territory, an argument with the girl I loved. Iris was slipping away. Summer was winding down, and I got the distinct impression that so were we. The thought of no more Iris made me feel sick to my stomach.

When I arrived at our spot, I sat on the log closest to the river. Iris walked over, straddled my legs, and sat in my lap. I wouldn't look at her when she draped her arms over my shoulders, but I inhaled deeply. Ivory soap and traces of wildflower lingered in the space between us. She wore a man's threadbare work shirt. Mr. Free had spoken to me of the power of woman. *Your base instincts are easily manipulated because young men don't question them; a young buck doesn't even know they're at work.*

Iris put her arms around my neck and placed her forehead against mine. "You're upset," she whispered.

"I love you, and I don't want to argue."

"You're still upset."

"When I came here the first day and saw you, I only knew what I felt. It was the easiest, simplest moment I've known with you. Everything else about us is complicated."

"George, I'm not arguing. You're arguing for me. Everything you've said is true." She kissed me on the forehead. "I'm trying to help you see that we have nowhere to go. This place in the woods by the river is all we can call ours, and it belongs to neither of us. School starts next Tuesday. You'll have your friends, and I'll have mine, but we'll be in two totally different worlds."

The magic we'd woven over the summer was quickly unraveling. The sick feeling in my gut wasn't solely due to the desperate fear of losing Iris. I felt in my bones that something big was about to happen, and it wasn't going to be good.

"Why do you say we have nowhere to go?"

"You know why I say it. Your people won't accept me, and mine won't accept you. Can you imagine yourself at one of my family reunions?"

I sighed. "The family reunion nightmare again? We don't have to go to any damned family reunions. My father likes you. That means a great deal, more than a great deal."

"Okay, your father likes us. I guess it's a start."

"You're too pessimistic. They've passed laws."

"I passed gas yesterday," she said and giggled. "All the laws in the world aren't going to make people like us, George."

"Saying things like that isn't ladylike."

"What I've been doing at this river with you all summer isn't ladylike either."

"Iris, stop it. We aren't about that stuff."

"You mean, you don't like it?"

I grinned. "I love it," I said, "but we're about so much more. We read one another's books and talk about them. You showed me how to catch catfish like a pro. I showed you about comics and Brains Benton."

She smiled at the mention of Brains Benton. "You know what? I like that Brains Benton stuff."

"There's a new one. I saw it at the dime store yesterday, *The Case of the Painted Dragon.*"

"I'm going to miss you and your strange taste in literature," she said, pulling herself into me. I put my hands on her waist and felt the warmth of smooth bare skin beneath the thin shirt. She was about to make me cry.

"You can't make this decision on your own. I deserve a say."

"I don't want to ruin your life."

I looked into her eyes. A tear rolled from the left one and paused on the curve of her cheek. I kissed it away. "This isn't going to work. *We* should say what happens to us, not others."

"I am saying it."

"You're saying it because you aren't willing to fight. You aren't willing to look the world in the eyes and tell it that your life is yours to live."

"My goodness," she said. Her smile was beautiful, and I realized with more power than ever before that I would not, could not live without her. "My knight has found his courage," she teased. She wrapped her bare brown legs around my waist, and I put my hands on her thighs. "What should we do, Sir George? How do we conquer the small-town society dragon? It's a vicious, devious creature."

"Come to church with me."

She pulled back and gazed at me with her mouth open. "Are you crazy? Isn't that the dragon's lair?"

"What better place to face off with her? Maybe I am just a little crazy, but I've had a lot of help this summer. I bought you a dress. It's a beautiful dress with shoes and a hat to match."

"Oh, George, you bought me clothes—and a hat? Men don't buy women hats." She was crying again, but a smile threatened at the corners of her mouth, then blossomed. She was so damned beautiful. I wanted to kiss her, take our clothes off, wade into the coolness of the river, and drown in her.

"Mr. Hugh helped me. You'll be the prettiest girl there."

"I'll be the darkest girl too. Your dress won't be very pretty once they drag me out by my feet."

"It's a church, Iris. It's perfect. It's not like we're showing up at the Harvest Festival dance or something. They're obligated to welcome you. It'll put them in the perfect spot."

"The perfect spot? What in the hell is the perfect spot? I can't see anything perfect about it. What kind of spot are *we* going to be in?"

"One where we can tell Eden that we are going to be what we want to be, and they'll be listening in the house where they've been taught to love everyone since they were old enough to go to Sunday school. *That's* what perfect spot. If they can't hear us and see us in there, they can all go to hell."

"You won't be able to live in Eden after we pull a trick like that, George, and I don't know if I'll be able to stay in my mother's house."

"Iris, you're worth it to me. The question is, am I worth it to you? Will you stay, or will you go? Sometimes all it takes is the will to fight. If you start giving up now, you'll be giving up the remainder of your life when things get tough."

"Mrs. Thrower will kill us herself."

"Maybe something in her head will pop when she sees us sitting in *her* church."

"What about your parents?"

"I think Pop will be with us. I don't know about Mom."

"I know about Mom."

"You do?"

"Yes, Mom might be close to having a stroke, too, but she won't let her baby go down by himself."

"Then, you'll do it."

She gazed over her shoulder, her eyes a long way off. It was an expression I'd seen on Mr. Free quite a few times over the course of the summer. "When?"

I thought about the coming full moon and how I suspected that its wane would bring big changes in my life, as well as in the lives of others. "Sunday, the twenty-fourth."

"What's so special about that day?"

"I don't know, Iris. Something is going to happen during the next full moon. Something that's going to change our lives."

She gazed into my eyes. "There was a chance that you were going to take my offer and run. It would have been a wonderful summer for you to look back on, something to brag about over beers with the boys one day."

"No, there wasn't, Iris."

She frowned. "No, there wasn't what?"

"There wasn't a chance that I would've taken your offer and drifted away. Mr. Free says that a gentleman should always bow out gracefully, but only when doing so will leave his character intact."

"I kinda like Mr. Free, George."

"It's Sir George to you, milady."

17

School started, and the magic of summer immediately began to fade. I sat in silence near the group that always gathered beneath the small oak tree in the playground, inhabiting my usual fringe position. When I got home, I could tell Mom that I ate lunch with all the right people: the Oak Tree Club, as all the wannabes and social outcasts called them.

The crowd talked about summer adventures that had seemed fascinating last year, but now bordered on making me yawn. I wouldn't trade watching Francois shoot a moon into the sky— and then tint it—for three trips to the Grand Canyon, a hot air balloon ride, or a view of New York City from atop the Empire State Building.

The stories were told to collect maximum social currency. Sully Blake recounted a summer of swimming, being chased by surfers, and learning to hang glide from the giant dune at Nags Head. I thought about Francois and his flying machine and, before I could stop myself, I laughed. Everyone turned to glare at me. I sipped from my Coke with wide eyes, hating the feeling of my face flushing red.

"And what did *you* do this summer, George Parker?" asked Elizabeth Conley. She had just related her summer in the Smoky Mountains where she visited her aunt in Pisgah. They enjoyed high tea at the Grove Park Inn with Asheville socialites who found her attractive, witty, and charming. Boys cuter than sin and richer than Croesus had lounged by the poolside and sneaked drinks from rich, jaded parents for her and the other attractive, witty, and charming girls pretending to be her new best friends.

Elizabeth (Lizzy, if you were a friend) had also learned to play tennis at the exclusive Biltmore Golf and Racquet Club with an attentive, divine instructor who could have been James Dean's double and was every bit as cool. He'd pleaded for a moonlight rendezvous, but Lizzy had begged off for propriety's sake. I was betting that her virginity was long gone.

Lizzy knew that I knew I didn't belong in her little group, and she never tired of reminding me with her sweet Southern subtlety. My expression must have indicated in ways I didn't understand that something about me had changed, because Lizzy stopped smiling her artificial smile. The condescension she honed daily and wore so well floated away in the warm breeze. Discomfort flashed in her blue eyes.

I gave her a bright smile and looked at the faces around her, playmates from my past whom I'd once yearned to love and be loved by before understanding that the pecking order was formed early in a small-town world. I was ashamed of myself for having been that person.

The social minions didn't have me completely figured out. Lizzy had lost her smile because she had more sensitive radar. The remainder of the pack was eager to hear that, once again, I'd done nothing over the summer but read, fish, and go to church.

I made eye contact with each in the way I'd now make it with Butch Sinclair, without a semblance of intimidation. It was a fine feeling, realizing that Lizzy wasn't the only one who looked smaller. My smile broadened, and I stood from my longtime place on the periphery of the Oak Tree Club and brushed off the seat of my stiff new jeans.

Summer had been special beyond my ability to describe, but a valuable truth had dawned on me as I listened to the exploits of my classmates. I felt something I'd never felt before—a calm, mature superiority. I could tell tale after tale that would sound unbelievable, even to me, tales that would bring envy and resentment to some and disdain to others.

"Wasn't a whole lot going on in the big city without you guys here, Elizabeth," I said and turned to walk away.

"That isn't what I heard," Greg Matthews said.

I stopped in my tracks. *Here it comes,* I thought. Greg Matthews was Lucille Thrower's grandson.

I turned and gave him a level stare. "Yeah, Greg? What, exactly, did you hear?"

"I heard you took up with a nigger over the summer."

My smile vanished. I studied Greg with the confidence that I had all the ball sack necessary to turn his first day back at school into a memorable but miserable event. I dropped my Coke on the ground, made fists with both hands, and relaxed them, then I repeated the process. I stared at Greg, giving his words time to run around in everyone's head, and then I took a couple of steps toward the group.

"I heard he kicked Butch Sinclair's ass too," one of the guys in the group said.

Greg continued to gaze up at me with a stupid grin, too proud to let on that I was bothering him even if I was, but I saw his grin falter ever so slightly, and a near-invisible flash of concern in his eyes when Butch's name was mentioned. I took four or five more quick steps, like I was going to kick a football from a tee. Greg crabbed backward a few feet, knocking over his soda and spilling his crackers. The Oak Tree Club made room for what looked like the first fight of the school year.

I turned and walked away, my grin returning full and bright.

Lee Roy lumbered down the halls in his new school clothes with a grin that no kid at Eden High could wipe off, no matter on which side of the railroad track he or she resided. He couldn't have cared less about the Oak Tree Club, and when we met in the hall, he gave me a great big bear hug for the benefit of everyone to see.

"School is great, George. Guess what happened?"

"What?"

"Coach Sutton asked me to come out for the team. I can't believe it. That's the best thing that's ever happened to me." His brow furrowed and he added, "Except maybe for the summer."

I laughed. "Don't get too excited. You didn't make the team yet."

"I don't care if I don't make the team. Being asked is the greatest thing ever. Coach Sutton is one of the nicest people I ever met." Lee Roy slapped me on the back, the pleasure in his eyes so intense I nearly cried.

Even if Lee Roy didn't make the team, Coach Sutton would let him down easy. The great big tow-haired man had a heart as large as a football helmet. He was a decent football coach, but his most valuable talent didn't lie in his coaching prowess. Instead, it lay in his unique ability to steer the iffy adolescent onto the road that leads to a fine young man.

Pop viewed Coach Sutton as Eden High's number one asset but I had a mind that Mrs. Lawrimore, our English teacher, might be tied for the spot. Throughout the years, student after student had returned from their college experience singing praises for her mastery over the calculus that is English. Eden didn't graduate too many college football players.

Butch Sinclair and the entire Bangalang Gang avoided me like the plague and regarded Lee Roy as Satan incarnate. It's amazing what a proper stand with a shovel and a wild man trip through a haunted hospital will do to a kid's perspective.

Joe Lee, our history teacher, asked Lee Roy if he had any brothers. Joe was the assistant football coach—an avid fan of chewing tobacco, a snappy dresser, and lusted after by half the girls in school. He teased Eden's pretty flowers and young men mercilessly, especially if he liked them. He could out-cuss anyone on Bangalang and possessed a wit sharper than a barber's razor.

Joe also had an eye for talented athletes. He looked at Lee Roy and said, "I think I'm gonna call you Bull."

Lee Roy gave the tobacco-chewing teacher a great big country grin. "I right kinda like that," he said with a nod. Before the day was out, Lee Roy was Bull the entire school over. I thought he was going to explode.

The first day of practice, Lee Roy nearly killed seven of the seniors. The three thousand miles we logged on our bikes over the summer served him well in the conditioning department. Coach Sutton was looking for big things out of his new running back.

Two weeks passed. The Bull was my best friend, the Butch Sinclair legend had embellished and grown, and I realized that I was being regarded not so much as someone who should be accepted, but someone who should be respected. In my humble opinion, respect trumped acceptance hands down.

Lee Roy worked at the department store with Mr. Hugh on Saturdays and trained for the first big game on weekday afternoons. I continued to fall deeper in love with Mrs. Lawrimore and ran to the library in quest of whatever book she so much as hinted might be worthwhile. I wrote Iris every night and marked each day off the calendar until September 18th, the first day of the full moon.

18

Until school started, I'd been dreading the arrival of a new full moon. Life was complex enough. I didn't want to sneak into Miss Ginn's house again. Lots of things can happen to a kid when he sneaks into someone's house at night, and most of them are bad. Then there was Pug. It was disheartening to see Pug sitting in his wheelchair on the porch, drooling on his bib when we raced our bikes by on summer evenings.

With the exception of Mrs. Lawrimore and Joe Lee's classes, I was once again teetering on the precipice of boredom. Due to my attitude of indifference toward most of my classmates, the boredom had come quicker this year, and with more power. I was left craving a summertime adventure the way a sailor freshly returned to port craves women and drink.

As I stood just outside my window, listening to Pop's light snore mingle with the whirring and chirping of doomed insects, I felt night caress my skin with the indescribable sensation of a cool, soft kiss. Tingling shivers of pleasure traced the length of my spine with such intensity that I shuddered. Autumn was whispering its arrival.

The definitions for pawn aren't distinguished, and I had no doubt at this point that I was one. All I had to do was crawl back through my bedroom window and forget about Mr. Free and his world of mystery, but where would be the fun in that? I had finally developed a firm grip on a spine and had no intention of letting it slip.

I believed in my heart that Mr. Free loved me, but I didn't know it for a fact. Sometimes you want someone to love you so badly that you make their love up, and you endow that someone with qualities that he or she doesn't have because you've convinced yourself that what you want will eventually outweigh the facts.

Buster rounded the corner with one ear pointing toward the sky and the other flopping like a broken wing. He stopped, raised his right front paw, and growled softly. Even beneath a bright moon, he wasn't sure about who'd entered his domain. "It's me, knothead," I whispered.

He lowered his head and ambled over, his drooping tail wagging a gentle apology. He sat at my feet and looked up at me with bright, adoring eyes.

"You stay here. I don't want you getting shot too. Somebody's gotta take care of Mom and Pop." For my effort, I got another Lassie whimper.

I started off toward Miss Ginn's, stopping to check out Mr. Free's place. The silver-white light was there again, escaping from every crack and fissure in the second story. I could hear the big band music from where I stood.

Eden slept quietly, oblivious to the fact that the supernatural danced in her streets like carnival revelers. I scanned the rooftop, but this time there was no Francois. I thought about taking Francois and one of his gadgets to school for a good old-fashioned round of high school show-and-tell beneath the oak tree at lunch and smiled. Francois would beat tennis lessons in the mountains hands down.

I crept toward the back of Miss Ginn's house, wondering how on earth I'd be lucky enough to waltz right into Pug's company again. While I was tiptoeing and stretching for a peek into a window, Buster stuck his cold nose to the back of my bare leg.

"Shit," I blurted, falling over into the shrubbery. I grabbed Buster around his neck and pulled him into my lap. "I thought I told you to stay home, you big lug," I whispered. He licked my cheek and eye as we sat waiting to hear Miss Ginn either investigating, dialing for the police, or cocking her shotgun.

Black and white shadows flitted about inside the den like fireflies caught in a Mason jar. I looked in the window again but saw nothing, so I moved toward the end of the house. Her room was empty.

She'd heard me, or Pug, the last time I'd entered her house. The front door had been unlocked then. Surely, being old, virtually alone, and quite possibly now a bit paranoid about intruders, she'd locked the door. However, I made my way toward the front door. Pug was sitting quietly in the library, staring out the window. Miss Ginn was nowhere to be seen.

The knob turned without protest, and I slowly pushed the door open. Relief was colored immediately by suspicion. Buster whimpered. I looked down at him, placing my index finger to my lips. He moved his big head in an oval orbit, his disapproval clear. The head movement was Buster for, *Don't do it, George. Don't do it.* When I looked back at the door, Miss Ginn was standing there with her shotgun. The barrels looked like two lengths of one-inch pipe.

She cocked both triggers and grinned. The sound was distinct and capable of demanding and holding the attention of even the most wayward high school student. Unlike Mr. Free, she was not brandishing a cigarette lighter. I raised my hands in the air, just like in the cop shows.

"I thought you were in the Boy Scouts, George."

"Um, no, ma'am. I was in the Cub Scouts. I didn't make it long in the Boy Scouts. I could give them another try if you'd like, though."

"They teach you things in the Boy Scouts, like how not to break and enter into the homes of defenseless old women."

"Miss Ginn, no offense, but you don't look a bit defenseless from where I'm standing. Now would be a good time for you to renegotiate your lawn-mowing fee. I'm open to just about any offer you might have in mind." I was amazed at the fact that my voice hadn't broken yet.

"This is no time for a comedy act, George. I knew it was only a matter of time."

"Ma'am?"

"Before peeping in windows wasn't enough."

I'd heard Doc use the word *karma* at least a thousand times. It looked like I might have peeped in one too many windows. Miss Ginn's eyes were cold and hard. She wasn't fooling around.

"It was you the last time, wasn't it?"

I looked from her eyes to the twin pipes. "Don't you lie to me, George Parker."

"Yes, ma'am. It was me."

"Just what in the hell do you want in my house, son?"

I swallowed, but it wasn't easy. The truth was going to sound so damned fantastic that I felt like a lie would surely be better, but I couldn't think of a good one. Heck, I couldn't even think of a bad one. If I told the truth, she was liable to shoot me for verifying her suspicion that I had graduated from Peeping Tom to something more sinister. In her mind, she would be doing Eden a favor. I was screwed.

"He was looking for me," Pug said. Miss Ginn went stiff with fright. My eyes moved from the barrels to her face. Over her shoulder, I spied Pug in his chair. It was a miracle she hadn't squeezed the trigger. Buster let go with a mournful, award-winning moan. I guess he felt like begging was the better of his two options.

"Put the gun away before you hurt someone, Doris."

"I'll second that," I added.

There was fear in Miss Ginn's eyes when she looked back at me. "Am I crazy, too, George?" she asked softly.

"No, ma'am, you aren't crazy. At least, no crazier than any of the rest of us." She lowered the gun, and I reached for it. I eased the trigger down and placed the shotgun in the corner behind me. Pug rolled himself into the hallway.

"Pug, honey, what's going on?" she asked in a small voice.

Pug opened his mouth to answer, but before he could utter a syllable, Miss Ginn crumpled toward the floor like a coat slipping off a hanger. I moved to her in time to keep her from hitting her head.

"Sorry about that," I said, laying her gently on the floor.

"It's probably for the best, George. Close the door and come into the library."

"But what about Miss Ginn?"

Pug looked at his sister and shrugged. "Leave her there. I'll explain it all when she wakes up."

"What if she doesn't wake up?"

"No such luck," Pug said with a grin.

I looked at Buster. "Thanks for the rescue, Rin Tin Tin," I said and slammed the door. A muffled whimper slipped from the other side.

Pug had rolled his chair back up to the big window in the library. The moon was framed in one of its panes. White light glittered off the gold and silver titles of book bindings. "It's good to see you again," he said.

"You, too," I lied.

He studied my face, waiting for me to continue. I suppose that for someone like Pug, small talk was difficult to come by. It was difficult enough for someone like me as well. I swallowed again and rubbed my palms on my pants. "Francois sent me. I'm supposed to give you something."

"That crazy little Cajun is a man of his word," Pug said, extending his hand to me with the barest hint of a smile. Miss Ginn still hadn't trimmed his fingernails, and I looked at his wrinkled hand in much the same way I'd eyed the last water moccasin I stumbled upon on the river.

"What?" I said. I sounded stupider than one of the perpetually truant Bangalang kids.

"Take my hand, George. Do what you came to do." I stared at his age-spotted hand and yellowed fingernails.

I took a step or two, hesitated, then took another. I was close enough to take his hand, but I couldn't do it. I'd watched him stew in a pot of his own making my entire life. I didn't want a matching wheelchair. I looked from his extended hand into his eyes again. He was amazingly calm for a man who knew the kid with the key to his cell was scared out of his wits.

"I'm not going to make you do it. It's your decision." We studied one another's faces, looking for different things but wanting the same result. Instead of pupils, I saw matching images of a full moon.

"No, it isn't my decision," I managed to say, my voice quivering.

"What do you mean?"

"I mean, there's no decision to be made. That time has come and gone." With this I took one more step and grasped his hand. I squeezed my eyes shut against a flash of hazy white light, and with a couple of ticks of the second hand, I found myself sitting in a misty rain.

An enormous football field, overgrown with weeds, lay before me. A muddy clay track, as wide as a regular football field is long, ran the field's perimeter. The air was clean and smelled of wet grass. Thunder rumbled and clouds pregnant with rain darkened the sky.

We sat on rickety wooden bleachers that stretched for a mile on either side. A matching set of bleachers, sparsely populated with people, was located on the opposite side of the field. Giants had once played football here, behemoths struggling toward the huge, crooked goal posts.

Apparitions, forms almost human in appearance but lacking clothing and true physical definition, packed the track. Bright almost-white forms ran out front while those of a darker color, almost silver, ran behind them. The participants grew darker still as the distance from the frontrunners grew. Those running last were crawling, their color as flat and black as charcoal.

The moans and groans of the crowd of faceless participants filled the air. Many talked as they passed by: the lighter the apparition, the more pleasant he or she seemed. The darker ones argued fiercely with someone only they could see, sometimes screaming in rage and gnashing their teeth.

Occasionally, one of the near-white forms would yell out, "Hallelujah," and a defined, beautiful face and sleek, hairless, genderless body would appear. At this point, the form would become a translucent white color and soar over the nearest goal post, rocketing through a glowing gold ring that hung in the stormy sky like a moon.

As the numbers on the track diminished, blobs crawled from beneath the bleachers on both sides of the field and flailed in the grass at the track's perimeter, howling with pain and fear, like wounded soldiers on a battlefield. Eventually, the immobile ghosts of grieving black were drawn by the noise of the running crowd. They dragged and rolled themselves into the mud where they were immediately trampled and nearly buried by the upright runners. Some remained this way for lap after lap, eventually emerging from the muck wailing in agony and pain only to be trampled again. Finally, the tormented crawlers would rise to became walkers, their dull black color moving toward gray.

Pug pointed out one of the morphing black blobs. "At some point, they learn to run."

"What in the hell *is* this place?" I asked, my heart thumping and thudding like Mom's worn-out Hoover.

Pug smiled. "I call it the Purgatory Plane."

"The Purgatory Plane," I repeated. "You think you could elaborate a little for the first-time visitor?"

"Well, it's just a guess, of course, but I've sat here for hours on my way to history and suspect those crawling from beneath the bleachers are the souls of the newly dead. I posit that they're wrestling with misdeeds committed during their lifetimes. When they vanquish the darkness residing within—the twisted being that they spent a lifetime deceiving with lies and illusions—their work is done, and they move on through the ring."

"It's awful. How long does the process take?"

"Until they grow enough to accept themselves and the consequences of everything they did and said while living. I think some have been on that track for thousands of years, if one measured the duration. Time doesn't really exist here."

"How'd you find this place?"

"Whenever I slip through, I always wind up here. Sometimes

the weather's a little nicer, but there are times when the rain's pouring so hard you can hardly see the track."

"I don't like it here at all, Pug," I admitted.

"That's telling. I think the good people pass right by."

"You mean the Christians?"

"Some of them," Pug said with a laugh.

I looked around at the people sitting in the bleachers with us. "Why are these people in the bleachers?"

"They've chosen not to go that route," Pug said, nodding toward the track. "I don't know why they're doing what they're doing. They either can't talk to me or choose not to. Things don't get simple even after we're dead. Nothing is ever simple, George, especially if it's important."

Footsteps approached from our rear. I turned to see a huge colored man clothed in overalls. He looked like a lean, muscled oak tree. In his left hand he carried a bulging crocus sack. He stopped, looked down at us, and smiled.

"Oh my God," I said. He tugged at the brim of a worn fedora by way of greeting and moved on.

"Pug, I've never seen a more beautiful smile in my life," I whispered. "Who *is* that?"

"I don't know his name. He never speaks. He stops, tugs at his hat, and moves on. I call him the Bottle Maker."

"What does he do here?"

"He does favors," Pug said.

"What?"

Pug smiled. "You'll see soon enough," he said, and reached for my hand. The enormous track and its tormented body of runners evaporated into whiteness.

A series of tremendous explosions shook the earth beneath my feet. I blinked against bits of dirt and the acrid smoke of black powder while my eardrums screamed a high-pitched plea for relief. Artillery rained down around us with ruthless destruction, ripping through the fabric of the air, dislodging trees and blasting the earth and living bodies to vapor.

We were standing on a hill, staring in utter amazement as

Confederate cavalry stormed a gun emplacement on an opposite hill. The temperature had risen in a breath from the cool of a misty autumn day to what felt like a hundred degrees. Butternut-clad infantry attacked Yankee positions with a frenzied devotion to conquer or die. Astride a giant stallion, a Confederate general shouted orders. The enormous horse reared, lending a clear view of its rider. I'd seen this very moment frozen in a portrait in Joe Lee's history class. We had front row seats at the Battle of Manassas. The giant of a man astride the giant of a horse was Colonel Wade Hampton.

Suddenly, the battle scene was replaced by screaming peasants surrounding a deadly device with a sharp, angular blade. The blade hissed toward the pretty neck, loose lips and all, of Marie Antoinette. Poor Marie's head fell, speechless and devoid of dignity, into a waiting bloodstained basket.

I opened my mouth to comment and nearly walked into the whirring blade of the Wright brothers' famous invention. Sand attacked my abused peepers and I shut them against the onslaught. The odd clang of a bell replaced the noise of the whirring propeller and I opened my eyes just in time to see the Liberty Bell crack. As the bell's last ring faded into the silent past, Lincoln's words filled the void in a place called Gettysburg.

Lincoln was replaced by men dressed in colonial garb standing in a dark room around a table lit by candles. A document lay on the table. I stepped in to get a closer look. One of the men, a good bit taller than the rest and dressed in dark blue, appeared to recognize me and motioned for me to join him. I walked over, expecting to see the Declaration of Independence. Instead, Francois's ancient parchment with its strange symbols and figures awaited my curious eyes.

"Take it," the tall man said.

I looked up at him. "Mr. Jefferson?"

He nodded and motioned toward the paper. "The document, George, take it," he repeated. I reached for the tattered parchment and held it toward one of the candles to study it more closely. When I grabbed the parchment with my left hand to steady it, the circuit was complete, and I found myself where I'd begun—standing in Pug's moonlit library.

The parchment hovered in the air between us, emitting a soft amber light that painted Pug's tired face with wonder. He released my hand and plucked the paper from the air. With a slender fingernail, he constructed one of his moonlight frames, and an equation similar to the one on the parchment filled the frame, although Pug's equation had missing variables here and there. He fitted the parchment with Francois's formula into the frame, and it vanished in a flash of amber, leaving a complete formula glowing before our eyes.

Pug opened a sketching pad on the desk by his side. The formula fell into the pad like a maple leaf fluttering toward the ground in the fall and my job was done—the key to the lock that Pug had struggled to pick for decades was finally his.

"Mathematics and imagination," he said with a contented smile. He looked at me and winked. "You should probably go before Doris wakes up. I have a bit of explaining to do."

"The Civil War battle, was that real?" I asked.

"Yes, as was Marie Antoinette, the Liberty Bell, the Gettysburg Address, and the meeting of the Founding Fathers. I could have just made Francois's formula appear, but wasn't that a neat ride?"

"I could have done without the Purgatory Plane," I said.

"I don't think you could," Pug replied, his smile fading.

I stepped over Miss Ginn, opened the door quietly, and gave Buster a pat on his head. "Thanks for rescuing me from certain death." He grinned up at me with lolling tongue and bright eyes, his tail thumping wildly. Buster wasn't good with the sarcasm thing.

As Buster and I ran across the Ginns' back yard toward the hole in the ivy at Mr. Free's, I realized that Pug knew things no living soul would ever know. We dove through the ivy at the corner of the wood fence. The big band, raucous as ever on the second floor, was growing louder by the minute.

I rapped the secret knock until my knuckles ached but got

no answer. "Stay here," I said to Buster as I pulled the door open. I made my way through the kitchen, past the study and den, and into the big foyer where the stairs rose to the second floor. When I stepped upon the first riser, the music stopped. I stood in the dead silence, listening for the voices of partygoers or conversation between band members, but there was nothing. A door opened and closed, footsteps approached, and Mr. Free appeared at the top of the stairs. He had a glass of champagne in his right hand and a cigarette smoldering from the holder in his left. He wore a white dinner jacket with a red carnation pinned to the lapel. He looked better than Rick Blaine on his best night.

"You're a sight for sore eyes, young man," he said, his smile as bright as his jacket.

"And why is that?"

"Why, you're my favorite guest, that's why."

"But you don't have any other guests."

"Your point being?"

I waved his remark away. "You're going to get arrested."

"Arrested for what?"

"The neighbors can hear that band like it was in your back yard. Heck, the town can hear it like it was in your back yard."

"I don't think so."

"What do you mean, you don't think so?"

"I mean that only you can hear it."

I gazed up at him and shook my head. "You're a strange man."

"And you, Spy Boy, are a strange neighbor. Anyone else would have stopped coming over here a long time ago."

"You mean, maybe I finally got me a ball sack?"

"You had one all along. You just didn't know how to find it."

"You said I had to grow one."

"I say a lot of things."

"Are you drunk? It's one o'clock in the morning."

He raised the champagne glass in my direction, took a sip,

and peeked at his wristwatch. "No, but I *am* celebrating, and it's almost two."

Two o'clock: a lot more time had passed at Pug's than I realized. "What are you celebrating?"

"A trade has been made, has it not?"

I shrugged. "I guess. What are you doing upstairs?"

"Preparing for a party—a homecoming party."

"Who's coming home?"

"Someone special, Spy Boy. Someone special indeed."

"Will I be invited?"

"That's hard to say."

His answer hurt my feelings and I looked away, my cheeks flushing crimson.

"It's not like that, Spy Boy," he said, his voice soft.

"It's not like what?"

"You don't have to be invited to a place when you belong there. This house is not home to an Oak Tree Club. It's home to you."

It was a perfect answer, a Mr. Free kind of answer. I didn't ask how he knew about the Oak Tree Club. Some questions got straight answers, and some didn't. I was beginning to know which was which before I asked.

I drank a little Coke with Mr. Free while he finished off a bottle of champagne. He told me about the time Francois stole an entire steam engine and drove it to Baton Rouge. He got away with it because the police could find no trace of the 'accomplice' who was capable of operating a locomotive.

Mr. Free fell asleep in his wingback, and Buster and I went home. Before I turned the light out, I wrote Iris a letter, an invitation, if you will.

Friday afternoon finally came, and I was stashing my books in my locker for safe weekend keeping. Reverting to traditional form, I decided not to take anything educational home except Mrs. Lawrimore's *American Literature* book. I was having a difficult time with public education's curriculum. School simply wasn't for me, and I doubted that I would ever accept the conventional wisdom that I was supposed to be better for it.

I felt a tap on my shoulder, and when I turned around, there was Cindy Turner. She was tall enough to look down at me and she was intimidating as hell. Fire flashed in her eyes. She had slivers of green in her brown irises that I found fascinating. I liked her mouth, too, and the way freckles sprinkled a path across the bridge of her cute nose, scattering themselves over her cheeks.

"Hear you got yourself a little girlfriend."

"Maybe." I was amazed at how dedicated Lucille Thrower had been to keeping the stones of the rumor mill turning.

"You ashamed of her?"

"No, I'm not. Despite what people obviously think to the contrary, I see Iris and me as my business. Maybe I'll stand up and tell everyone about it in church on Sunday and clear things up."

This brought a hearty laugh. "That'd be a hoot, wouldn't it? I'd love to see Lucille Thrower's face." Cindy's smile disappeared as quickly as it had come. "You peep at your girl with your sick little ass?" she asked.

I saw something in her pretty brown eyes that set me at ease. I was getting better at dealing with these female creatures. I didn't bother with an answer. I just kept looking into Cindy's strange-colored eyes and smiling.

As she stepped in a little closer, I noticed she was wearing the lemony stuff that the girls had taken to this year, and I loved it. "It doesn't matter anyway," she said, her voice lowered. "I just wanted to tell you that I think the whole thing's kinda cool. Some people in this town could use a good dose of medication for their self-righteous hypocrisy."

In a move that surprised the heck out of me, she gave me a kiss on the cheek. "And I'm glad your eye's better. I was sorry about that after I cooled off." She turned and walked away.

"Cindy?"

She stopped and looked back, her shoulder-length auburn hair shining beneath the fluorescents. "Yeah?"

"Why didn't you tell?"

"'Cause you're kinda cute, George. After I thought about it for a little while, I figured it was sort of a compliment."

The smile she brought with this statement was short-lived because it wasn't returned. "Don't try any repeat performances," she said, narrowing her eyes and pointing at me. "Next time, I'll let Daddy shoot you out of that tree."

Even though I'd hidden the smile, it was hard keeping it at bay. Suddenly, my next-door neighbor was prettier than ever.

19

"Lloyd, put that paper down and get ready," Mom said. "Look at George. I'm so proud of him. He's all ready for Sunday school, and you haven't even made a move yet." This was the Sunday morning ritual. Every Sunday morning, my father was as close to late as he could get without calling it late.

I gave Mom a great big loving-son smile. "Thanks," I said. "I don't want to be late for Sunday school, so I think I'm gonna go ahead and take off."

"Are you sick, George?"

"No, ma'am. For some strange reason, I'm excited to be going to church today."

She smiled and reached over to pinch my cheek. I felt a rush of guilt. "Mom?"

"Yes, George?"

"I love you," I said, my smile gone, my expression serious and genuine. I needed to make this as right as I could. I was never going to forget that muddy clay track.

Pop lit a cigarette and grinned. He liked it when I told Mom I loved her. "I'm glad George is chomping at the bit. I get too much of your organized religion as it is, Nancy. You think Jesus got up and went to church every Sunday morning?"

"I wouldn't know," Mom said, clearing his plate. She hated my father's condescending attitude about church and churchgoers; she secretly harbored the belief that he might be an atheist but was too afraid to ask him outright. Some things a wife just didn't need to know.

"Well, I think they called them temples, but I got an idea that Jesus was in church every day and everywhere he went. Wouldn't hurt the Eden crowd to pick up on that philosophy, don't you think?"

"You were two sips from drunk last night, Lloyd. I don't want to hear any of your preaching this morning. Perhaps I'll raise my hand this morning and ask Reverend Paul if it's okay for you to walk around in a drunken stupor every Saturday night."

My father looked at me and arched his eyebrows. "She's a bit snippy this morning, isn't she?"

I looked at Mom at the same time she looked at me. She had no idea how much I appreciated the fact that Pop didn't think the way the average male Edenite thought, or how much I was counting on his maverick attitude.

"Sometimes I guess we're a handful, Pop," I said.

Mom gave my father a triumphant look and threw her hands over her head. "Hallelujah, out of the mouths of babes."

Pop laughed. "You wouldn't know what to do without us, Nancy."

"That might be true, but I wouldn't spend nearly as much time worrying about my sanity."

I gave Buster a pat on the head, then climbed aboard Lightning and rode down to Mr. Free's, where I entered through the small gate to the left of his garage. Iris was already there. Mr. Free was drinking champagne and reciting the now familiar story of a dogfight he survived in the skies over Germany, only without the Francois part.

"Of course, dear Iris, each battle seemed to have the surreal quality of a dream capable of ending my life, and I spent a great deal of time pondering my ability to outmaneuver German fighter pilots and their faithful steeds. But an even more confounding conundrum was the fact that a race of supposedly superior humans would attack a country capable of producing the city of Paris and the elixir known the world over as champagne. It seemed a concept more ludicrous than ridding the world of flowers and pretty girls."

Normally, a comment like this from Mr. Free would bring laughter, but I could barely acknowledge the fact that he was speaking. Iris's beauty had struck me speechless. Dodie was pinning a carnation to Iris's dress.

"Oh, George, isn't it just beautiful?" she asked when I walked into the room. "And *you*, just look at you."

Iris had no idea how beautiful she was, nor did she realize that I was dressed the way I dressed each and every Sunday that Mom dragged Pop and me from the comfort of our beds to attend church. I stared at my girl with watering eyes.

"Ah, Spy Boy," Mr. Free said, rising from his wingback. "Good to see you on a fine Sunday morning, young man."

"Good to be seen," I said, unable to take my eyes off Iris.

"She's a beauty, isn't she? I hope you don't mind. I asked Dodie to come over and assist. I must say, Spy Boy, that you and Hugh McVey know how to dress a lady."

Dodie looked at me, her face a puzzle of different emotions. I suspected that Dodie thought we were all just a tad crazy, but Mr. Free paid her well. "George," she said with a nod.

"Miss Dodie," I responded with a slight bow of my head.

I looked at Iris again. "Iris...I...you're... You're beautiful."

"We'll make a fine couple indeed, don't you think?"

"Indeed, I do," I said, my voice quivering with pride, and more than just a tad of fear. It was happening.

Mr. Free raised his glass. "To youth and good looks."

Dodie rolled her eyes. "Y'all are crazy," she said, confirming my suspicions. I didn't blame her. I was thinking the same thing.

"Too crazy," Mr. Free added with a laugh. "You know, Dodie, crazy isn't that bad. One could be mean, or moody, or just plain small-minded."

"Crazy is bad enough, Mr. Free."

Mr. Free opened another bottle of champagne, and we all drank except Dodie. "I can't believe you children is going to church with alcohol on your breath."

"I don't think the alcohol will be a problem once they decide to lynch us, Dodie," Iris said.

Dodie sat down and wiped a fine spray of perspiration from her forehead. "You ought to watch what you say, young lady."

"There'll be no lynching today, Miss Dodie," Mr. Free said with a wink. "You have my word on this as an American fighter ace and a Southern gentleman. As my cousin Boudreaux was fond of saying, 'Don't start no shit, and there won't be none.'" He looked at Dodie and Iris, then said, "Please excuse my French, ladies."

"That didn't sound like French to me, Mr. Free," said Dodie.

I'd given the church appearance a lot of thought. In Eden's First United Methodist Church, and probably in churches all over the world, the members come to adopt certain places in the pews. With rare exception, they sit in the same seat their entire churchgoing lives. I'd chosen the place for us to sit accordingly. The center of the front row at Eden First United Methodist was always vacant, except for when the little kids were called for children's time.

When Iris and I walked through the doors, nearly all of the First United Methodist regulars had taken their places. Debbie Norton was at the organ, doing what she was born to do. She was the real thing, a Christian who believed that it was about "walking the walk, not talking the talk" as Pop was fond of saying.

Her eyes were closed, and she was funneling the power of divinity through keys of ivory and ebony with her very soul. Despite the stirring beauty and power of Debbie's work, some members whispered the prior week's news and events and others strained to hear them.

We stopped at the entrance to the nave where Craig Davis, the editor of the *Weekly Observer*, handed us a bulletin and looked at Iris as if he'd never seen a woman before. I took Iris's right hand in my left, and we stepped through the threshold. We slowly passed row after row, leaving each one as silent as pillars of salt. The weight of eyes I'd grown up with, eyes that I'd known my entire life, fell on our backs.

I squeezed Iris's hand. Her courage wasn't lost on me. Despite the near-overwhelming power of the moment, I smiled. In my mind, I saw the eyes of each man in the congregation tracing the fabric of Iris's skirt as it clung snugly to her rear. The dress ended just below her knees, where impeccable calves were being exercised by high heels.

We walked to the front of the church and took our places on the vacant front pew. I motioned for Iris to sit, then I reached over the back for a hymnal, scanning the respectable crowd behind me as I did so. I flashed them a great big grin and gave a little wave of my hand. To my amazement, someone waved back, someone named Cindy Turner. When my eyes fell on hers, she winked and gave me a thumbs-up. I'd never heard my church so quiet before the beginning of a service in my entire life.

It hit me that my planning had centered on getting to where I was now. I did have an emergency exit plan, but I had no idea how I was going to handle anything less than physical danger. Debbie stopped playing the organ in mid-hymn and turned her attention to the rear of the nave.

I heard Mom say, "What on earth? What's going on here?" There was a long pause while no one answered, then she spoke again. "George—George, is that you up there?"

I turned around so she could see that, yes indeed, it was her only son. My father was standing just behind her, grinning like he'd just won first place in the annual fishing tournament. Either he didn't know what was going on and had decided to take things one step at a time, or he'd figured everything out at first glance and reached for his own ball sack. My guess was the latter.

I gave Mom another tiny wave. "Hi, Mom," I said and turned back around. Iris was staring straight ahead with the look you see on the faces of people who just realized that the roller coaster wasn't such a great idea after all.

Mom's hushed footsteps approached at a quick pace, her heels punching into the carpeted floor with an intense, choppy rhythm. She turned the corner, quick-stepped it to where we were, and stood staring at Iris and me with her mouth open. Pop followed at a leisurely pace with his hands in his pockets.

"You look nice today, Mom," I said.

"George, what on earth is going on here?"

Pop strolled up behind Mom and put an arm around her waist, his grin never faltering. "Mom, Pop, this is Iris," I said.

"Hello, Mr. and Mrs. Parker," Iris said. Her face was as pale as Iris's face could get, and her eyes had that frightened deer look.

"It's a pleasure to see you this morning, Iris," said my father, winking at me.

"Iris," my mother said, looking from Iris to me, then back to Iris, finally resting her gaze on me. "George, this is…a surprise," she whispered, finally realizing that the church had quite a few people in it besides us.

"Why is that, Mom? You knew I was going to be here."

She looked past me at the attentive Sunday morning crowd, then she bent close to me. "I'm going to kill you and your father," she whispered and took a seat beside me. Pop sauntered over to Iris's side, reached over the pew, grabbed a hymnal, and sat down.

"Church is going to be exceptional today," he said.

I caught movement from the corner of my eye and assumed it was one of the ushers arriving to ask us to leave and never come back, but when I turned, there was Mr. Free. He was standing tall and proud with a brilliant smile, a cream-colored three-piece suit with a powder-blue shirt, a dark blue tie, and a trademark red carnation pinned to his lapel. In his right hand he held a fedora with a ribbon matching his flower and a polished ebony cane in his left. I'd seen the cane before, resting in the umbrella holder in Mr. Free's den, and knew it was also home to a shiny sword of needle-like proportion.

Iris blessed him with her gorgeous smile. To show his appreciation, Mr. Free extended his hat and performed a bow worthy of royalty. He then rose, and much to my amusement and appreciation, smiled at the congregation and repeated the bow.

"What a handsome gathering," he announced to the awestricken Edenites. He walked to where Iris was sitting, stopped, and extended his hand. Without hesitation, Iris placed her hand in his and he gave it a kiss. Mr. Free, gentleman to the very end, moved next to my mother and extended his hand again. Mom was flustered. She gave him her hand, took it back, then gave it to him again. Her hesitancy struck her as funny, and she giggled like a schoolgirl. Mr. Free laughed, kissed her hand, then moved over so that he stood before my father. He extended his hand again, and my father took it without hesitation.

"Welcome to Eden Methodist," Pop said.

"Your son is of high caliber, Mr. Parker," Mr. Free announced. It was time for my cheeks to turn color. Satisfied that he'd rendered a performance that would have made Clark Gable proud, Mr. Free took a seat by my father.

The organ was still silent. I looked up to see Debbie staring at the entourage on the front pew with a look of shock. I stared back. Iris looked down at her nails, admiring the job that Dodie had done with a frost pink polish. My mother was praying quietly, her eyes closed and her lips moving nonstop.

"Please, madame, or is it mademoiselle?" Mr. Free said, "You play so beautifully, and you're a picture of desirable womanhood."

"Oh my God," Mom said.

Being spoken to directly by Mr. Free caused Debbie's pale cheeks to flush brightly. She flipped to the next hymn, cleared her throat, and after two false starts, found her unmistakable groove.

Hugh McVey appeared on Mr. Free's end of our pew. Hugh hadn't been to church in my memory. Mom told me that he hadn't been since the deaths of his daughters. In repeat of everyone else's entry thus far, he bowed slightly at the silent congregation and gave a wave before taking a seat by Mr. Free.

"Your taste in women's attire is beyond compare," Mr. Free said loud enough for Iris and me to hear. He and Mr. Hugh shook hands.

I was thinking that things couldn't get much better, when the last of our party arrived. Lee Roy, looking like a model in one of Mr. Hugh's well-cut suits, slipped into the pew beside my mother. "Ain't this grand, Mrs. Parker?" he said.

"Yes, Lee Roy," Mom said, her face so pale I was worried that she was going to pass out.

"The prettiest girls in this church are sitting right here on the front row, Mrs. Parker," Lee Roy said, beaming like a snake oil salesman. "I'm betting y'all start a new trend today."

Mom and Pop had pretty much adopted Lee Roy after I brought him by for the first Mingo fishing trip. He ate with us nearly every Friday and Saturday night and loved Pop's grilled burgers. Mom invited his entire adopted family over for dinner once a month.

Lee Roy liked to flirt with Mom, but he wasn't nearly as good at it as Mr. Free. I think one of the reasons Mom grew to love him so was because of his innocent attempts to make her feel beautiful: 'You're prettier than a flower, Mrs. Parker.' 'You look like sunshine, Mrs. Parker.' 'George and I saw a girl in the zombie movie that looked just like you, Mrs. Parker.'

Mom was tickled pink that I finally had a *real live friend*.

"We're starting something, Lee Roy. I'm not sure it's going to be a trend, though," she said dryly.

Lee Roy leaned over and patted Iris's hand. "I finally get to meet the sweetest girl in Eden. It's an honor." He looked at me and winked. Mr. Free had been doing some coaching.

I was attempting not to laugh at Lee Roy's wonderful entrance when Debbie stopped playing the organ again. This time she wore an expression of pure astonishment. I heard several "Oh my Gods," and a "What's happening in here today?" Mrs. Gladys Powell, the owner of Sadie's clothing store, screamed and ran out of the church.

I turned to see what was causing the uproar, and there was Pug and Miss Ginn making their way down the aisle. Miss Ginn wanted to sit in her usual place, but Pug was having none of it. Stiff in his movements but determined, he walked up the aisle, made his way to the front, and stopped before me.

"A fine morning to you, young Parker," he said, extending his hand.

"Likewise," I said, taking it and giving it three firm pumps. He walked down to Mr. Hugh's end of the pew. Hugh McVey was standing with tears in his eyes and his arms open wide.

"I thought it was a miracle when I decided to come today. Now I know it was." He and Pug embraced like lost brothers.

"Welcome, oh welcome back, my dear old friend," Mr. Hugh said, kissing Pug's ear and hugging him until Pug grunted.

My mother leaned toward me. "George, you have a lot of explaining to do."

"It's all about math, Mom," I said.

"Not your best subject as I recall," she said with a frown.

Mr. Free motioned with his cane for Debbie to get back to her playing, and play she did. Miss Ginn returned to her usual place, not about to sit on the front row, where the circus crowd had chosen to set up their act.

I sat in the comforting smell of the nave, perfumes mingling with traces of dry-cleaning, wood wax, hair spray, and the faint hint of tobacco that lingers from that last cigarette just before entering. I inhaled deeply, closed my eyes against the morning sun slanting in through the tall windows, and attempted to determine which had brought the most surprise and consternation to Eden's little church—Iris and me, Mr. Gerard Free, Hugh McVey, or the sudden appearance of a walking, talking, lucid Pug Ginn.

"If we was at my church, the folk would be talking in tongues about now," I heard Lee Roy say over the din of the organ.

"The service isn't over yet, Lee Roy," Mom said.

Mr. Free retrieved a round pewter flask from an inside coat pocket, took a long pull from it, and offered it in my father's direction. Pop reached for the flask.

"Lloyd Parker, don't you *dare*," Mom said, slapping Pop's hand.

"Thanks anyway, neighbor," Pop said with a shrug.

"Perhaps later," Mr. Free said, peering at my mother. "Madame, the good book advises on allowing the man of the house to make his own decisions. And might I add that you have excellent taste in clothes as well? I'm at a loss as to which of you ladies looks most inviting."

"You're quite outspoken, Mr. Free," my mother answered, her voice as frosty as the inside of our freezer.

"I sometimes feel obligated to give voice to truth, Mrs. Parker." Mom made a face and squirmed in her place.

"Mr. Free, you're going to get me into trouble," I said.

"You've already succeeded admirably in that department yourself, young man," Mom said, giving me a hard look.

"I suppose so," I humbly agreed. "But Iris *is* gorgeous, isn't she?"

Mom was silent, her expression a cross between frustration and pleasure, the one she often got when Pop was trying to explain why he gave gasoline to people who couldn't pay for it. "She's beautiful, George," she said; then she did something that made my heart swell. She reached across me and squeezed Iris's clasped hands. "Welcome to our church, honey," she whispered.

"Thank you, Mrs. Parker, thank you so much." Iris had been holding up admirably, but the kindness shown by my mother brought tears. I pulled a new handkerchief from my inside coat pocket and handed it over—more coaching from Mr. Free on display.

As far as I was concerned, we could all get up and go home now. I wasn't interested in what the Edenites had to say after the sermon, either in support or in condemnation. They did most of their lying in church anyway. It was when they got home and reached for the telephone that they would delve into moments of truth, assuming that the truth proved more interesting than a lie.

Reverend Paul swept into the sanctuary with arms open. "All rise," he said, and then he saw us. He stopped at the lectern rail and stared with his mouth open, most of his concentration centered on Pug. He recovered quickly and looked from our group over the congregation and his smile faded.

"This is something a minister rarely gets to do," Reverend Paul said, his gaze fixed on Iris. He pulled at his chin with thumb and crooked index finger. "Let me rephrase that. This is something hardly anyone gets to do." He looked at the congregation again, his eyes moving from one parishioner to the next: reading, acknowledging, and divining.

"Anyone know what I'm talking about?" There was no answer. The drama was unfolding, and everyone in the sanctuary knew who was directing the play. Reverend Paul waited for a long time, his eyes settling on mine. I moved to take Iris's hand.

"Three miracles," Reverend Paul said. "Who gets to walk into church to confront not one, not two, but three miracles on a Sunday morning?" Silence stalked the room like a hungry animal.

Reverend Paul ignored the quiet. "What have I done to be so blessed this morning?" he implored, glancing toward the ceiling, his voice booming out over the nave. He looked at Pug. "Pug, can you speak?

"Yes, Reverend, I can," Pug said, his voice cracking a bit but clear.

"Did you walk in here under your own power?"

"Yes, Reverend, I did."

"The good people of Eden and their ministers have prayed for you for decades. I have prayed for you."

"Thank you, Reverend," Pug said.

Reverend Paul looked at Mr. Hugh next. "What on earth got into you this morning, Hugh? How many times have I asked you to join us?"

"Let's just say I had a dream," Mr. Hugh said.

Reverend Paul smiled and pointed at Mr. Free. "Welcome, Mystery Man. To you as well, Bull," he said, using Lee Roy's beloved nickname. Mr. Free nodded, and Lee Roy blushed.

The man in whom my mom had placed so much faith stepped down from the lectern and walked over to stand directly before Iris. He opened his arms wide, his crisp black robe rustling. "And the best for last—courage," he said. "Welcome, young lady, welcome to this gathering of God's children."

He bent toward Iris and whispered. "Stand up and give me a hug." Iris didn't hesitate. Reverend Paul engulfed her and looked over his shoulder. "Debbie, a detour this morning. Would you please play 'Amazing Grace'?"

He released Iris and made his way to the sanctuary, singing with gusto. When the hymn was finished, he gave us a bright smile, shutting it off as quickly as it came. "Nothing like not having to resort to the week's notes," he said. He fixed a few of the members with a steady gaze as he tucked the prepared sermon into the big Bible.

He placed a hand on either side of the lectern and stared down at the Bible. "I've not been pleased with myself since I came here. It doesn't take long for a young minister to learn that preaching the Word is only a small part of his job. For so many, churches are about politics, business, and improving social status. Churches are often about doing things in God's name to which God would never assign His name. Churches are about the people who sit in them on Sunday mornings suffering the woeful state of the human condition. Unfortunately, for too few, churches are where we come to be better people and Christians."

Reverend Paul looked up from the Bible to survey the congregation again. Hugging Iris had been the point of no return and he knew it.

"A minister sees these things at his first church. Heck, he sees them before he ever answers the calling, and he detests them. If he isn't careful—if he takes his eyes off the prize and allows himself to lose sight of his calling, if he listens to the finance committee or a church elder instead of his Master, he can and will find that he's lost his way.

"After all, we ministers are only human. We like new cars and nice clothes too. Even better, larger churches and the prestige they can bring." He fiddled with the corner of a Bible page for a moment then looked straight at Mr. Maynard Cribb. "Sitting in obedient silence during closed-door meetings where Christians lay and hatch plans as if they were about to run headlong into battle can bring a comfortable life to a compromised minister." He smoothed out the Bible page and smiled.

"Look at this," he continued, indicating the front row. He lowered his voice to a whisper. "I walked in this morning with my usual fare." He held up the folded pages of his prepared homily. "This sermon is safe in that it's digestible without causing any lasting pain and serious self-reflection. I walked in feeling comfortable with today's message, but lo and behold, sitting before me—on the front row, no less—are three miracles and more courage than I've seen in years.

"Courage," he repeated, then allowed the animal of quiet thought and self-examination to prowl unfettered for a bit among the congregation. "Not only is it more courage than I've seen in years, but it's also far more than I've engaged personally." He began tapping on the lectern with his forefinger, looking at us, then the congregation as he drummed a beat. Reverend Paul had had his moments of fumbling and bumbling since coming to Eden, but he was knocking this one out of the park.

"Tell me, holier-than-thous," he boomed. Mom and I both jumped in our seats. "What am I to do about this message before me this morning, written with more eloquence through action than I'll muster if I live to ninety?"

He knew what was expected of him from the stalwarts, those who made the rules because, church or no church, they had the money. Although he'd never use the words, it was ball sack time.

"Well, I never," Mrs. Lucille said, chasing the animal of silence away. I didn't have to turn. Her voice was as unmistakable as my father's.

Reverend Paul fixed her with his dark eyes. "You never what, Lucille? Behaved the way decent folk behave in situations like this? If you watch me, I'll show you how it's done. If you don't want to see how it's done, you're welcome to go home and make preparations for the sure-to-follow character assassination of

Eden's First United Methodist minister, the most recent in a long line of unfortunate political church casualties."

The ensuing silence gave new meaning to dropping pins. Someone coughed, but other than that, we might as well have been sitting in a crypt at midnight in February. Twenty seconds passed by, feeling more like twenty minutes, and then Mrs. Lucille allowed the animal back in. She didn't say another word, and she didn't move. I waited with anticipation for the meaty, muffled sound that would indicate the explosion of her head.

As Reverend Paul continued to survey the landscape of faces he said, "Is it time for me to remind my fellow strugglers of a tenet: hate the sin, love the sinner? Look around all you please, but don't forget when you stand in front of your mirror next time to give the man or woman looking back at you the attention he or she deserves."

He looked down at us again, his eyes moving from one end of the pew to the next, then back to Iris. "Welcome, to our humble church, in the name of Jesus Christ our Lord."

I held tight to Iris's hand during the ensuing sermon, proud of her, proud of me, and proud of my parents and friends— but most of all, proud of the man who had chosen to stand by our side and his belief this morning. Mom had been right.

After the service, I realized that paying my second visit to Pug had brought huge reward. Church members hugged both Iris and me. Some of the smiles were as transparent as cheap plastic, and I saw things in the eyes of quite a few adults I'd known and loved that were unsettling. Many of these people would spend a long time on Pug's rain-drenched clay track. By and large, the congregation was interested in Pug. He was, after all, a walking, talking miracle.

"I don't know what happened," I heard him say. "I woke up one morning last week and felt fine. I sat up in bed, put my feet on the floor, and stood of my own accord. It was a wobbly moment, of course. Doris walked into the room, and I looked at her and said, 'Good morning, sister. Thank you for tending me all these years. What might I do for you this morning?' Doris fainted, and what I needed to do became apparent. I needed to find the smelling salts." Pug laughed and all around, church members laughed with him…except for Miss Ginn.

She was pretending to listen and find her brother's story amusing, but she kept looking at me as if I could change her into a frog. I shrugged, held up five fingers, and smiled.

"You do know that you've probably ostracized yourself and us from Eden society forever, don't you, George?" my mother asked over her shoulder as we walked home. "They're probably heating the tar and slitting pillows as we speak."

"Nancy, you should have been an actress," Pop said, lighting a much-needed smoke. "I don't know if I've ever seen a prettier girl in my life," Pop said, looking back and winking at Iris. "And I think Reverend Paul hit the nail on the head. I've never seen a braver one, either." He gave me a proud grin. "Hell, that's the first time I felt like I've been to church since George was born." He looked at Iris. "And Iris, Nancy—does that boy of mine have a backbone, or what?"

Since it was Sunday morning and we'd just left church, I didn't bother to tell him that I preferred ball sack.

Mom didn't want to smile, but she couldn't help herself. She was riding high on the adrenaline created by this morning's event. "I'm sorry," she said. "Lloyd is right. I suppose the four of us can form a leper colony of sorts, providing, of course, that your father keeps enough business to put food on the table."

"George and I pulled a fast one on you two," Iris said. "I was waiting to be dragged out of church by my hair. Instead, I found decency and kindness. I'll help Mr. Parker do whatever he needs doing at the station after school and on the weekends."

"I certainly like the sound of that," Pop said.

"Lloyd, please," Mom said, looking toward the heavens the way she often did when she could do nothing with Pop, or make sense of anything he said.

"Think about it, Nancy. No matter what all those old farts in church were thinking, they couldn't keep their eyes off her. I'll sell more gas than Esso. Iris, will you wear shorts?"

"God help me," Mom said, giving Pop a shove.

"I'm used to it, Mrs. Parker. It's not like I was discovered today. George is the only man I've ever met able or willing to see beneath the surface."

"Ouch," Pop said.

"At least you're honest, Mr. Parker," Iris said.

"Call me Lloyd, Iris. You make me feel old in more ways than one. Calling me 'mister' makes things worse."

Iris ate dinner with us, and it was obvious that, despite Mom's fears for our futures, she liked her son's girlfriend a great deal.

Pop's basic honesty and decency was more than Mom could do battle with, even had she been so inclined. He laughed with Iris, joked with her, made fun of her fancy books, and told her that his son always made the most sense when he was reading comic books.

A knock came at the door. Mr. Free stood there with two bouquets of flowers from his garden, one for Mom and one for Iris. Under his arm was a bottle of French champagne.

We had to drink from Mom's best glasses, bluish creations that came out of a box of laundry detergent. They were a far cry from fine crystal, but Mr. Free rendered the matter at hand far more significant than the embarrassment of cheap glasses.

He stood in our small kitchen, raised his blue glass, and winked at my mother. "To forgiving parents, the long view, and excellent friends." We touched glasses and drank of his delicious bubbly. Iris giggled and rubbed her nose.

"Please, Mr. and Mrs. Parker," Mr. Free said, "accept my heartfelt and humble apologies for the clandestine friendship that George and I have shared throughout the summer. I simply couldn't help myself. It's the way with us spies."

"Neither could I," I added.

"I think your friendship is the best thing that could've happened to George," Pop declared, holding his glass for more bubbly. "Are you a real live spy? Wait till the guys down at the barber shop hear that."

"Mr. Parker, I'm a businessman by trade, but not one of

the best, I'm afraid. Thus, my silent partnership. However, you have my permission to allow the fine folk of Eden to think whatever they please. A healthy rumor mill makes life more interesting, even when you're the brunt of its product."

"I don't know what to think," my mother said. Her looks had always served in giving her the sense of holding the upper hand. Mr. Free and the myriad of intoxicating traits that made the man were too much for her. She felt like a chorus girl trying to get lucky with the producer, and she didn't like it.

"I know what I think," Iris said, looking at me, then everyone else in the room. "I think this is the best day of my entire life."

20

School became an interesting pastime. I still didn't fit into a group, but I found that, more than ever, I didn't care to. The Sunday service had made us famous, or infamous, as had Lee Roy's prowess on the football field. As a result, Lee Roy and I had become a group, one many of the girls found fascinating. If you want to find yourself suddenly "belonging" in any social environment, the first order of business is to figure out how to get the girls to adopt you. Your male counterparts may continue to hate your guts, but it won't matter in the least. Lee Roy was taking serious lessons from Mr. Free, right down to the hand-kissing, and the girls ate it up.

Attention turned out to be something I could do without. Our newfound social standing and adoration were nice, but I was an introvert at heart and always would be. Lee Roy, on the other hand, loved it. He had his eye on Kim Mack. I'd had a crush on the sweet brown-eyed girl ever since trying to carry her books home from school in third grade and being rebuffed for doing so. But a first crush will always be a first crush.

"I think I love Kim, Patti, Susan, and the other Kim," Lee Roy confessed during one of our late-night conversations over a campfire and s'mores.

"That's a lot of girls to love," I said, grinning because of his seriousness.

"I can't help it, George. They're all just so sweet. I like that new girl, Emily, too."

"Well, you need to think about how you're going to spread all that love you have around. At least one of them will probably get jealous," I teased.

"You aren't helping, George."

We tolerated, at times even enjoyed, the good attention, but the negative kind was tough. I found a Confederate flag in my locker. True to Mom's predictions and fears, Pop lost business from one sector of town, but in short order the dollars were made up from another. No crosses were burned in our yard, and I wasn't tarred and feathered—at least, not physically. All in all, the good of taking Iris to church and publicly proclaiming her my girl far outweighed the bad.

"People aren't afraid of you and Iris," Pop explained one day. "They're afraid of what might come after you and Iris. They're just afraid, period. A long time and a lot of heartache went into building where we are now, George. It isn't easy to undo wrong, and there's plenty of that to go around. It's a whole lot easier to deny it and hope it'll go away, to do nothing. People don't like being reminded of that."

The first football game came, and Iris refused to go. She refused, not because she was afraid for herself, but because she was afraid for me. "Maybe someday," she said.

I hated her decision because Lee Roy loved her dearly, and she missed the packed stands yelling, "Bull! Bull! Bull!" as Lee Roy rumbled over defenses like a small tank through a field of sunflowers. At every home game, his name echoed between the stands and through the quiet fall night in Eden. The Eden Tigers finally had a football team, and its centerpiece was a hulking, unstoppable brute of a sophomore affectionately known as Bull.

I'd never enjoyed watching the game from the stands until I could stand and scream, "Bull!" at the top of my lungs. Lee Roy would pick me out of the crowd after an amazing touchdown run and point at me. Kids who never knew I existed slapped me on the back, and I knew for the first time in my life what a perfect high school moment felt like.

One Friday night during a full moon, I left at half-time because we were trouncing Johnsonville, a rival town about five miles up the road. I had no mysterious dates to make or promises to keep. I was living a normal life and it felt good.

The night was cool and the air stimulating. I'd come to understand that lurking in Eden's night shadows were things people focusing on work, families, churches, and living a normal life rarely thought about. I also saw, for the first time, that if you aren't looking for a certain thing, you aren't going to find it.

When I drew near Mr. Free's house, I spied the glow of a cigarette. He was sitting at his patio table with his back to me as I slipped through the gate. "Spy Boy," he said without turning.

"What're you doing?"

"Enjoying the sounds of youth at play and the jubilation of winning. Our friend's name brings a smile each time I hear the 'Bull' chant," he added with a chuckle. "What're you doing out and about while victory is being won?"

"Visiting my best friend."

"You shouldn't call another man 'best friend,' Spy Boy."

I took a seat opposite him. "Why not? I thought you'd like that."

He motioned to the six-pack of small Cokes, a spare glass, and a bucket of ice. "Please, share a libation with me." He smoked and waited for me to finish making my drink.

"I do like 'best friend', but it brings connotations I don't find pleasant, chief among them my sincere belief that you can have more than one best friend, but not a bevy of them. Lee Roy wouldn't care for you referring to me as your best friend in his presence."

I started to speak but he stopped me with a raised cigarette holder. "I know. You wouldn't do so in Lee Roy's presence. The point is, he's every bit as best a friend as I.

"This really isn't about Lee Roy's feelings," he continued. "At some point, I'm going to disappoint you. Disappointments are all the more bitter when delivered by the actions or words of a best friend."

"How could you possibly disappoint me after all you've done for me?"

"I've been known to find ways, Spy Boy. Humans are wonderful at forgetting past kindnesses when faced with present disappointment."

"I don't know what you're talking about."

He laughed softly. "That's a rather pleasant position to in-
habit," he said, his cigarette glowing as he inhaled.

"What's wrong, Mr. Free?"

"The moon talked, my dear young friend. I've waited years
for it to do so, pined away precious minutes of my allotted time
waiting for the moment. Now, the moment has come, and I
find many reasons to be sad about the occasion."

Bubbles tickled my nose as I sipped my drink and tried
to follow him. I often failed to understand Mr. Free's cryptic
observations and statements, but, almost without fail, time
brought clarity. I decided to sit quietly and enjoy the beauty of
an autumn night, the sounds of a Friday night football game
in the distance, and the treasure named Gerard Free. Answers
would come as they always did—in time.

21

The magic of summer ended the following Monday after school. As I rolled beneath the oaks toward home, I saw cars at Mr. Free's house. My heartbeat increased with pedal speed, and the closer I got, the more ominous the vibrations became. Something was wrong—something was terribly wrong.

The first car was Eden's only police cruiser, the second was the county coroner, and the third, the Morris Funeral Home hearse. Men were loading a sheet-draped body into the hearse when I rolled up with tears pouring down my face. I let Lightning clatter to the sidewalk and ran toward the hearse, but Ellis Morris stepped in front of me, his arms extended with hands up. I tried to dodge around, but he grabbed me and held fast.

"Whoa, whoa, George. This is far enough."

I struggled against his iron grip, then looked into his dark eyes, almost as kind as Mr. Hugh's. "What... What happened, Ellis?" He looked past me and let go of my arm, nodding at someone approaching from my rear.

Then I felt someone touch my shoulder and Dodie stood with red, swollen eyes. She pressed a spare handkerchief into my hand and shook her head. "Let's step in the house, George," she said. I turned and looked at Ellis. He nodded, his eyes conveying his sorrow. Ellis was a class act.

I followed Dodie inside, trying not to look at the hearse, but unable to help myself. Its rear door was open wide, and a pair of brown and white wingtips protruded from a white cover.

We sat down at the kitchen table, then Dodie reached across and squeezed my hands. "I come to clean like I always do on Mondays." Her voice was soft and soothing. "Mr. Free didn't come to the door. I don't know why, but I didn't hear the car running. That Caddy purrs like a little kitten, George. I went in and called for him but got no answer. Most times, when he didn't answer, he'd be upstairs, so I thought nothing of it."

Something crept into Dodie's eyes. "I don't go upstairs in this house, George. There's something up there that I ain't got no business knowing about." She shook her head to dispel the unease that had crept into her voice. "I got busy doing my work. When I took the garbage out to the curb, that's when I heard the noise in the garage. I don't know why I didn't notice earlier. Maybe a car was rolling by when I was knocking, or I wasn't supposed to notice."

Dodie's mouth quivered, then broke into an ugly grimace of grief. I tried not to cry but the effort was ridiculous. We stood up and hugged. She hugged me the way a mother hugs her hurt children, and we cried together until she could finally speak.

"I opened the garage door and fumes come rolling out. There he was, sitting behind the wheel of that great big Cadillac, dressed to the nines. He went out in Mr. Free style, ain't no doubt about that. He was wearing a pale-yellow suit, exquisitely cut, as usual, a white silk shirt, a blood-red tie, and his red carnation. He was a sport to see, George." She smiled and shook her head as more tears rolled.

"There was a half-bottle of that old demon rum, a six-pack of his little Cokes, and his cigarette holder was in the ashtray. I think he was in a good mood. He sure enough had a big smile."

I didn't know what to say. Of all the things I could've dreamed about Mr. Free, suicide would've been the last, and no matter how I felt about the act, Mr. Free was gone. I waited for anger, but it didn't come. He'd loved me and I'd loved him.

I walked home in a trance of despair, the foolish illusion that I'd grown into a man completely shattered. To say that I'd been unprepared for Mr. Free's death would be the understatement of my life. Not only was I not prepared, but I'd also never given a moment's thought to being so. Such is the blissful naiveté of youth before one understands that the only constant is change.

Mom would not always be there, neither would Pop, or my sweet old Buster. I thought about my grandparents. The wrinkles and the gray hair were undeniable and had been there since I could remember: God's signs, intended to prepare younger humans for the deaths of older humans. Gray hair and denial don't mix.

This was my first taste of loss—irreversible, utter, permanent loss. Mr. Free would never again flick his Zippo, mix us drinks, weave his unbelievable tales, or fill the night with smoke and laughter.

I stumbled up the back steps past my mother, who was at her post in the kitchen. "George," she said to my retreating back. I continued on my way, walking into my room, and burying my face in a pillow filled with the scents of my mother's clean, cared-for world, a world of comfort and safety that was as fragile as a bird nest in a dying maple. The gigantic, muddy track with the tormented souls slipped into my mind again. It was a horrible thought, but then I remembered Pug had told me that some souls flew right past the Purgatory Plane, and I smiled into my tear-soaked pillow.

There's no fooling a mom. I felt my bed give when she sat. "George, honey, what on earth happened?"

I pressed my face deep and screamed my agony into muffling softness. Mom rubbed the back of my head for a full two minutes, her presence and gentle touch priceless. Finally, I gathered myself and turned puffy eyes on her.

"Mr. Free's gone, Mom."

"Don't be silly. That man loves you. He wouldn't go anywhere without leaving word."

I shook my head. "Mom, he's not gone like that. He's gone as in dead."

Her hand went to her mouth. "Oh God...oh my God, George." She leaned down and kissed my forehead. "I'm so, so sorry," she whispered.

There's no cure for the grief of loss save time, but gentle words and the presence of those we love can move us from one tick of the clock to the next. I remembered Doc's words. "Even time takes time, son."

There was no funeral. Ellis called and told me that if I wanted to say goodbye to Mr. Free, I'd better get up to the funeral
home pronto. I called Lee Roy and Mr. Hugh. Pop drove us
to pick up Iris. We stood by Mr. Free's casket and cried like
children. Lee Roy, the biggest, toughest one of our trio, bawled
like a baby.

Mr. Free was as unperturbed by it all as he would have been
in real life, and as usual, he looked fantastic. As a matter of fact,
he looked better than ever.

"How can you be dead and look that damned good?" Iris
said through tears.

"It's called style," Lee Roy said, blowing his nose into a sog-
gy handkerchief. "I wish I had some."

Of all his fine garb and haberdashery, I always thought Mr.
Free looked best in his white dinner jackets. Dodie had chosen
his burial clothes and must have thought the same, right down
to the red carnation. Tucked inside the casket were his cigarette
holder, a pack of his fancy French smokes, the pewter flask
that had nearly given Mom a heart attack in church, and a small
Coke.

The next day, a tall, emaciated stranger from New Orleans
showed up. He introduced himself, wiped his clean-shaven head
with a limp handkerchief, and loaded Mr. Free into a gleaming
black Cadillac hearse that appeared to have been built in the
thirties.

I was standing on the sidewalk at the dime store when the
hearse rolled through and wasn't at all surprised to see a passen-
ger. A young man with bright red curly hair and aviator goggles
was riding shotgun. He grinned and gave me a thumbs-up. I
watched the big black car, one of the oddest sights I'd ever
seen in Eden, disappear, taking with it the world that had been
mine over the summer—but unable, thank God, to take away
the memories.

Mr. Hugh ambled up the sidewalk, smiling when he reached our
house. Buster and I were sitting on the steps, and he joined us,

taking a seat on the other side of Buster. He didn't speak. He just sat and scratched Buster's ears.

After several minutes I said, "I don't know what I'm going to do."

"You know. You just don't know that you know."

"Sir?"

"You get up every day and you do what you're supposed to do. It isn't fun. It isn't fun for a long time. Sometimes it isn't fun for a very long time, but you still keep getting up and going out there because that's all you can do. There's no giving up when you're still young and life is left to live."

"Don't some people die from the sorrow?"

"I'm sure they do, but that's mostly in movies and books."

"How'd you know I was taking Iris to church that Sunday? I didn't tell you."

"The girls told me. George, I know I said this before, but I want to thank you again for the summer, and I'm very sorry about Mr. Free. I didn't know him, but I keep having this feeling that he brought something good to Eden, something that'll last a long time."

"I ought to thank you, too, Mr. Hugh. All I did was show up with a couple of Iris's grandmother's fancy hooks. You took us to fish, you gave Lee Roy a bike, then school clothes, that killer suit he wore to church—every day since I can remember, you've walked by here with a smile whether you felt like one or not."

He reached over and tousled my hair. "You're special, George. You ever stop to think that might be why Mr. Free took you under his wing?"

I watched him walk down the street toward his house, tall and graceful and every bit a slowly vanishing constant. I thought about businesses that'd been on Front Street forever but were now closed. A ghost was all that was left of the old Hemingway Hardware where Pop and I had bought my shotgun. Doug's jewelry store was gone, Powell's auto parts, and Dr. Curtis's wonderful old drug store.

Fine old homes were gone, the children who once ran through their rooms swallowed by colleges and life, never to return to our little town with their smiling, happy faces. What was the use? Why struggle? As Butch was once fond of reminding me right before a beating, "Life's a bitch and then you die."

22

On the first full moon after Mr. Free left me, I watched my parents prepare for their supper club. Pop was in a fine mood, excited about the prospect of seeing his buddies, and Mom was gorgeous and happy. I realized that an excellent response to the "why struggle" question was standing before my eyes—two beautiful human beings, glowing with health and filled with love for one another.

Supper Club made Mom beautiful, which, as I've noted, wasn't a stretch in the first place. Pop also lost about twenty years of birthday candles when it was time to hang out with his cronies.

"They're my brothers, George. I grew up with them, played baseball and football with them, drank with them, and chased girls with them. Even got the crap beat out of me in the principal's office with them."

I watched my parents laugh across the porch, down the steps and over to Pop's old '57, where he plopped his aluminum Pepsi cooler—filled with Pabst Blue Ribbon, Seagram's Seven, and Canada Dry ginger ale—into the trunk.

"I wonder what Jeff and Ricky are drinking tonight?" he pondered as he opened Mom's door.

"Whatever it is, it'll be too much," Mom said, rolling her eyes. "You're going to church tomorrow, Lloyd Parker."

"Church has gotten right interesting, to tell the truth, Nancy," Pop said, sticking his tongue out at her after she sat, and then he shut the door.

"I'm tellin'," I said.

"No, you won't," he said with a laugh, his face flushed with drink and cheer. "Stay out of trouble, George."

"Yes, sir." I smiled at Mom and waved.

I was almost finished with *Eddie Rickenbacker*. Mrs. Lawrimore had recommended an O. Henry collection next, and it waited on my bedside table. Sometimes, when Mom and Pop were gone, I'd let Buster in. Buster loved to stretch out on my bed more than I loved grape ice cream. I spread an old towel at the foot of the bed and gave him the "it's okay" expression. As Buster snored and chased dream cats, I read. A full moon cast its glow outside my window, and the last of Mother Nature's diminishing nighttime symphony tuned up in the cooling night air.

I don't know how long I was asleep when the horn woke me. At first, I thought it was a car horn, then I recognized "In the Mood." Mr. Free would have had it no other way. The clarinet's fine, smooth notes, backed by the four saxophones, was unmistakable. I sneaked out of bed, careful not to wake a comatose Buster. As I stood gazing down at my big dog, Mr. Free's laughter rang inside my head, followed by something he once said: *I mean that only you can hear it.*

I pulled on my clothes and left Buster to his dreams of rabbits and pretty girl dogs. After a short sprint, I was slipping through the ivy at the corner of the Great Wall. I stood in Mr. Free's backyard for a moment, just listening. The light that had poured with such hypnotic allure from the upper floor was back, and there was no one to caution me about being careless.

I hadn't forgotten Mr. Free's words of warning or the promise I'd made. I hesitated for all of three seconds. I'd grown a ball sack that had developed the habit of speaking louder than my little voice. I walked across the back yard, the wet grass beneath my bare feet a cool reminder that summer was gone until next year.

The back door was locked, so I retrieved the key from the little mailbox and let myself in. When I opened the door, the music stopped. I was an intruder, and Mr. Free no longer lived in this place. No matter how many nice things people gather over the years, a home loses its soul when its owners pass away.

I stopped in the kitchen and gazed at the small table where

Dodie had told me about Mr. Free. It was the last time I'd been in the house. I grabbed a Coke out of the refrigerator and walked through the dining room and into the study. The lamp between the wingbacks cast the only light in the house.

I took my seat in the chair on the left and stared at the dark fireplace. I'd been looking forward to sitting in the chair before a crackling fire, discussing life and philosophy with Mr. Free for years to come. Tears began to well.

An envelope with my name scrawled across the front lay in the bottom of the bombshell ashtray. Well, not exactly my name, but close enough: *Spy Boy* appeared in Mr. Free's hand. I sipped my Coke again and stared at the note as if it were a scorpion. Where had it come from? It wasn't here when Mr. Free left. It wouldn't have gone unnoticed under the circumstances.

I wanted to rip it open, and I didn't want to rip it open. The envelope contained the last of Mr. Free that I would ever get to experience. I decided to listen to the music and savor the moment.

I got up, walked over to Mr. Free's sideboard, and opened the drawer on the top left. A spare Zippo lighter and a package of his Gauloise lay inside. I returned to my chair, tapped the cigarettes against the palm of my hand like Pop always did, and opened them. I studied the envelope and Mr. Free's penmanship.

I thumbed the lid of the Zippo and closed it back several times, savoring the familiar snick-click that reminded me of Mr. Free and my father. I lit one of the Gauloises, took a deep pull, and immediately began to hack my lungs out. I studied the smoldering stick with wonder, then crushed its life out in the green-stained bottom of the brass ashtray. When my eyes cleared of tears, I picked up the envelope and the music started back.

The paper was heavy Crane stationery. I touched it between my nose and upper lip, closed my eyes, and inhaled. Traces of Old Spice, rum, and tobacco teased my memory and senses.

I burrowed into the chair, relishing the feel and smell of the supple leather and the beat of the band upstairs. The realization that his place would soon slip from my life was heartrending.

A tall, pale stranger, with a large, ravaged nose and who looked like death itself, had shown up in black tails and top hat with a white feather tucked in its band. Dr. Death, as Ellis later called him, had whisked Mr. Free's body away in an ancient black hearse. No doubt, someone would show up to haul away his worldly possessions as well. Despite this possibility, I felt good for the first time since Mr. Free died.

Earlier, I'd used the words *killed himself* during a conversation with Pop. "*Died* will work just fine, George, or *passed away.*Anything but *killed himself.* I just can't imagine a man like that killing himself. Something terrible must have happened to him."

Though I'd been forbidden to seek Mr. Free's company by both parents, I realized that Pop's part in this consisted solely as support for Mom's wishes. Pop had taken an instant liking to Mr. Free, shark and all. I opened the envelope.

I knew you'd be back. You've not let me down yet. I've known many men, both young and old. Never have I known a purer heart or a more loyal friend. You believed in me when there was no reason whatsoever for you to do so, when everyone in your realm was telling you to stay clear of the stranger. Thank you for the privilege and honor of your friendship. Stay true to yourself and remain on course, Spy Boy. g

I rose from the wingback with a smile on my face. He was taunting me. The note wasn't a warning; it was an invitation.

When I reached the foyer, I climbed the first step and stopped, waiting for a whispered caution, for someone to tell me to go home where I belonged. I waited for a strong hand to fall upon my shoulder. There were only the sounds an empty house makes, mostly overridden by the steady swing of Glenn Miller's horns.

It was dark at the top of the stairs, except for a white glow emanating from beneath the only door on the left side of the hallway. Despite the adrenalin, I stepped slowly, waiting for

Francois to pop out of thin air and stop my heart, but I reached the door without interruption from Francois or anyone else.

When I touched the knob, a tingle ran the length of my arm, curling up around the back of my neck and nestling behind my left ear—the exact sensation I'd experienced the first time Mr. Free and I shook hands. It was my last warning. I paid it no heed. I wanted one more grand adventure to top the summer off. Words from the past made an unwelcome entry.

George, promise me that as long as I live in this house, you won't go up those stairs.

I waited for my little voice to take up the cause of promises broken, but this one was easy. I'd crossed my fingers, and Mr. Free didn't live here anymore. The knob turned smoothly, and the big door swung open of its own accord.

It occurred to me that I might have gone to sleep in Mr. Free's chair. Hell, for all I knew, Buster and I were fast asleep in my bed. But the scene before me was too real for a dream. I could see every detail, smell every scent, feel every vibration.

There was no spare bedroom, no billiard, sewing, or reading room. Instead, there was, to my amazement, a huge dance floor. To my right was the Glenn Miller orchestra, sixteen pieces of precision-operated musical instrumentation flashing beneath the spotlights. I knew who the man and his band were; Mr. Free had shown me many pictures. The rich, powerful sound of their music rolled over me in waves of synchronous brass magic so hot it crackled. The tin can preservation of their sound on vinyl seemed ludicrous, like calling a broken piece of soda bottle a diamond.

"Oh hell yeah, you can *ride* on that, Spy Boy," Mr. Free said inside my head. The boys were smoking brass with mighty lungs.

Behind the stage, the wall was painted in a huge, life-like mural. Mr. Free's Caddy pointed toward a two-lane blacktop with ancient live oaks lining either side. In the distance a full moon rose between the trees. It was an amazing piece of work, lending the impression that one was gazing through a window, not at a painting.

To my left, pale blue and white neon bathed the black lacquered surface of a large bar. Behind the bar, a mirrored wall, fitted with glass shelves filled with adult libations of every description and color, promised a taste of heaven and escape to people who didn't know better—or didn't care anymore. A younger man in a snug-fitting tuxedo with a fighter's body manned the bar, polishing its shimmering top with a cloth in slow, circular motions.

Tables were placed around the perimeter of the room, each draped with a white linen cloth and adorned with a tiny oil lamp, its yellow flame flickering against the blood-red petals of a rosebud set in a slender crystal vase.

I turned to look behind me. The door had vanished. In its place was a wall of black, dappled with twinkling stars. I didn't care. My ball sack had conquered the urge to fly the second I mounted the first step downstairs. I was going nowhere.

Empty champagne glasses rested on one of the tables, the remainder unoccupied. Glenn and the boys worked their magic for one couple only, the dapper Mr. Free and his painting come to life—the beautiful, enchanting Jolie.

Jolie wore a sleeveless yellow dress with a full skirt, ideal for dancing, a dress that allowed a perfect pair of legs to move unencumbered. She and Mr. Free were destroying the dance floor with the Lindy. For once, Mr. Free was barely noticeable in a flawlessly-cut black tux.

I looked toward the orchestra, but the band members, intent on the task at hand, either couldn't see me, or chose not to.

"Welcome to the Pompano, kid," the bartender yelled over the din of the music. He motioned for me to join him, and I walked over and slipped onto a leather stool.

He extended a large hand. "Name's Jake. A pleasure to meet you, Spy Boy." His smile exposed short, stubby teeth. His hair was parted down the middle and slicked neatly back with some sort of hair tonic—or maybe Vitalis, the stuff Pop used. I reached for his hand and felt the latent power in his firm grip.

He was handsome in a sharp, dangerous way, the sort of man who didn't start trouble, but who was quite capable of ending it in short order. A slender mustache adorned his upper lip, and his black eyes glittered like the sun-kissed ripples on Black River. He wore a white dinner jacket, and, like Mr. Free, sported a red bow tie with matching carnation.

I eyed the shelves of multicolored poisons on the mirrored wall, and, to my pleasant surprise, saw that I was handsomely dressed in my own tuxedo. I smiled at the tough-looking bartender, and he winked. "How about a little Coke?" I hadn't shaken the possibility—probability—that this whole thing might be a dream. As far as I was concerned, the sweet taste of a little Coke would pretty much lay things to rest.

I watched Jake's fluid movements as he dropped ice into a tumbler, added a shot of Bacardi, popped the top from a small Coke with a church key, and filled the tumbler the remainder of the way. He placed the glass on a small white napkin and slid the drink over.

"Courtesy of Mr. Free," he said with an admirable blend of confidence and calm. I gazed into his shining black eyes, not quite sure what to do. If this were only a dream, then what harm would it do to have a drink?

"Go ahead, Spy Boy," he said. "Nothing's gonna happen to you here, and you ain't going nowhere."

You ain't going nowhere. The words struck a chord. I looked from the suave bartender to the glass of fizzing soda and rum. I glanced at the place where the door once was. The star-spattered sky twinkled on.

The concoction was delicious. I'd once sneaked a taste of Pop's beer while he labored on our Chevy on a hot Saturday afternoon. The warm beer was bitter and left a terrible taste in my mouth—nothing like the delicious, ice-cold zing of sugar cane juice and Atlanta's finest on the rocks. I smiled and took another big swallow.

"'Atta way to do it, Spy Boy. If you're gonna drink, drink like a man. The Pompano is the finest dance club in the world. Any friend of Mr. Free's is a friend of mine."

The elixir invaded my inexperienced system like the Mongol hordes sweeping into Europe, and I began to float on my bar stool. I drained the glass and slid it over. "Fillerup, barkeep," I ordered, feeling like John Wayne with an extra-large grin.

"You ought to take it easy on that stuff, Spy Boy," a voice said from behind me. I turned into Jolie Benoit's incredible smile, meeting her mysterious dark eyes only a second before the creamy contours of her breasts demanded my undivided attention.

My obvious lack of control didn't faze her. "The spirits can be quite habit forming. Ask me how I know." Her slow, Southern-flavored words came from far away, scarcely penetrating the hypnotic spell cast by her ample blessings. If ever there was cause for nonsensical blinking, this was it.

Until this moment of truth, the title of most beautiful woman I'd ever known had belonged to Iris. It was no wonder Mr. Free had dismissed my jealousy when he and Iris met, and that my mother had amounted to nothing more than a moment of pleasurable entertainment.

My hungry eyes traced a path over her shoulder and up the line of her slender neck as I made a half-hearted attempt to remember what she'd just said. Her hair was piled up on her head, loose strands curling at the nape of her neck. Full, luscious lips parted slightly and she smiled.

"Here I am, sweet thing," she said, redirecting my wandering eyes with a gentle touch to my chin, guiding my attention to her face and her smoldering dark eyes. I should have been guilt-ridden over Iris, but guilt was nowhere to be found in this place. Reverend Paul would have a thing or two to say about how beautiful sin could be.

I was being seduced, perhaps bound in the Pompano for eternity, but I was filled with a sense of wellbeing, running headlong toward my fate with a willing, bewitched heart. My little voice finally managed a feeble word from a past fast fading from memory—*Iris.*

In answer, I fell into Jolie's glistening black eyes. She moved the small hand that had directed my chin to my shoulder, and I shivered from the exquisite sensation.

Mr. Free sidled over just in time to see my reaction to Jolie's touch and he laughed with warm appreciation, but I ignored my loyal old friend. I'd proven to be easier than free candy in Aunt Nee's kindergarten and wasn't the least bit ashamed of the fact.

I traced the path of a thin scar above her left eye that ran to her hairline. It was an old injury, well healed and noticeable mostly because it was slightly paler than the smooth brown skin it flawed. With rum-fueled confidence, I ran the tip of my finger along the path of the scar.

"What happened?"

"Just a little car accident, my darling. Nothing for you to worry your handsome head about." Her sparkling eyes roamed my face much the same way mine had just roamed hers. "Gerry said you were cute."

"Gerry?"

"Gerard, honey—Mr. Free." Her pert nose wrinkled when she smiled. I was in love with two women.

"How are you, Spy Boy?" Mr. Free asked, sipping from a glass of champagne.

Words were becoming difficult to find. Mr. Free was supposed to be dead. Jolie was supposed to be dead. Only a summer of fantastic experiences could have prepared me for this. I wondered again if I was asleep in Mr. Free's wingback or truly in this place, where everything looked and felt more lifelike than reality.

"I'm doing great, Gerry. Just great," I said as an unhappy thought occurred. My indestructible smile betrayed a fracture. "I ought to be pissed at you, though. How's it feel to be dead?"

Mr. Free's smile faded too, and he shook his head. "You have a right to be angry, Spy Boy, and I thank you for not succumbing. As far as being dead, as you can see, it feels heavenly—absolutely heavenly."

"I'd like a hug from the young man who brought me my lover." Her voice was rich with Southern magic, magic that chased reservation into a deep crevice and slammed a door on it.

A hug from this woman could cast a spell from which there would be no escape. I *knew* this the way I knew I couldn't fly. She moved closer, placing a hand on my other shoulder then pulling me into a hug that left me swimming in desire for more. I closed my eyes, inhaled her deeply, and prayed for time to stop.

I'd felt this only once before, on the bank of Black River.

Mr. Free laughed again and Jolie, much to my dismay, released me from the divine embrace. She turned, leaving me tottering on the stool like a faltering top. "Gerard, please," she huffed, resting a hand on a sensuous curve of hip.

"Of course, my darling," Mr. Free said, adding a slight bow.

"I'd love to dance with you, Spy Boy." I looked at Mr. Free, arching my eyebrows in question. He raised his glass and nodded, as cool and poised as ever.

Jolie extended her hand, her bare arm a perfectly rendered part of a near-faultless whole. She pulled me from the stool, and I floated along behind her in a cloud of rum vapor and desire. Glenn and the boys began the perfect song, "Moonlight Serenade."

When we reached the center of the floor, she moved in close, the faint perfume of wisteria enveloping me.. She guided my left hand to the small of her back.

"I can't dance," I confessed.

"Just relax," she said.

I searched her eyes, probing for who she was, for what made her tick with such stunning perfection. The most eligible bachelor and accomplished man I'd ever known had pined and waited while beauty after beauty longed for his hand.

She gazed back in a quest of her own, giving completely

of herself. For this song, I was the only person on earth—or wherever it was we were dancing.

Conversation was out of the question for me. Fortunately, she led in that regard as well, smiling and forming words that made little sense to my intoxicated mind, but the rhythm of her speech, the kindness that radiated from her, were much more important than understanding.

After a time, she bent her head toward me and rested it on my shoulder. The fine, almost translucent curls at the base of her neck glowed in the dim light. "You're sweet," she whispered.

The white heat of Puerto Rican rum pulsed in my veins, firing my brain and heart with crazy ideas and longing. I didn't want this to end. I'd lived all the life I needed to live. I was convinced that there was nothing finer to be had than what I was having at this ineffable moment.

You may get lost and never come back. The words made me open my eyes and blink a few times, but Jolie's warmth and smell moved with me, into me. I wanted this spirited woman to devour me and keep me close to her heart forever. I closed my eyes again and breathed deeply. She had me, heart, mind, and soul.

My little voice whispered one word, *Iris* just as a light tap landed on my shoulder. I turned with monumental reluctance to see Mr. Free. Ever the gentleman, he bowed slightly. I did my best to return the bow, but stumbled clumsily, libation-induced haze having reduced me to a near-catatonic state.

"May I, Spy Boy?" Mr. Free asked, ignoring my coordination problems. "I believe someone is looking for you."

I didn't want to let go…ever. I looked back at Jolie, and she smiled, an apology in her eyes. "There'll be time later, George—time for me to thank you properly." She removed herself and I could see that no matter how grateful she was to me, no matter how flirtatious and playful she became, her heart and soul belonged to Gerard Free—in more ways than I could imagine

I turned to see who on earth could be looking for me. About

halfway down on the opposite wall from where I'd entered, sat Francois. His aviator cap and goggles were gone, as was his flamboyant attire. Mr. Free must have dressed him. Like me, he wore a tux, but with a black jacket. He'd not opted for a lapel flower.

I noticed as I drew near that the flickering light on his table didn't find its source in a candle wick. A clear glass ball with a flat bottom sat before him. Inside the ball, a creature resembling a butterfly fluttered about, its intricately patterned wings glowing with a golden yellow light much the same color as a candle flame.

Francois pushed a fresh rum and Coke across the table and offered his hand. I looked at the hand, then at Francois. His eyes were as vibrantly green and scary as ever. "Come on, Bubba," he said, "give it one more try. By the way, you clean up real nice, Mr. Spy Boy," he added as he squeezed my hand with warmth.

"So do you, Mr. Dulcet."

I sat down, took a big gulp from the fresh drink, and smiled. "I could get to liking these things," I said, smacking my lips. "Heck, I *already* like them."

"Alcohol is nothing but trouble, George," Francois advised, turning up a glass of some bluish-looking liquid and draining it. He showed his missing tooth and its intact brothers. "Then again, as Gerard would say, sobriety is an appalling state of mind."

"You're truly crazy, you know that?"

"Me? Look at you. Look around you. Who you gonna tell about this? Not even Iris will believe it. Lee Roy will help the men in the white coats get you into a straitjacket when they show up. Speaking of Iris, you ought to be ashamed of yourself."

The distance between Jolie and me had cleared my head ever so slightly, but I knew better than to pretend I didn't know what Francois was talking about.

"What's that?" I asked, pointing at the glass ball with the butterfly critter inside.

"Oh yeah, right. Change the subject, cheater."

"I didn't cheat."

"Like you weren't about to."

"It isn't fair."

"What isn't fair?"

"Just look at her. Are you queer or something?"

"No, I ain't queer. Just loyal."

My cheeks burned. "Is that why you called me over, so you could lecture me about loyalty and devotion? There's something about this place. It's like she has some sort of magic power. Is she a witch, Francois?"

"This place ain't no excuse for what's going on in your head and heart, least of all what's going on in your pants. And that ain't no girl, Spy Boy," he drawled in his Crescent City dialect, leaning his head in Jolie's direction. "Keep in mind that Iris ain't a woman yet. You're blind if you can't see how much alike they are. And, no, Jolie ain't a witch. That right there's a witch," he said, pointing toward the sphere.

I looked at the winged thing. "I'm not blind. I'm fifteen," I said.

"Touché," he said, shaking his glass in Jake's direction. "And you're right about the magic power. Jolie had magic in your world, too, big-time magic. It's why Tante Evangeline wanted her so bad.

"Women like Jolie can make a Pentecostal preacher throw the Good Book at his wife. She can get anything she wants from any man she wants. In case you hadn't noticed yet, young men included," he added, winking at me. "When Jolie rebelled, Tante Evangeline orchestrated her death. She used Gerard to kill her and then captured her soul."

That name again. I never had learned who Tante Evangeline was, but it didn't take rocket science at this point to know she was bad news. "What in the hell are you talking about, Francois?"

"Jolie reneged on an agreement with a voodoo priestess.

That's pretty much as bad as reneging on the Mafia if you get my drift—worse even."

I didn't get his drift, and I didn't know what to say—a voodoo priestess? Things were at work far beyond my ability to comprehend. The winged thing beat against the glass of its prison, catching my eye. "You gonna tell me what that is, or not?"

"Or not," Francois said, turning to raise a finger at Jake. He pointed the finger at his empty glass. Jake nodded with the patience of a true professional. Francois could be quite the pest.

"Wonder if I'm bugging him. He's a right healthy specimen of a man, ain't he, Spy Boy? You reckon I could take him?"

"I reckon I'd like to watch you try."

Francois laughed. "Yeah, I just bet you would." I watched Jake make Francois's drink. His routine was as fascinating as Pop's preparation to smoke a Lucky. I had no bar experience, but I knew that Jake was good at what he did.

"It's what you helped me trade for," Francois said.

"What?" In typical Francois fashion, he was jerking me all over with what passed for him as conversation. For all I knew, he'd disappear like smoke right in the middle of this fascinating exchange.

He pointed at the glass ball with the butterfly thing inside. "That—that's what you helped me trade for."

I studied the ball and the butterfly more closely. The winged creature was beautiful, but beautiful in a sinister way. A stinger curled from its rear, ending just over its head. The stinger was tipped with a tiny, spear-shaped diamond that glowed emerald green now and then. The creature's eyes, tiny round mirrors of pale blue, locked on mine. It crashed against the wall of its glass prison in an effort to get at me, its stinger jerking left and right with blurring speed. It pointed the stinger directly at me and the diamond winked a beautiful golden hue a couple of times.

The glass ball encasing the mean-spirited bug was imperfectly shaped, with tiny bubbles suspended in its smoky surface.

The unevenly blown glass appeared to be completely sealed, lending the impression that its evil contents had been born inside.

I looked at Francois. "And what did *you* get in the trade?"

"Jolie. I got Jolie back for Gerard."

"Where was she?"

"Her soul was trapped inside Tante Evangeline's chest of power."

"How exactly did that happen?" I asked, grateful for the rum and Coke to calm my nerves and unsteady heart.

"Jolie traded her beauty and freedom to get Gerard back, George."

"Back from where?"

"The war, a dogfight in the cold night sky over France, to be exact. When Gerard came back, Jolie found she couldn't fulfill the requirements of the trade."

I clearly remembered the dogfight, and what Francois had said to Mr. Free on that night. "What requirements?" I asked.

"Tante Evangeline traded her for other things to put in her chest, things that men who lust for rare beauty will willingly trade when the moon is full and the drink is flowing. Some will trade eternity for one night of bliss, as you now know."

Francois' expression was rife with mischief, mockery, and accusation. I rolled my eyes and opened my mouth to defend myself, but he interrupted. "A year or two went by, and Jolie decided that she'd paid enough. She escaped into Gerard's arms, but Tante Evangeline had different plans.

"They hit a bridge abutment on a moonlit night. A child appeared in the road as they rounded a curve. The car passed right through the child, but Gerard, quite drunk, had taken evasive action he couldn't correct. Jolie was killed.

"He buried her three days later and, for months, he struggled to live a normal life. One day, he woke with the unshakable conviction that his days of normalcy and magic were over. He couldn't go on. After a long night of New Orleans jazz and quite a few glasses of his favorite poison, he stuck one of his war toys to his head and pulled the trigger. He was in the hospital for six months, in a coma for four of them.

"While he was waffling between life and death, I came to him. 'You can't die,' I said, 'Evangeline has Jolie's soul. Death won't reunite you.'"

I looked from Francois to the butterfly. "What on earth does this thing have to do with Jolie and Mr. Free?"

"That *thing*, as you refer to it—and I gotta admit, *thing* is as good a word as any—is Tante Evangeline's soul."

"What?"

It was Francois's turn to roll his eyes. "I don't know how in the hell Gerard ever figured you were so special. You act and sound like a dumbass."

"Thanks, I've worked hard at it." I drank more of my rum and Coke and thought about kicking his ass. I'd shaken his hand. In this place, he wouldn't disappear into a cloud of pixie dust. I hadn't yet realized that the concoctions mixed in a barroom were capable of highly exaggerating the weight of one's ball sack and physical ability.

"Tante Evangeline was good at what she did. In the Netherworld, you hear many calls for help from the dark people. When I heard the voice of Tante Evangeline, I knew who it was."

I thought about the amazing trip I'd taken with Pug, the blobs crawling from beneath the bleachers, crying out desperately for help. Francois had sat in those very bleachers. He may have been there the night I went with Pug.

"As children, Gerard and I had slipped beneath the lip of her tent on many a Mardi Gras night to listen while she told fortunes to people inclined for such things. She shopped for 'clients' this way. Some have their fortunes told for the sake of novelty. Some come with secret desire lurking in the fine lines of their palms.

"Dealing with spirits in the Netherworld is dangerous business, Bubba. I had no intention of being wrangled by Tante Evangeline. I wanted her destruction. I wanted to help Gerard and Jolie. I owed Gerard for my brother, but I'm powerless in your world with the exception of illusion.

"Your friend, Pug Ginn, passed through the gray of the Netherworld of what he calls the Purgatory Plane on the way to exploring the past that intrigues him so much. Often, before he returned to the consciousness of his wheelchair prison, he'd stop and sit on the wooden bleachers, watching and listening as the souls reaped the poison fruit of seed they sowed during lives of evil.

"Pug wasn't dead, yet he could travel through a place that only the dead could go. He'd managed this feat with magic every bit as powerful as Tante Evangeline's. He had the keys to reversing Jolie and Gerard's fate. I needed an intermediary. You know what an intermediary is, Bubba?"

"Do you know what an asshole is, Francois?"

"Excuse me?"

"Sorry. It's just that you're a bit condescending at times. I'm pretty sure that the definition of intermediary is me."

"I don't think you'd talk to me like that if you weren't drinking."

"I would too."

He gave me a disdainful frown. "You want to hear about the trade, or not?"

I wanted to kick his freckled, redheaded ass is what I wanted, but his story was too irresistible. "Why me, Francois? Out of all the kids in the world, why me?"

"When I followed Pug back to his place, I could feel someone else on his side: one George Parker, lurking, willing, and bored. That day you decided to ride your bike and look for a new fishing hole because you were afraid of Bangalang, I did what troubled spirits do. *Bam*, there I was, standing in the top of that pine tree, using the same tool that you've used your entire life when things weren't going so hot."

"What tool?"

"Don't you know, George? Pug mentioned it to you. Teachers have mentioned it to you. It's at the root of every wonderful invention man has ever created."

"Imagination."

"Yep, I could do anything I wanted once I passed through the portal into your world, and I used your imagination to do it. Once I appeared to you, once I had your attention, I had a way to communicate with Pug—a way to trade."

"Why couldn't you just ask him yourself, for Pete's sake?"

"I couldn't pass anything directly to him except words. I told him that you'd lost your dog. I told him if he'd help me, I'd help him. The rest, as you know, is history."

"That sounds like a total crock of manure."

"Bubba, I don't understand everything about where I am and what I can do. It ain't much different than when I was alive. I'm figuring it out as I go. Some of us don't have to go to the track to confront our sins of the quick. Some of us do."

I looked around the room. It was a magnificent reproduction of a 1930s-era New Orleans ballroom. "Well, where in the heck did this come from?" I asked, waving a hand in a sweeping motion.

"Let's just say I'm learning the tricks faster than others."

"But why? What did Mr. Free do to deserve loyalty like this, Francois?"

"Bubba, you know who Ralph Waldo Emerson was?"

My mind flashed to Mrs. Lawrimore scrawling this great man's name across the blackboard. "Of course," I said.

"'A friend may well be reckoned the masterpiece of nature,'" Francois said, pointing a finger toward the ceiling. "I believe Gerard told you what he did."

"I know he took a bullet for your brother, but to choose to linger in that gray world like you did. I don't know if I could do that."

"We were dear friends, Bubba, true friends. It's a love difficult to describe to those who've never known it. I think you'd do it for Iris or Lee Roy."

"I don't know why you needed me for this," I said, pointing toward the vicious little bug in the ball.

"You remember when I gave you the formula that day outside the department store: the day you talked Mr. Hugh into the clothes and the job for Lee Roy?"

"Yeah, I remember."

"The formula was a mathematical roadmap to escape, directions that eventually led Pug to the awareness that mathematics weren't the way for him to see what he needed to see, to discover what he needed to discover. Pug didn't need intellect to recapture his life; he needed imagination. Of course, he already knew that. What better way to deliver this gift than with a boy he trusted and his dog?"

"And what did he give you?"

"He gave me the Bottle Maker."

The Bottle Maker. I'd not forgotten the muscled colored man and his beautiful smile.

"Pug didn't allow you to remain in the bleachers that day to watch the Bottle Maker do his magic, and he lied to you about talking to him. They know one another well. The Bottle Maker refused to acknowledge my existence. He speaks to no one in the bleachers, only the dark people circling the track and to Pug.

"At Pug's request, he agreed to meet me. After hearing my story, he fired up his kiln and blew me this glass ball. *She will die on the next full moon,* he said when he handed the ball over.

"I was right there waiting when the old bat took her last breath, standing on the foot of her bed like the angel of death itself with that glass ball in my hand. When she saw the ball, her eyes filled with fear, but there was nothing to be done. If she could've screamed, she would've let go like a wounded hyena.

"Her soul left her body, a tiny glow of purple light that, instead of treading on that muddy track for eons, headed straight to the glass in my hand. The wicked little soul began to orbit and poke at the glass like a crazy moth to a flame. The ball opened and sucked her in like a Venus flytrap and she turned into the creature you see."

"Who in the heck is the Bottle Maker?"

Francois waved the question away. "He's for another time and place, Bubba, a story yet to be told, but you can take this to the bank. You're going to have dealings with him again one day soon."

As I pondered this ominous announcement, Francois continued his fascinating narrative. "Evangeline's power chest passed from her to her apprentice, but Jolie's soul was allowed to escape. Tonight, perhaps tomorrow night, I'll break the ball and set Evangeline free."

"Why? Why would you do that? Mr. Free has Jolie back, and that lady right there is evil," I said. The freaky butterfly thing threw itself against the ball, winked its diamond, and made a chattering noise. I backed away from the table a little.

"It's very simple, Spy Boy. A deal is a deal."

Jake arrived with Francois's blue drink. "Mr. Dulcet," he said, placing a fresh napkin and more blue poison before Francois. "How are you fixed, Spy Boy?"

"Getting better all the time, Jake. Thanks."

"One more song and I believe we'll be going," Mr. Free said from behind me.

I turned to see him and Jolie smiling down at me. "How's it hanging, Gerard?" Francois asked, winking at Jolie and flashing his crazy smile. "Lord have mercy, they don't come no finer. You look like the first sunrise after a Cat 5 hurricane, darling."

"You're one of my all-time loves, freckled one," Jolie said with a laugh.

The single horn played again, Glenn and his clarinet. I knew the notes instantly. Saxophones joined in with strings following close behind. It was "Moonlight Serenade" again. Jolie extended her hand toward me. I looked at Mr. Free. "Of course," he said, looking at Jake. "My man, a rum and Coke with a road service, please. We have some traveling to do."

"Coming right up, Mr. Free," Jake said, hustling off to the bar.

I strolled out onto the floor with Jolie. Before we began dancing, she put her arms around my neck and gave me another incredible hug. A sense of peace spread through my consciousness like an ink drop colors a glass of water. I wondered if it was the way a black widow's mate felt as its last seconds ebbed away. The song ended all too soon and Jolie stepped away, her eyes on mine.

"This Iris girl, she loves you a great deal, Spy Boy. You and me—perhaps another life, another time."

The mural had changed during the dance. The moon had risen higher, the blacktop looked like a silver ribbon. The Caddy sat idling with deep-throated power, plumes of gray rising from its dual exhaust pipes. Glenn and his band were gone.

Mr. Free shook my hand, then dropped his dented old Zippo into my palm. I slipped the lighter into my pants pocket, tears filling my eyes. Jolie hugged me, and Francois punched me playfully on the shoulder. I watched them load into the Cadillac with the wicked butterfly fluttering and glowing in its glass prison. They rolled into the mural with the honk of the horn and a roar of the pipes.

From a distance, Mr. Free raised his glass of rum and Coke in the air and blew the horn one last time. I wondered again, as I knew I was supposed to, who the hell the Bottle Maker was.

When I got home, I rode Lightning down to the river with Buster tagging along behind. I fondled the Zippo in my pocket and watched as the moon sank. I wanted to see if it had anything to say.

ACKNOWLEDGMENTS

Writing is a lonely pursuit, but one doesn't achieve even a small amount of success without the support and encouragement of others. My heartfelt gratitude to the late Mrs. Joycelyn Lawrimore, who opened my eyes to what my mother, Frances, class poet and bedtime storyteller, quietly passed to her eldest. To Margie Horton Cooper, steadfast friend for decades, a superlative reader with an encouraging word at just the right moment, time after time. To Rick 'What-Did-You-Write-Me' Foshee, his years of unwavering backing, and our time on the enchanting Black River. To Charles Spain Verral, who introduced me at an early age to the power of words. To Steven Mayfield, for talking me down when I needed it (numerous times), for his rock-solid advice, as well as for his amazing generosity, and to Carolyn Jack, a Regal House stablemate and angel who calls herself friend. To Ms. Cappy Hall Rearick, Southern Belle of Southern Belles, amazing fellow writer, Conroy devotee, and adoptive mother. To Betty Jean Franklin, for her keen eye, and Matt Franklin for the wonderful artwork. And, of course, to Rhonda, for sending that first story out into the world so many years ago.

Special thanks to Paige Sawyer Photography. Paige is a magician with a camera and a wonderful man all around.

Sincerest gratitude goes out to Jaynie Royal, Regal House founder and editor-in-chief extraordinaire, for her faith, trust, guidance, and for believing in *Moon* and me. *Moon* would not have happened without Jaynie.

Finally, to everyone who encouraged me and helped with a kind word or genuine show of interest. You know who you are.